SHADOWS IN T

The car, a black sa
side them, powerin
tained shock and K drew a his-
sing breath, for the car was dangerously close. Worse, it was angling, cutting in on them. It happened so fast, the powerful burst of speed, the violent assault on the Bentley and the angled thrust, that catastrophe loomed. The black saloon was a hideous menace, threatening to batter them off the road, over the edge and down to the rocks and the sea below . . .

Edward knew he could not have been the target of that murder attempt. It had to be Katerina. Mystery encompassed her existence . . .

Also by Robert Tyler Stevens
in Hamlyn Paperbacks

THE FIELDS OF YESTERDAY

SHADOWS IN THE AFTERNOON

Robert Tyler Stevens

Hamlyn Paperbacks

SHADOWS IN THE AFTERNOON
ISBN 0 600 20740 4

First published in Great Britain 1983
by Hamlyn Paperbacks

Hamlyn Paperbacks are published by
The Hamlyn Publishing Group Ltd,
Astronaut House,
Feltham,
Middlesex, England

Printed and bound in Great Britain by
Hazell Watson & Viney Ltd
Aylesbury, Bucks

In January 1919, when the Red Army was advancing on Riga, seaport and capital of Latvia, HMS *Princess Margaret* steamed out of the harbour and headed for Copenhagen. Aboard were four hundred refugees, all fleeing from the Bolsheviks. Among them were seven people in peasants' clothes – a middle-aged man and woman, four girls and a boy.

On arrival in Copenhagen, the captain of the mine-layer was presented with a silver epergne engraved with the words: 'Four hundred refugees of all nationalities assembled in Riga will always retain a grateful remembrance of their deliverance from the Bolsheviks in January 1919 by the gallant captain of HMS *Princess Margaret*, officers and men.'

Once ashore in Copenhagen, the refugees dispersed.

1

The isle of Formentera, veined by dry gullies and patterned by Mediterranean shrubs, lay like an uncut stone of brown and green in a setting of oceanic blue. Although it was close to Ibiza and not far from the Spanish mainland, it had escaped the rampaging development that had smothered so much of the Balearic islands. It had even escaped an airport. Its principal town, San Francisco, was tiny, its scattered hamlets were few, and its people, for the most part, were still compulsive tillers of its baked soil. Formenterans looked after their own business and each other. Holidaymakers were a race apart, a species of sunseekers accepted and politely indulged.

On slopes and lowlands the almond trees were dusty, the olive trees laden, the fall of the fruit still some way off. The isle was as quiet as a slumbering monastery, except for the Playa d'es Pujols in the north and the Playa de Mitjorn in the south. There the eccentric holidaymakers disported in skimpily-clad fashion, swamping their bodies in oil.

East of Es Calo, the sun-splashed cliffs showed their brown, barren face to the shimmering sea. The single-storeyed villa, lapped by almond trees and overlooking the cliffs, was enclosed by a bougainvillaea hedge, the shrubs explosive with bursting colour. The large garden was an enchantment, its beauty the consequence of being lovingly tended from the time, fifty years ago, when it had first been won from the intemperate ground.

There were no holidaymakers in this area save for the family which had just arrived at the only other villa, two hundred yards from the first and a short walk from the village. Kate Matthews, slipping off her jeans and T-shirt, put on a yellow dress, combed her dark hair and hurried downstairs.

'A dress?' said her mother.

'Oh, well, you know,' said Kate, with a fifteen-year-old's natural ambiguity.

'Where are you going so soon?'

'I thought – well, to see the Señora,' said Kate, raven-haired, blue-eyed and pretty. Romantically disposed, she could wander dreamy-eyed while others rushed into life's pursuits.

'You spent most of your time last year with her.'

'Strange girl,' smiled her father.

'And the year before,' said her mother. They came to the villa for a month each year, renting it from mid-July to mid-August. There was no beach. There was only sun, peace and a restful inclination to do nothing.

Kate smiled a little shyly and sidled out. It was hot. The light breeze fanned her face with heat. But, young and alive, she ran on quick feet down the path and over a hard little track that wound through scrub. Reaching the white-walled villa, festooned with hibiscus, she found the Señora sitting at a table on the tiled patio that overlooked the garden. A blue umbrella shaded her aged body from the fierce sun.

'Señora?' said Kate. That was what she always called her dear and treasured friend, even if she wasn't Spanish.

The lady looked up. She was very old, white of hair and slender of figure. But her eyes were still quite magnificent, a clear, unveined grey, and no deep lines furrowed her face. The fragility of age was apparent, but not its wrinkles or its bent back. Her eyes regarded Kate out of a mind full of dreams.

'They've all gone, all my loved ones,' she said in English.

'Señora?' said Kate, puzzled. The Señora had a son and daughter, and grandchildren, and although one family lived in England and the other in America, they would all come to visit her before the end of August and stay for some weeks as they always did.

The lady came to her feet. She rose slowly, but with grace, as if she had been born in the court of St James or another.

Her white dress was a lightness around her slender, fragile body, and she was upright, not stooping, and to Kate quite beautiful. Kate had spent tranquil hours with her since the age of eleven. They had an affinity, these two, the very old and the very young.

The dreams slipped, the lady's eyes opened and she smiled in pleasure and affection.

'Why, it's Kate. You've come again. Has another year gone? Another one? Yes, but how good to see you, sweet child. Your letters are precious, but not more than you are." She kissed the girl on the cheek, and Kate hugged her.

'Señora, oh, I came as soon as we arrived, to see how you were.'

'Well, I'm old, Kate, that is all.' The lady's smile was warm. Kate in her bright yellow dress was a reminder of her own sweet youth of long ago. 'How pretty you're getting. How very pretty.'

'You look super,' said Kate. She had put a dress on because she knew the Señora did not consider girls in jeans to be at all acceptable.

'I am super?' The lady smiled. 'But I'm so old, Kate. I will tell you. I'm almost a hundred.'

Kate, staggered, gasped, 'You're not, you can't be.'

The lady laughed softly.

'Well, I'm eighty-three. That's near to a hundred, isn't it?'

'Eighty-three?' Kate calculated. 'Señora, you were actually born when Queen Victoria was still alive?'

'Yes, when Queen Victoria was still in command of almost every royal family in Europe, and I, old as I am, was only a contemporary of her great-granddaughters. You'll stay a little while, my sweet?'

'Oh, I should like to.'

'Then let us have lemonade.' The lady picked up a little silver bell from the table and rang it. 'Maria? Maria?'

Maria, her servant, appeared. She was a middle-aged Formenteran.

'Señora?'

'Lemonade, please. You see, Maria? Kate is here again.'

'I see, I see,' said Maria, and smiled at Kate. She brought

the lemonade in a jug covered with a white napkin. Ice tinkled as she filled two glasses, and the lemon slices spilled and splashed. It was always the same, always made from fresh lemons, always cool and delicious, with a little bite to it. The lady served no other drink to young people.

She sat and talked with Kate. Kate was quick and energetic in her speech, the lady mellowly articulate, and each was receptive to the other. The bees buzzed on gossamer wings, the sun cast heated light, and the colours of the garden danced before the eye. Kate was fascinated by the graceful woman she had met five years ago, on her family's first visit to the adjoining villa. The Señora often told stories of her youth, of her years as a girl, and Kate sometimes wondered what stories there were concerning all the other years.

The lady became quiet. It was age, of course, which often transported her from the present to the past. Her eyes were full of dreams, her face serene. There was always serenity about her, as if the magic of life was a beatitude. This year, thought Kate, the serenity was more finely drawn.

The Señora broke her temporary silence to ask Kate about her schooling. Kate told her of the struggles and problems she had with subjects like science and mathematics.

'Science, child? Mathematics?' The lady sighed. 'What is the world doing to girls these days? Has it forgotten that girls grow into women, and that women relate to compassion and caring, not to infernal things? Science and mathematics are the essence of the infernal. Everything one reads or listens to these days tells one so.'

Quite earnestly, Kate said, 'Then I shall do my best, Señora, to give them up.'

The lady smiled and shook her head.

'No, no, Kate. I shouldn't say such things. It's your world you have to live in, not mine, and if your world is in desperate need of women scientists and women mathematicians, then you must continue to struggle with the subjects.'

'Do you think so, Señora?' said Kate, who would have been quite happy to have had nothing to do with them at all.

Again the lady smiled, and again the grey eyes dreamed.

'Such a world, such an unhappy world,' she murmured. 'I

know Edward would have said it was no better than a factory, into which every woman, as well as every man, was being pushed.'

'Who was Edward?' asked Kate.

'Edward?' said the lady, as if it had been Kate who had plucked the name out of the day. She looked at the girl, at her dark hair, her blue eyes and her vivid youth, and because Kate was so remindful of another the dreams returned to possess her. 'They are all gone, my loved ones, all gone, Celeste.'

Kate's susceptible heart missed a beat.

'Señora, I'm Kate. Who is Celeste?'

The lady came to.

'She's gone, my sweet, but you are so like her.'

'Oh, I think you've a story to tell,' said Kate.

'Stories are like life, Kate, always to do with the past.' The lady put a hand under Kate's chin and lifted her face. The fine grey eyes searched the unclouded blue. 'Life is always a memory of moments just gone and years long past. Cling to each moment, if you can, for each is so precious, yet so fleeting. Only love defies time. Time robs us of all else, of all whom we cherish, but it can't rob us of love. God gives it, and it is His greatest gift to people. But so many people, so many, never understand it. Be sweet, my child, as Celeste was,and then you'll come to know that love means giving, not receiving.'

'Tell me about her, Señora.'

'About Celeste? But then there was also Edward, you see. I could only tell you part of the story. The rest only they could tell. And they are gone, Kate, all of them, all whom I loved so much.'

'Oh, tell me, Señora, tell me your part.'

Fragile old age took on the serenity of treasured dreams.

2

The small hotel, painted white, gleamed in the warm October sunshine. Half a mile from the little village of La Roche, it fronted the winding coastal road and its sign said it was the Hotel de Corniche. It could not, of course, be compared with the grand establishments of Nice and Cannes, but set in an environment of peace and tranquillity, with a breathtaking view of the blue sea, it had its own appeal.

Unlike other small hotels, it remained open all the year round, which said much for its desirability. Madame Heloise Michel, the owner, valued the patronage of guests who provided her with an income during the out-of-season months and enabled her to keep a few of her staff at work. Times were hard in 1928. One heard that exiled Grand Dukes in Nice had to sell their valuables to pay their hotel bills, or did not pay them at all, creating embarrassment for managements instinctively disinclined to throw the exalted into the street.

A pre-war Bentley, approaching the Hotel de Corniche from the west, rounded one of the thousands of bends at a moment when some idiot leapt into the road from the right-hand verge. It was an idiot of the male gender, a man clad in a blue flannel shirt and blue serge trousers. The driver, handling the car carefully, was able to stop in good time. The man flashed a startled glance, showing a ruddy face and a dark, untidy moustache. He did not, however, apologise for his suicidal stupidity, but ran across the road and disappeared into the shrubs and trees of the ascending terrain. The sound of a rifle shot followed him. It was, to the driver of the car, unmistakably a rifle shot. He had experienced a surfeit of rifle fire during the war. He stood up in the car and looked around. He saw no one. He heard no one. Silence prevailed. The sky was clear, the afternoon warm and bright. The south of France lay in quietness under its October sun.

'Extraordinary,' said Edward Jonathan Somers. He got out and peered at the trees and shrubs crowding the gentle ascent. He detected neither movement nor sound. He turned and inspected the downward slope on the other side of the road. Scented pine trees covered the ground. He advanced. One did not shrug off a running man and a rifle shot. Somewhere, fairly close, was the person who had fired the shot. Because he was curious and intrigued, he began a slow and cautious ingress into the profusion of pines. Caution was commonsensical, slowness a necessity.

The descent was not steep, but even so he could not go too far because the return would be a climb, which would mean an uphill effort for him in more ways than one. Reaching a break in the trees, he saw the high stone wall that bounded the Villa d'Azur. The villa itself, nestling amid palms at a distance of some seventy yards, showed only its pink roof tiles. He noticed the jagged array of broken glass cemented into the top of the wall. Villa owners were not usually inclined to seal themselves off as uncompromisingly as that. Intruders intent on burglary or pillage were rare in the quieter areas of the Riviera, although confidence men and gigolos operated with smooth efficiency in Nice and Cannes.

Edward turned at the lightest of sounds and saw, not a rifleman, but a slender and quite lovely woman, a brimmed white hat in her hand. Her silk dress was also white, and with it she wore black silk stockings and white shoes. She came to his eyes as a vision unexpected and enchanting. Her hair was a mass of dark, rich auburn; long lashes framed eyes of deep, clear grey, eyes that were startled as she beheld him. He thought her about thirty, but there was something of the magic of never-forgotten youth in those eyes of striking clarity. They held him mesmerised. He was as silent as she was. It was a moment when his tongue lay still, a discovery more fascinating than anything which might have been said. But he spoke when the silence began to bring a slight flush to her oval face.

'I heard someone fire a rifle,' he said with a smile.

'M'sieur,' she said, 'you are regarding me with so much earnestness that I fear you think I am the guilty one.' Her voice was warm and mellow, with an undercurrent of amusement, her responsive English so fluent that she might have been a compatriot. But he had a certainty she was not English.

'Have I been staring?'

'Indeed, m'sieur, and earnestly.'

'I do apologise – ' Edward broke off as a man appeared.

Tall and strong-looking with an iron-grey beard and an impassive countenance, he was dressed in a white shirt, grey tie and black trousers. Without either jacket or hat, he looked as if he might have been interrupted while relaxing in the sunshine. He turned dark eyes on the slender woman. She, taller than average, lifted her chin and Edward thought he glimpsed a flicker of imperious defiance. The bearded man said nothing. He merely shook his head in reproach. She turned without a word and walked away, elegant and graceful, to become a flutter of white amid the pines.

The bearded man regarded Edward sombrely.

'This is private property, m'sieur,' he said in French.

'Are you sure?' said Edward in the same language. 'It isn't fenced.'

'It is private property, m'sieur. Please go.'

'My only reason for being here is that I heard a rifle shot,' said Edward.

'A rifle shot?' The bearded man was unresponsive.

'I think it was fired over the head of a running man.'

'I'm not that man, m'sieur. Nor, as you see, do I have a rifle.'

'Even so,' said Edward, 'I'm sure one was fired, and that isn't something which happens every day.'

'I think, m'sieur, you will find rifles being fired every day in many parts of the world. Please have the goodness to go on your way.'

'Very well,' said Edward, and left, making a slow climb back to the road. He was breathing a little heavily by the time he reached his car, but he was thinking more about the striking vision of elegance than his chest.

The doors of the Corniche swung open for him a few minutes later as he pulled up outside the hotel. Jacques, the porter and handyman, came down the wide steps to take care of his luggage.

'Welcome, mon Capitaine. You are well?' That was how Jacques, an old soldier, always greeted him.

'I'm in excellent health, Jacques.' That was how Edward always responded, although it was never precisely true. He was no longer in the British Army, and nor was he resplendent with health. He had been gassed in Flanders in 1917. Any exercise in advance of a slow walk put a strain on his poisoned lungs. He had not been as badly gassed as some, but he had breathed in enough of the deadly stuff to reduce him from a vigorous man to a disabled one. His doctor assured him he was not in danger of dying unless he indulged in activities fatally foolish, like mountain-climbing or hundred-yard sprints. All in all, anything of a robust nature was out. Providing he walked where others ran, providing he paced himself, he could live his allotted span – and providing he escaped the hazards of severe and foggy winters. So he spent his winters at the Corniche, where there was neither fog nor snow to endure.

At thirty-five, he considered he had already enjoyed eleven years that might have been denied to him. To live at the Corniche during its out-of-season periods was an added enjoyment. Its comfort, peace and quiet made him feel he could not count himself an entirely unfortunate man. He always stayed until April, returning then to England and an appreciation of its burgeoning spring, and the endearing vagaries of its summer, in his little cottage near Guildford.

He had been invalided out of the army in 1919, but someone had taken an interested note of the fact that he had a degree in history, for he was invited to become a member of the team responsible for preparing the official history of the Great War. This entailed absorbing research work, which fascinated him. The department concerned was accommodating, not minding where he was as long as he was doing what he was drawing his pay for.

As usual, he had brought a trunkful of material that would

enable him to complete his current assignment by May. This was an account of the first battle of Ypres. While the weather remained warm he would be able to work outside, to do his writing by the little summerhouse in the garden at the rear of the hotel. Young Celeste Michel, daughter of Madame Michel, would bring him coffee or Pernod from time to time. He had acquired a taste for Pernod.

He mounted the steps to the open doors, leaving Jacques attending to his luggage. In the cool, shady lobby, with its strip of carpet leading to the stairs, a girl came from behind the little reception desk, a delighted smile on her face and her blue eyes alight.

'Monsieur Somers! Oh, how happy I am to see you.' And Celeste Michel, Latin-black hair bobbed, flung her arms around him in welcome. He planted a kiss on her cheek. They were old friends. He had known her for eight years. Celeste, sixteen now, was devoted. Edward was her confidant, recipient of her imaginative outpourings concerning the hotel, the village and herself.

'Sweet soul of innocence, how you've grown,' he smiled. 'You're up to here.' He touched his chin.

'But of course. Almost I'm fully grown. I'm sixteen.' Celeste, quite without inhibitions, stood back so that he might better observe what she had accomplished since he had last seen her in April. She had put two inches on her height and acquired roundness where she most desired it. Having every French girl's unashamed consciousness of physical development, she was extremely proud now that she had a figure. She wore a neat black dress, stylishly short, with a white collar and white cuffs. 'I've left school and am now Mama's invaluable help. I'm in charge of the reception desk, the telephone and the allocation of rooms. Do you wish me to call a number for you?'

'I can't think of one at the moment,' said Edward.

'Never mind,' said Celeste, 'but I'm at your service whenever you're desperate to communicate. Did you have a good journey? The roads were not too bad for you?'

'My journey was very good.'

Jacques entered the lobby with a trunk weighing

down his shoulders.

'To room three, Jacques,' said Celeste.

'I know, I know,' said Jacques, and hefted his way through the lobby.

'M'sieur, you have your usual ground floor room,' smiled Celeste, 'and Marie has put it into perfect order for you. Oh, I'm so happy you've come again. Mama herself says it's a pleasure to have you.'

She looked him over with care and affection. He was thin, of course, he was always thin, and a little hollow-chested because of his complaint. His light salt-and-pepper tweed suit was the same one he had arrived in last year, and the year before, but it was very well cut and good-tempered. His face was lean, with hollows, but he did not look ill. Indeed, the sun had touched him during his drive in the open car, and there was colour in his cheeks. With his tweed cap removed, his thick dark-brown hair showed its widow's peak. His eyes, brown, were those of a kind and amiable man. Celeste felt sad that he had no wife to look after him. She thought very little of all the unmarried Englishwomen who must know him, for not one of them, apparently, cared to take him on. Or perhaps he had not asked any of them. She had spent the last two years casting around for a suitable French lady, one who would make him an affectionate and caring wife. Her interest had pointed her in the direction of the only two ladies in La Roche who were eligible. After some consideration, she dismissed both of them. Whether either of them would have suited Monsieur Somers was not a point uppermost in her mind, for she was quite sure they did not suit her. She thought one too stupid, the other too gushing.

Celeste smiled. She accompanied him to his room on the ground floor. It was square and spacious, with a shining floor of *parquet à l'anglais* and a colourful bedside rug. Double casement doors opened out on to the well-kept garden. He always had this room, so that he did not have the stairs to negotiate. He did not mind stairs, he said, but what was the point of making him walk up and down unnecessarily? Her mother, who was fond of him, would not have that at all. Since she was a war widow, her mother could have made him a very good wife, but perhaps she was rather old at forty.

'This is splendid, Celeste,' said Edward, regarding the room with satisfaction. Its furniture and walls were friendly and familiar to him. Jacques had deposited the trunk and gone to fetch another.

'It's as you like it?' said Celeste.

'It always is. So is everything else, including you, my angel.'

She laughed.

'Oh, for you, m'sieur, I will even grow wings.'

Madame Michel entered through the open door. Running to matronly fullness, she was a handsome woman, her black hair parted down the middle and braided around her head. She extended a warm hand to Edward, who took it.

'I am happy of your arrival, Monsieur Somers,' she said in English. She was proud of her English, though not always accurate with it. 'It is most of a pleasure to see you again. How well you are looking, but you must take care when the evenings become cold. You need not say when you are needing to be on fire. Marie will light it each evening from next month.'

'Ah, my very good Madame Michel,' said Edward gravely, 'I'm in contented expectation that all will be taken care of, including when I'm needing to be on fire.'

Madame Michel smiled.

'M'sieur, I'll bring you tea,' said Celeste, 'and then Marie will fill the bath for you.'

She knew he liked to take baths. Celeste was satisfied to soak herself once a week, as was her mother, but many visitors had acquired the habit of bathing every day. There were sixteen guest rooms, and when the hotel was full a glut of daily bathers put a great strain on the old boiler. During the winter season, however, when the hotel averaged only half the number of summer guests, the boiler made few complaints.

Celeste lingered after her mother departed. Jacques brought the second trunk and Edward tipped him. Celeste still lingered.

'M'sieur—'

'Tea,' said Edward.

'Oh, yes, at once.' She sped away. In a little while she took the tray to him, in the garden, where he sat relaxing at a table near the summerhouse. Blooms festooned the poinsettia bushes with colour, and the afternoon was still warm and sunny, though the evening might bring a touch of coolness when it arrived.

'Thank you, Celeste.'

'You will inspect the pot?' she invited, lifting the lid. He peered. The tea leaves swam in the steaming water.

'I think it'll do,' he said.

'It would be calamitous if it did not do,' said Celeste, very aware that Edward was as critical as all English people about the quality of a pot of tea. 'May I pour, m'sieur?'

'Please do, my infant.'

Celeste poured.

'Oh, m'sieur, what do you think? I am now friends with Madame. You remember her?'

'I remember you telling me of her. I remember you were very inquisitive.'

'No, no, interested, that's all,' she protested. 'You aren't too tired to talk?'

'I'm not too tired to listen. I feel you've got a thousand words on your tongue. If you're not too busy, entertain me, Celeste. I made my journey in wise stages, and have only motored a hundred miles today. I'm ready to be entertained.'

'It's always been so intriguing,' said Celeste.

'My motoring?'

'No, m'sieur, the mystery of Madame, who came to live at the Villa d'Azur two years ago and hid herself behind its walls, even though she was so beautiful. I saw her only twice, each time through the *pylône grille*.' That was the wrought iron gate that fronted the road at the beginning of the villa's drive. 'She smiled at me. But three months ago, you see, the little green gate in the wall overlooking the sea was open. I couldn't resist peeping, and there she was, m'sieur, gathering flowers from her garden.'

3

She looked up and saw the young girl, black-haired, pretty and blue-eyed, standing just inside the green wooden gate.

'Child, what are you doing there?' Her French had what Celeste thought must be the attractive accent of a well-educated citizen of Paris.

'Oh, nothing at all, madame, nothing at all.'

'You're just looking?' She smiled, and Celeste was entranced.

'Many pardons, madame. Please forgive me.'

The woman hesitated, casting a glance over her shoulder. The wide garden was a picture of lushness and colour. It was also quiet and empty. No voices, no people, no children. So very empty. And here was a child, here was a child who looked sweet and delicious, a young girl with blue eyes.

'What is your name, child?'

'Celeste, madame, but I'm almost sixteen.'

The woman smiled again.

'Oh, many many years ago I too was sixteen,' she said.

'Many years ago, madame, many?' said Celeste in wonder.

'Many years, Celeste.' The clear grey eyes reflected memories of joys and innocence. 'Where are you from?'

'The hotel. It's owned by my mother. I'm Celeste Michel, you see. Goodbye, madame. I'm sorry to have been so inquisitive.'

Again the woman hesitated, then said, 'Would you like some lemonade? Yes, you would. In summer, there's never too much lemonade when one is sixteen, do you agree?'

'I'm always avid for lemonade, madame,' said Celeste earnestly.

'Come,' said Madame. 'Please close the gate first, and bolt it. Thank you. Come.' Carrying a trug filled with blooms, she walked along the garden path with Celeste, her white dress waisted by a narrow belt of black velvet, the skirt slightly flared, so that it whisked and whispered, flirting with the shrubs.

Celeste felt excited and enchanted. As far as she knew, no one in the area of La Roche had ever been inside the high walls of the Villa d'Azur. The extensive garden, with its lawn still green after the protracted heat of summer, was beautiful. The villa rose a pale, washed pink above the terrace.

Madame, with Celeste beside her, crossed the lawn towards the terrace steps. She had the grace of a woman and a natural vitality. There was a little air of defiance about her, as if she was ready to meet any challenge to her wisdom. Celeste sensed it. She knew it was to do with herself and her presence here.

The terrace was magnificent with its colourful tiles, its steps and its walls, its flowers and its hanging baskets. It looked out over the lawn and the deep blue of the sun-kissed Mediterranean. The vista was a grandeur, an unparalleled gift of nature. Man's handiwork in all its genius could never match such splendour.

The dry warmth pervaded the terrace, and the shutters of the villa's windows were closed to resist the infiltration of heat. The large French windows were open, however.

'Please sit down, Celeste,' said Madame. Celeste slipped into a seat beside a white ornate garden table, above which was a huge umbrella. Madame put her trug down and clapped her hands. 'Anna?' A servant appeared at the French windows. She was a stout woman with a broad homely face. Madame said something to her in a language foreign to Celeste. The servant disappeared.

'Madame, it's beautiful, your villa,' said Celeste.

'Thank you, child.' Madame's smile was warm, if a little strange and wistful. 'I shall now pray that the lemonade is not less than perfect. It wouldn't do to serve indifferent lemonade to a guest who considers my residence beautiful.'

'Oh, but—'

'Ah, you see, when I was sixteen and indifferent lemonade was served, we did not send it back, of course. Papa wouldn't have allowed us to. But the disappointment could be quite tragic.'

Celeste laughed. Madame's eyes sparkled. She saw the quick, vivid eagerness for life in the girl, the responsiveness. She removed her wide-brimmed hat, and the mass of looped auburn hair took on tints of fire in the sunlight. That light made the grey eyes so bright that there was a hint of palest blue in them. She sat down with Celeste and under the shade of the umbrella the fiery tints died and the hair softly shone.

'Madame – oh, such beautiful hair,' said Celeste, who was neither shy nor inarticulate. 'Truthfully, I'd give my fortune to have hair so lovely.'

'You have a fortune, child?' said Madame, smiling.

'I have forty francs, I think,' said Celeste.

'Yes, that's a fortune without doubt to one who is only sixteen,' said Madame. 'I had no money at all to speak of when I was your age. That is, I was never aware of having any. It seemed not to matter. I'm very aware now that money is of no consequence whatever to people who have always had too much, and that it's only the poor who are honest enough not to despise it. Ah, here is Anna with our lemonade.'

It came in a tall jug, with two glasses. Anna, clad in her black-and-white servant's habit, stood with her hands clasped at her lap as Madame poured the liquid. Slices of lemon floated. Celeste tasted the drink. It was cool and sweet, yet contained the little bite of the fruit that lingered on the palate. Madame smilingly awaited her comment.

'Oh, it's quite perfect,' said Celeste.

Madame's grey eyes again sparkled in evidence of her participation in the girl's enjoyment of life.

'You are sure, Celeste?'

'But yes, madame.'

Madame spoke to her servant, again in the language foreign to Celeste. Anna said something in return, then smiled cautiously at the girl and retired.

'Anna agrees that there are always times when the lemonade should be just right,' said Madame.

'I must confess, madame,' said Celeste ingenuously, 'that until now I've always thought lemonade was only lemonade.'

'What a discussion we're having about it,' said Madame, eyes dancing. 'But it's true, lemonade is only lemonade on ordinary occasions. It becomes memorable only when the occasion is memorable. I must tell you, Celeste, that the summers in my country aren't what they were. When I was young, the summers were such that every day was memorable, and therefore so was the lemonade – except when it was indifferent.'

Celeste laughed. Madame smiled.

'You aren't French?' said Celeste in interested enquiry.

'It isn't important, child. After all, I live in France now and am grateful—' Madame checked herself. 'It's beautiful here in the Riviera, and you are a dear girl to sit and talk with me.'

'Oh, I'm happy to have met you, madame. I've often wondered what you were like.' Celeste was not given to the art of dissembling. She still had some way to go before she was a woman. 'You've lived here two years and no one—' She stopped. One could not be inquisitive to the point of impertinence.

Madame's expression was a little rueful.

'Everyone is curious about me?' she said.

'A hundred pardons, madame. I didn't mean to—'

'No, no, it's perfectly natural,' said Madame gently. 'But I have to live a quiet life. I cannot entertain, for I've little money and I also suffer with my heart.'

Celeste found it difficult to believe that anyone who lived in such a beautiful villa could be short of money. Nor was it easy to accept that any lady with so creamy a skin and such an air of vitality could have a weak heart. But it was possible, of course.

'Madame, how sorry I am,' she said, and Madame let her lashes fall.

'It's difficult, you see, Celeste, to live as other people do, to bustle about, to entertain and participate in excitements.

One must do as one's doctor advises or become a victim of one's foolishness.'

'Oh, that's what Monsieur Somers says.'

'Who, pray, is Monsieur Somers?' asked Madame.

'An English guest of ours,' said Celeste. 'He was gassed in the war, madame, and his lungs don't permit him to endure winters in England, so he spends them with us. Mama allows him favourable terms, of course.'

'Ah, during the war I worked in a hospital, and it was so sad to see—' Again Madame checked herself. 'Continue, child.'

'He's a deserving man, madame, and very charming and kind. It's a worry, yes, that he has no wife to look after him, although he's told me he would be more of an affliction than a husband.' Celeste smiled reminiscently.

'That's very wry in a man who has breathed in poison gas, isn't it? To make jokes of that kind about himself? Men with a sense of humour are the most tolerable ones, aren't they? It's always good to laugh, Celeste, even in the company of a man with crippled lungs. He's a better man for making his jokes.'

'Oh, yes,' said Celeste with feeling.

'And you have other guests who are interesting?'

Celeste, who enjoyed observing people and talking about them, said, 'Well, there are often some ladies and gentlemen who are unattached, and one cannot help noticing how the ladies become more ladylike and how the gentlemen gradually become trapped. One follows developments as closely as one can, for it's always terribly interesting, isn't it, to watch and to wonder? One can find oneself *most* interested in a certain lady and a particular gentleman, and wonder if they're falling in love.'

Madame's laugh was rich with amusement.

'You are incurably romantic, dear child, as most of us are,' she said. 'We weave our dreams about those we observe. Do you dream, perhaps, about your charming Monsieur Somers?'

'Madame?'

Madame's smile was teasing.

'You are in love with him, perhaps, and dream of looking

after him yourself later on?'

Celeste blushed.

'But he's old enough to be my father, madame. Well, almost.'

'Ah, yes. Almost. It's a sensitive emotion, the feeling of being too young.' Madame's eyes filled with memories, and she looked like a woman who dwelt in companionship with the past. 'My own papa was – yes, a Bulgarian count and was appointed to the household of a most high and distinguished family. Naturally, I spent many hours each day with the children. There were five of them, four girls and a boy, and I was just two years younger than the eldest girl. She was the eldest, yes, but also the shyest of all of us – that is the shyest of the family. I was almost one of them, of course, for we were all very close, though I wasn't shy myself. We had such fun, such wonderful days, and when the eldest girl fell in love she was desperate to be older than sixteen. I could tell you many stories—' Madame halted.

Celeste looked up. At the open French windows of the villa stood a man, tall, bearded, and middle-aged. He was frowning.

'Your husband, madame?' asked Celeste impulsively, and then, glancing instinctively, saw that Madame wore no wedding ring.

'My doctor.' Madame's voice was a little vibrant. 'Please excuse me a moment.'

'I must go—'

'No. Please wait a moment, child,' said Madame. She rose to her feet, walked over the terrace and disappeared into the villa with the bearded man.

'This is foolishness of a mad kind, Katerina Pyotrovna.'

'It is not.' She spoke firmly and defiantly.

'I absent myself for a brief moment, to go to the village, and no sooner is my back turned than there are strangers in the place.'

'There's a young girl here, that's all. And she's hardly a stranger. Her mother owns the hotel. Boris Sergeyovich, am

I to wither away? I will if I'm to be denied all communication with people. I might as well be in a convent.'

Tall, slender and straight-backed, chin high, she was in elected confrontation with the bearded man. And he, for all his severe reproach, was in admiration of her.

'Residence in a convent can be arranged, as you know,' he said, 'and indeed was suggested years ago.'

'I do not have the disposition to make a suitable nun.'

'Countess—'

'I'm not a countess, I'm a nobody.'

'You are not,' said Boris Sergeyovich Kandor.

'I'm a nobody turning into a cabbage. Is there a more dreadful fate?'

'Yes, Countess Katerina, there is,' he said.

She winced. Shadows darkened the clarity of her eyes.

'Boris Sergeyovich, see, I beg you – let me make a few friends, discreet friends.'

'You cannot command discretion of curious people. They will go away and talk about you. They will describe you. I'm not sure that you shouldn't dye your hair.'

'Never! Oh, don't you see, one can dispel the curiosity of people by mixing with them?'

'Madness,' said Dr Kandor. 'Am I to let you cast yourself into revelation and destruction?'

'One friend only, then,' she begged. 'The girl. She's so sweet, she has eyes so like—'

'I know her, I've seen her. As you say, her mother owns the hotel.'

'They are our closest neighbours,' she said, 'our only neighbours.'

'How did she get in?'

'The wall gate was open. I stepped outside for a moment, to look down at the beach. People are sometimes on the beach, and my eyes are hungry for any kind of people. I'm frequently of the feeling that people have disappeared from the world.'

'You should not show yourself. If you're recognised, who knows what would follow?'

'Boris Sergeyovich, you speak as if the whole world would

recognise me. But who would recognise me here, in the south of France? It's a place my family never visited.'

'That's why we thought this villa very suitable,' said Dr Kandor.

'Boris Sergeyovich?' She was wheedling, beguiling, and casting her magic over a man who she knew held her in stern but affectionate guardianship, a man who would give his life to protect her. 'One friend, please? To reject all people will invite curiosity as dangerous as accepting them all. I've been here two years and have met no one, no one.'

Dr Kandor sighed.

'One friend, then. The girl. No more. And remember, you are Bulgarian, you are Countess Katerina Pyotrovna of Varna.'

'That's what my passport says, yes. I don't find Katerina unacceptable, though my own name is very dear to me. But I will remember. And I've already told Celeste I live quietly because of my weak heart.'

'Yes, that is what I tell people myself when I can't avoid questions. Looking at you, I wonder, however. A weak heart?' He took her wrist and felt her pulse. 'Katerina Pyotrovna, you are an abundance of health.'

'My incurable affliction is loneliness,' she said.

'The girl may visit every two weeks.'

'Every week,' she said.

'Every two weeks.'

'Am I to decide nothing for myself?'

'It's my responsibility to decide what is best for you,' he said, 'as other men must decide what is best for the scattered ones. You are precious to us, all of you. It's the only way, this way, to keep you separated and therefore safe. I must obey orders and so must you, for your own sake and the sake of those you love. Discovery of one will provoke a search for all.'

'It's safe, Boris Sergeyovich, but it isn't quite the same as being alive. However, you've made a concession and I'm grateful. I'll tell Celeste she may visit once a week.'

'Katerina Pyotrovna—'

'I'm not Katerina Pyotrovna,' she said with a flash of imperiousness.

'You are to all who have ears. It's the only name I must ever call you, whether we are alone or not alone. Your young friend, then, tell her she may visit.'

'Once every two weeks,' she conceded.

'Yes.' He smiled. 'To prevent you turning into a cabbage.'

She went outside to tell Celeste.

Celeste, having finished her account of her first meeting with Madame, who had declared herself to be Countess Katerina Pyotrovna of Bulgaria, waited for Edward to comment. She had told him, the previous year, of the mysterious lady who had come to live at the Villa d'Azur, but never appeared, never went to the village and never entertained.

'One thing is certain, my angel,' said Edward. 'You've described her perfectly. I cherish the aptitude of your tongue. Yes, she does have magnificent auburn hair, beautiful grey eyes and captivating grace.'

'M'sieur?' said Celeste.

'I too have met her, only half an hour ago,' said Edward, and told her of the incident.

'A running man who was fired at?' Celeste was incredulous.

'The shot was aimed over his head, I think. To warn him off, I imagine.'

'And you saw her? She was outside the villa?'

'In the little pine wood that stands between the road and the walls around the villa. But she wasn't carrying a rifle.'

'I simply can't think why anyone would use a rifle so dangerously,' said Celeste. 'The village gendarme would be very annoyed, and it wouldn't do the Countess's weak heart much good, would it?'

'No, it wouldn't,' said Edward, 'and there speaks the uncluttered mind of the young. Adults dissemble. Young and innocent angels never do. But it's mysterious, isn't it?'

'I'm quite fraught with curiosity,' said Celeste. 'Do you think her beautiful, m'sieur?'

'I think her quite the most beautiful woman I've ever seen.'

Celeste smiled. She was most anxious to find a wife for

him. She was sure that the Countess, for all her weak heart, would be a delight to Edward.

'I may tell her that?' she said. 'I'm visiting tormorrow. Mama allows me time off every fortnight to spend an afternoon with her. She has told me so many stories of the years she spent with the children of the high and illustrious family her father served.'

'You haven't said which family this was. The Bulgarian royal family?'

'Oh, for the sake of discretion, she won't say,' said Celeste. 'It might have been a royal family, yes, and one perhaps which is in exile now.'

'In return for the stories she tells you,' said Edward, 'you tell her stories about us?'

'Us, m'sieur?'

'Your guests,' smiled Edward.

Celeste blushed.

'Oh, never malicious, m'sieur, I assure you,' she said. 'But I must tell her about Madame Knight and Colonel Brecht.'

'I know that English lady. She's been coming here for the last three or four years. But who is Colonel Brecht?'

'Oh, he's a German officer, and it's his first visit here. You'll be able to see how proud and polite they are with each other, and yet he looks at her when he thinks she's unaware, and she casts her eyes at him in the same way. It's so intriguing, oh, yes.'

'I may not see them as you see them, terrible infant,' said Edward.

'Alas, that's because you're a man,' said Celeste. He laughed, and his thin face took on some reflection of the bright, vigorous handsomeness she was sure it had shown before he inhaled poison gas. And Celeste decided that if he had found no wife by the time she was eighteen, she herself must contrive to marry him. The decision induced warm pleasure. 'M'sieur, I must return to my work.'

'You must, or I shall have your mother beating me over the head.'

'As if she'd do that. Sometimes, m'sieur, you are very amusing.'

'You're always delicious,' said Edward.

'I do my best,' said Celeste. 'M'sieur, we are friends, you and I?'

'I like to think we shall always be friends.'

'Then—' For once Celeste was hesitant. 'Then when we're together, may I – do you think I might call you Edward? Not before guests, of course, only when we're together.'

'Since I've always called you Celeste and never mademoiselle, and since we're such good friends, why not?'

'I am so glad,' said Celeste, and kissed his cheek with warm impulsiveness. But one must begin to take steps, she thought, if one was thinking about marrying a man. Of course, if he and the Countess – yes, that would be wonderful.

Katerina Pyotrovna sat at her dressing-table. Outside, the night was flooded with silver. A single light only, that from her bedside table lamp, cast its glow over her bedroom. The reflection of her face in the mirror was shadowed. The hairbrush in her hand was still.

One clung to life, even when life was so empty. Because there were always memories, she was never completely divorced from what life could offer. She thought of those she loved. She thought every day of them. Her mind turned on the man she had seen, the man who appeared so quietly out of nowhere, with his face lean and drawn, and his eyes very intent. He had looked at her and the pine wood had suddenly become a place of breathless silence for long moments. Then he had smiled and spoken of the rifle shot.

Boris Sergeyovich had fired that shot, to warn off a creeping intruder. Boris, seeing him from a distance, had gone to get his rifle. The intruder, knowing himself discovered a minute later, had run, with Boris in pursuit. Boris had been furious with himself afterwards. It had been the impulse of a fool, he said, to loose off a shot. And he had not been very pleased with her for venturing into the wood.

The other intruder, the man with brown eyes and a fine, firm mouth, was not a creeper. He came like a brightness into her mind. Such a man would be so interesting to know and to talk to. He had smiled, and his smile had shed the lines from his face. She felt sad. He represented only a moment of time, a moment that had come and gone. Boris had carefully followed him, had seen him climb into a car and drive away, and had concluded he was merely a motorist who, having heard the shot, had stopped to investigate and then retreated from her confined world to return to his limitless one.

Celeste was coming tomorrow. That was a sweet something. She loved the girl. She would talk to her about the man, and Celeste would weave an imaginative story about him, and they would laugh together.

But she still felt sad, and very lonely.

4

He had retired early last night, after meeting the other guests before taking dinner. Tired after his three-day journey, he had slept well. He had done a small amount of writing after breakfast, and this afternoon he had his work on the table by the summerhouse, his pencil between his fingers. He always wrote his rough drafts in pencil, his finished drafts in ink. For once, the pencil was indeterminate. It idled. He lacked concentration. His mind was not attuned to the first battle of Ypres. His mind was on a woman of singular enchantment. A Bulgarian countess, Celeste had said. He had never met any Bulgarians, but he imagined the women to be broad-faced and Slavonic, not slender, elegant and breathtaking.

It was warm again today, the French Riviera basking in its sunny autumn, and conditions could not have been better for the completion of a chapter. But her image was a floating disturbance.

'Herr Somers, do I interrupt you?'

The voice was deep, the accented English slightly guttural. Edward looked up. Colonel Franz Brecht, stalwart and upright, a retired forty-five-year-old officer of the Brandenburg Grenadiers, and still an inveterate user of a monocle, smiled enquiringly down at him. Edward had met him last night and they had exchanged a few civil words, then several friendly ones.

'Since I haven't written a thing yet, no, you're not interrupting me, Colonel Brecht.'

'Ah, a few moments together, then?' said Colonel Brecht.

'By all means.'

The handsome, stiff-haired German took a seat. He viewed the garden with approval and then turned interested eyes on Edward.

'One cannot complain,' he said.

'One doesn't, I hope, when one is fortunate enough to be able to spend time here.'

'True,' said Colonel Brecht. 'But other people do, poor devils.'

'The unemployed?' said Edward. Unemployment was rife all over Europe. Britain and France, the victorious nations, were suffering almost as much as Germany, the vanquished.

'They have good reason to complain,' said the Colonel. 'It's a damned disgrace, the inability of governments to find work for the men who survived the war. You spoke last night of the work your government has given you. May I ask what you are writing about now?'

'The first battle of Ypres, from 19 October to 22 November 1914,' said Edward.

'The nineteenth?' Colonel Brecht screwed in his monocle. 'You must forgive me, Herr Captain—'

'I'm no longer a captain.'

'Ah, so? But active or retired, your rank applies.'

'It's not important,' said Edward.

'It is an honour to know a man, Herr Captain, who was once my opponent.' The German was distinctly a gentleman of military form. 'But may I point out, in respect of the first battle of Ypres, that our Fourth Army, commanded by the

Duke Albert of Württemberg, had already begun its advance on 18 October, and our Sixth Army, under Crown Prince Ruprecht of Bavaria, was already making its initial feint.'

'Your English is superb, Colonel, your memory faultless,' smiled Edward. 'However, I'm writing this strictly from the British angle. All events and movements prior to the nineteenth have been covered by a separate account. My terms of reference compel me to begin with the commencement of the battle which, as far as we were concerned, did not open until the nineteenth. There were no actual engagements on the eighteenth.'

'You don't consider an advance into a tactical position part of a battle?' asked Colonel Brecht.

'Oh, yes. Battle preliminaries can't be discounted. I am, however, commissioned only to cover the opening of the battle proper, and to continue until it ended on 22 November.'

'You will conclude with conclusions?'

'I've not been asked to,' said Edward. 'Conclusions will come from a higher plane, but I'd only say this was the battle that led to four years of trench war.'

'The real conclusion, Herr Captain—'

'Look here,' said Edward amiably, 'since we'll see a great deal of each other here, let's dispense with formality.'

'Quite, quite,' said Colonel Brecht, and coughed. 'But let me say that I think the war hammered the heart out of the nations. France, Germany and Britain are shattered, their wealth destroyed and their people in tatters. It was not a war at all, but a suicidal madness, provoked by the warlords of Europe.'

'You sound like a Bolshevik,' said Edward.

'*Himmel*, I hope not,' said Colonel Brecht. 'However, not everything was destroyed. Look at this beautiful garden. How good it is to still be alive.'

The Colonel watched the gardener at work, filling a wheelbarrow with dead blooms and dry leaves. Something else drew his eyes, the emergence of a woman from the hotel. Her parasol floated above her handsome head. He came to his feet.

Edward, having seen the lady also, said with a smile, 'You're off?'

'Ah – yes – must leave you to your work before I become a bore.'

Aware of the majestic advance of the lady, Edward said, 'There's no need to dash off. Stay and share a pot of tea with me.'

'Good of you, but must be fair to you,' said Colonel Brecht. 'Perhaps a game of billiards this evening, after dinner?'

'A pleasure,' said Edward. The Corniche boasted a billiards room, its ancient table still remarkably playable.

'Excellent,' said Colonel Brecht and strode briskly away. Unable, however, to avoid crossing the path of the approaching lady, he halted, clicked his heels and gave her a politely stiff bow. She, in a dress of blue with a matching hat, inclined her head in gracious acknowledgement, but without stopping. The Colonel disappeared into the hotel through the open French windows of the lounge. The lady approached Edward, who was comfortably clad in a white cricket shirt and grey trousers. He came to his feet.

'Rosamund,' he said, 'what are you doing to Colonel Brecht?'

'Who is Colonel Brecht?' said Mrs Rosamund Knight. She was forty and owned an hour-glass figure of Edwardian majesty, full-bosomed and wasp-waisted. She was handsome and she was well preserved. Her husband, killed in the war, had left her comfortably off. A healthy, normal woman, she felt her bed very empty and incomplete at times, but she was not a woman to decline into apathy or self-pity. She made the most of things. She had begun to winter at the Corniche four years ago, and she and Edward knew each other well. They also liked each other. Childless, she had only her garden to provide her with a major interest, and that, when she was abroad, was efficiently taken care of by an ex-soldier who frankly would have preferred her to leave it to him all the year round. Rosamund resolutely refused to be intimidated, and throughout the spring and summer fought a running battle with the veteran of Flanders. It was a battle in which craft and subtlety were exercised by both sides, and in which most skirmishes were won by Rosamund, for to craft and subtlety she added a dash of feminine ingenuity. She was already succeeding in making Colonel Brecht pursue paths of retreat.

'He seems a decent enough fellow,' said Edward.

'Of whom are we talking now?' asked Rosamund.

'The same gentleman. The one to whom you've just given a queenly nod.'

'That was Colonel Brecht?' Rosamund looked surprised. 'Do you know, I thought I'd seen him before somewhere, but I can't recall knowing his name. Is he staying here?'

'He's been here several days, I believe,' said Edward, 'and certainly he was at dinner last night and breakfast this morning.'

'Really? One wonders,' said Rosamund, 'why Madame Michel takes in German guests. The Germans are responsible for the disastrous state of Europe. I'm amazed that any of them can visit France without being conscience-stricken at the devastation caused by their plundering armies.'

'Tut tut,' said Edward.

'Tut tut? Not at all.'

'Come now, Rosamund, the war is over and done with.'

'The consequences are still with us, Edward.'

'And with Germany too.'

'You're very charitable, you dear man,' said Rosamund. 'I'm rather unforgiving, I suppose.'

'It's understandable,' said Edward. 'Sit down, won't you, and I'll ask Madame Michel to serve us some tea.'

'How nice.' Rosamund looked pleased. She folded her parasol and sank flowingly into a chair. 'That's one of the miracles of this charming French establishment, the serving of highly creditable tea. Are you sure I'm not disturbing you? You've brought your work with you as usual, haven't you?'

'Yes, but it can wait until I'm more in the mood for it. I'm in no mood at all at the moment. Tranquillity has enervated me.'

'Then I'll impose on your kindness for a while,' said Rosamund, 'but will go as soon as my chattering begins to pain you.'

Edward went to order the tea. On his return he caught sight of the gardener. It was not old Pierre, who had worked for Madame Michel for years. It was a man with a sun-browned face and a large untidy moustache. It was, without doubt, the running man over whose head a shot had been fired.

They were drinking tea with lemon, the Countess and her friend Celeste, at the table on the terrace. The blue sea was a shimmering expanse of sunlit ripples, and the air at three thirty in the afternoon was dry and balmy.

The Countess was entertaining Celeste with an anecdote concerning the children of the illustrious family her father had served. It was one of many similar anecdotes and featured a trip in a sailing boat during a holiday at the family's mansion close to a Black Sea resort on the Bulgarian coast. The Countess called it a dacha, which Celeste thought was what the Russians called their country or seaside houses. Oh, the Bulgarians too, the Countess had said.

The little boy, Nikolai, had of course insisted on taking charge of one and all, including the Bulgarian sailor deputed to be responsible.

'One could never resist Nikolai, however,' smiled the Countess. 'We girls solemnly assured him that his sailor cap alone was a masterful headpiece of authority, signifying his command and compelling our instant obedience to his orders. He gave only one order, as it happened, and that was more of a warning than an order. "Sit down, you girls, or you'll fall overboard." I begged him not to keep repeating it, saying I was sure repetition would cause us tremulous girls to do exactly that, to fall overboard and disappear into the dread seas. We turned about after a while and came sailing merrily along adjacent to the beach, from where Mama and Papa waved to us.'

'Your mama and papa?' asked Celeste.

'Oh, mine and theirs too, my sweet. Disaster struck, naturally.'

'I know,' smiled Celeste, 'all you girls stood up to wave

back and you all fell into the sea.'

'No. Nikolai did.' The Countess laughed, her face alight at the memory. 'The sailor fished him out quite quickly. He streamed water over everyone, and we shrieked. Natasha, the youngest, told the sailor to throw him back. But Nikolai, taking his ducking very well, made the coolest comment. "Who pushed me?" he said.'

Celeste sat back and laughed, and the Countess regarded her appreciative young audience with delight.

'Oh, madame, that's so funny.'

'For days we went around asking the same question of the heavens. "Who pushed Nikolai?" And Natasha would cry, "He wasn't pushed, he fell from grace." You are laughing, Celeste? Yes, it was very funny.'

'There's always much to laugh about or to interest one,' said Celeste. 'A gentleman who was a German officer during the war is staying with us for the first time. He's been with us a week. There's also an English lady. Like Mama, she was widowed by the war. She and the German officer, Colonel Brecht, are so polite and distant with each other that I'm full of quivers, for I'm sure one or the other will depart from our doors in a sudden rush of disdain. But then – oh, it is very piquant, madame – they cast many glances at each other.'

'Furtively?' said the Countess.

'Oh, furtively beyond question, madame. Do you think that means they're secretly taken with each other?'

'We must hope so, Celeste, indeed we must. There's no joy in life for the observer unless he or she can see romance lurking.'

'People are so interesting,' said Celeste, and slipped in a casual rider. 'Monsieur Somers is as interesting as anyone. He arrived yesterday, and as usual is staying until April.'

'I think you've mentioned the gentleman before, yes?' said the Countess.

'He's the Englishman who was gassed in the war,' said Celeste, and could not hold back what she really wanted to impart. 'He's immensely impressed.'

'I'm sure he is, my sweet. You're a delightful girl, and now that you've left school may count yourself a young lady. Let me see, I think you said he was almost old enough to be your father. Almost is the important word. Celeste, I think you're in love.'

'Oh, no, madame, it's you he was impressed with,' said Celeste.

The Countess's fine eyes opened wide.

'Me, child? He's impressed with me?'

'Immensely.'

The Countess laughed.

'I'm enchanted, naturally, to know this,' she said, 'but must confess I can't think how I impressed him, for I've never met the gentleman.'

'But you have, madame,' said Celeste, 'you met each other yesterday, and he recognised you.'

'Recognised me?' The Countess sat straight up, her grey eyes startled, her face registering shock. Her voice vibrating, she said, 'Recognised me? What are you saying, dear child?'

'I was telling him about you after he arrived yesterday,' said Celeste, wondering why Madame was actually agitated, 'and he said oh, yes, he had met you only half an hour before. He recognised my description of you.'

The Countess let out a long sigh and her taut body relaxed. Interest of a very feminine kind gladly took the place of shock.

'He was wearing a tweed suit and cap, Celeste? He's a little thin, with brown eyes?'

'Yes, madame,' said Celeste. Her elegant friend had requested her not to call her Countess, just madame. One usually only called a married lady madame, but mademoiselle would not quite have suited the Countess.

'So he's Edward Somers, your most cherished winter guest, and the one you sigh about, my sweet?'

'Oh, I only sigh because he has no wife to care for him.' Celeste by now had matched Edward and the Countess, and whether a wife with a weak heart could look after a husband with infirm lungs did not seem too important.

'Celeste,' smiled the Countess, 'he did not to me look like a man who is going to fall into disuse and die of self-neglect. Quite the reverse. You know, people who feel sorry for themselves look sorry for themselves. Monsieur Somers did not seem at all in need of care or pity.'

'No, madame,' said Celeste, 'but it's a shame he—'

'My sweet,' said the Countess gently, 'you must take care or you'll go through life shouldering the worries of everyone you like, and your shoulders will bend under the burden and your bones will crack, one by one. You must avoid the pain that will give you.' She paused, took up her glass of tea in its silver container and sipped it. 'Tell me, why was he immensely impressed with me? Was it to do with my unsurpassable beauty?'

'Yes.'

'Celeste, I was joking.'

'I know, but all the same, Edward said you were the most beautiful woman he'd ever seen.'

The Countess put her tea down and her lashes fell to hide her eyes.

'That was a rather hasty judgement, wasn't it?' she said.

'Oh, I don't think so,' said Celeste. 'I don't think he would make hasty judgements of that kind. It's the first time I've ever heard him speak like that about any lady. He's more inclined to say ladies are dear creatures, without whom men would find life very dull, though rather more peaceful—'

'Oh, the wretch!' But the Countess laughed. 'There, now you've intrigued me very much. You've made him sound the kind of man who would provoke conversation quite stimulating. But I must ask you, is he given to exaggerations? I can't believe I can possibly be the most beautiful woman he's ever seen.'

'Well, that's what he said,' smiled Celeste, 'and he was most definite.'

'Heavens,' said the Countess lightly, 'we can only assume he's seen very few. He hasn't, for instance, seen the daughters of the family I've spoken about so much. Now there were young ladies truly beautiful – Irina, Louisa, Nadia and Natasha. Perhaps Natasha didn't quite have the classical beauty of her sisters, but she made up for this by being an incorrigible show-off.'

'I suppose you have photographs of them, madame?' said

Celeste.

The Countess examined the glittering reflection of the sun on the rippling sea. She appeared to find it dazzling, for she shaded her eyes with her hand.

'No, I've no photographs, Celeste.'

'Oh, it doesn't matter,' said Celeste, 'for I think my friend Edward has made up his mind that you stand alone.'

'Ah, he has now become Edward and not Monsieur Somers?'

'It's because we're old friends. Madame, is it possible you'd allow me to bring him next time I visit you? I'm sure he'd be very happy to meet you formally.'

'No, dear child.' The Countess looked rueful. 'No, I can't receive people.' She turned her eyes on the sea again to hide the longing, the longing to have friends, to enjoy company. She was basically an extrovert, loving light and colour and conversation. 'I'm sorry, Celeste. Oh, I couldn't do without your visits, I look forward to them so much. But I must do without visits from others.'

Celeste found it difficult to understand why a woman who seemed to have so much vitality could have a heart so weak that she was unable to receive more than one visitor a fortnight.

'I'll say nothing to him, madame. I haven't mentioned I would ask you.'

'You're very sweet, Celeste.'

Celeste bumped into Edward when she returned to the hotel. Her entrance into the garden coincided with his retirement from it, a portfolio under his arm. His eyes brightened. He had a warm affection for the French girl, who gave him a great deal of care and attention, all of which he frankly enjoyed.

'A happy visit, Celeste?' he said.

'Oh, yes. She's always so sweet to me. M'sieur, what a shame she has a weak heart. It prevents her receiving and entertaining. I'm sure she would like to fill her villa with people sometimes.'

'She looked radiant with health to me, but I suppose that doesn't necessarily mean she's as vital as Diana.'

'Diana? Who is Diana?' Celeste was sure she wouldn't like her, whoever she was.

'The Roman goddess, the huntress.'

'I am astonished, m'sieur, that you can compare Madame the Countess with a marble statue.'

'A hideous blunder, Celeste, but one can't always be brilliant.'

'Oh, we all have our uninspired moments,' said Celeste. 'I have to tell you that at the end of my visit Madame asked me to give you her compliments. She also ventured to suggest your judgement is a little faulty.'

'Really? Enlighten me, my angel. What faulty judgement have I made?'

'Well, she's sure you're quite mistaken in thinking her as beautiful as you said.'

Edward shook his head at her.

'Oh, you terrible infant,' he said, 'you shouldn't pass on remarks of a highly personal nature. Think of the red face of embarrassment.'

'But no woman would be embarrassed at hearing a man has been deeply affected by her beauty,' said Celeste. 'Her sensitive soul would be touched.'

'What about my sensitive soul and my embarrassment? And what do you mean, deeply affected? Now what are you imagining, you imp of the heavens?'

'Nothing, m'sieur, nothing at all.'

Edward smiled at her demure look.

'Celeste, what's happened to Pierre, your gardener?'

'Oh, he's retired, Edward.' His name came blithely to her lips. 'We've a new gardener. Gregory. He's a White Russian, and has been with us for two months. Mama is most pleased with him. Poor Pierre grew too gnarled and bent for the work, and retired quite happily.'

'I see,' said Edward. 'Well, I miss old gnarled and bent Pierre, and whenever you see him in the village, tell him so. What does he enjoy most in his retirement?'

'His pipe and tobacco,' said Celeste.

'Then I'll walk into the village and buy some.'

'I'll ask Mama if I can come with you,' said Celeste.

'I shall enjoy your company,' said Edward. He did not tell her that the new gardener, Gregory, was the running man. The matter was something to be thought about, for it did seem as if there was a mystery indeed surrounding the exquisite woman who could not receive visitors and whose villa was guarded by a high wall.

'M'sieur—'

'Celeste, your Countess has a companion, hasn't she? A dark, bearded man?'

'He's her doctor.'

'Her own personal physician?'

'Yes.'

'I've heard of royalty having personal physicians attached to their households, but not countesses.'

'It's pleasing to know you're so interested in Madame,' said Celeste.

'Boris Sergeyovich?'

Dr Boris Kandor eyed Katerina Pyotrovna with the wariness of a man who knew her strengths and his own weaknesses. He knew her resilience, her resolution and her beguilement. Her smile at times was enough to melt the walls of Troy. She had been spirited and fascinating as a girl, the most fearless of the daughters. As a woman she was a superb creature. And she was right in what she so often said. She would wither away without doubt unless she was fulfilled. But how could she find fulfilment unless she went into the world outside? And if she did that the world would come to know her and she would lose her beautiful head. Her enemies would lop it off.

'You're going to ask me to make another concession, Katerina Pyotrovna.'

'I only wish to have one more friend,' she said, 'only one more. Then I'll ask for nothing else.'

'Life is sweet, even for people in our situation,' said Dr Kandor. 'We're locked away, yes, but not in a grey prison or a hovel. We have a house, a sky and a sun. Neither of us would willingly exchange this for a running troika, a frozen trail and the sounds of the red wolves. So, one more friend, that's what you wish now. And next month, another one?'

'No,' she said, 'I promise. Let me have two friends, sweet Celeste and an English officer, crippled by the war.'

'What mad request is this?'

'It isn't madness, dear friend and protector. Nor do you think so. You're frowning because you want to hide your pleasure in the idea. You remember Riga and the British warship which took us and other refugees aboard, risking the lives of their sailors to save so many of us from the Bolsheviks. You've had a soft spot for the British since then.'

'For their brave sailors,' muttered Dr Kandor. 'Who is this English officer? Have you met him? If so, how?'

'Oh, Boris Sergeyovich, shame on you to imply that during your occasional absences I venture to creep out of this place to meet people.' Katerina Pyotrovna shook her head. 'You know that isn't true.'

'You ventured outside yesterday.'

'But not behind your back. And only to take a little walk in the wood. You were there too.'

'I was there, yes,' said the doctor, 'but not with you. I was on the track of a prying man, whom I'm still uneasy about.'

'We mustn't quarrel about it,' she said. 'The English officer is a guest at the hotel, and Celeste's most cherished friend. He was gassed in the war. That's dreadful, isn't it?'

'Not as dreadful as a prowler who might have been prowling because he's an agent of your enemies. If they suspect you're here, if he was trying to get a good look at you—'

'He did not get a good look,' she said, 'he saw nothing of me. I concealed myself as soon as I glimpsed him. Boris Sergeyovich, you'll permit Celeste to bring her English friend, won't you? He's only staying at the hotel for the winter. He'll come, and then go. So one more friend, please, just one?'

It was not wholly a wish for another friend, he thought. There was something else, something perhaps to do with the longing of a woman who had never known the love of a man.

That was dangerous. But she had been denied ordinary communication with people for years. An Englishman with crippled lungs, a friend of the entirely charming young French girl, perhaps that need not be very dangerous.

'I must protect you, Katerina Pyotrovna, yes,' he said, 'but can't bring myself to starve you. It's I who have a weak heart, not you. But you've never asked for the impossible, nor made my responsibilities too difficult, although sometimes I've suffered a little worry. Very well, invite him to call. In two days. With the girl.'

Her expressive eyes were quite moist with gratitude.

'I'm sure it will not put me at risk,' she said. 'I'm sure we're sometimes too sensitive about the dangers of recognition. There can only be a few people outside our own country who know me.'

'Our sensitivity, Katerina Pyotrovna, is something that tells us the world can be a very small one at times.'

'Yes, I agree,' she said, 'but I am in need of friends, friends who will be a pleasure to me, not a danger. These two friends, Celeste and the Englishman.'

'Merely a pleasure?' he said, watching her.

'That is all,' said Katerina Pyotrovna. But her heart and her blood were already affected, and had Dr Kandor felt her pulse at that moment, he would have found a flutter, a flutter that had nothing to do with physical weakness, but with emotion.

A note arrived at the hotel, delivered by a servant and addressed to Mlle Celeste Michel.

Dear Celeste, I am happy to tell you that Dr Kandor has diagnosed an improvement in my condition. Therefore, if you wish, you may bring Monsieur Somers to see me in two days' time, on Thursday at two thirty. I hope your mama will be able to spare you the time. I shall not assume that Monsieur Somers has nothing else to do, of course, but if he would like to call then I shall receive both of you with pleasure. I am, your most affectionate friend, Katerina Pyotrovna.

5

The click of billiard balls made Rosamund Knight open the door and walk in. At the table, Colonel Brecht was practising a few shots. He straightened up. Rosamund, gowned in shimmering green, was not disposed to retreat.

'Good evening, Colonel Beck,' she said.

The Colonel coughed.

'Ah, good evening, madame. It's – ah – Brecht, Colonel Brecht.' He made a stiff bow.

'I'm sorry to have disturbed you,' she said.

'No – not at all – I am waiting for Herr Somers.'

Edward appeared then. His dinner jacket was sleek on his lean frame. He smiled at Rosamund, full-bosomed in her gown and her bare shoulders lightly powdered. She looked extremely handsome.

'Rosamund, you're here to play billiards?' said Edward.

'I looked in,' she said.

Colonel Brecht cleared his throat.

'Naturally, if you'd like a cue—?' It was an awkward invitation.

'You've arranged a game with Colonel Beck?' she enquired of Edward.

'An after-dinner perambulation at slow speed around the table to a hundred up,' said Edward, 'but if you'd care to take alternate shots with me, then do join us.' He whispered in her ear, 'Brecht, Rosamund, not Beck.'

'I'll watch, if I may,' said Rosamund.

'But do you play?'

'A little,' she smiled. 'My husband taught me.'

'Good,' said Edward, 'then you shall play the winner. Are you game?'

Rosamund's smile was a little wicked. She essayed a glance at Colonel Brecht. He was standing at attention, eyes fixed on the tip of his cue.

'If that's agreeable to both of you, I accept,' she said.

The German took a silk handkerchief from the inside pocket of his dinner jacket and courteously dusted a chair for her close to the scoreboard. She murmured polite thanks, then sat with her eyes on the green baize of the table.

Colonel Brecht broke off, leaving his white and the red in baulk, close together. Edward very neatly brought his ball back up the table, hit the red and gently kissed the white.

'Bravo,' said Rosamund.

Colonel Brecht coughed. Edward smiled. Rosamund, who knew gentlemen did not encourage comments from spectators, gazed innocently into nowhere. Edward made a break of nineteen. Rosamund rose and put up his score. Colonel Brecht retaliated with a break of twelve. Edward, pacing himself, chalked up a dawdling eleven. Colonel Brecht failed. Edward failed. The Colonel, concentrating, put some neat cannons together, plus a couple of reds, and compiled a useful twenty-six. Rosamund kept the scoreboard moving. Edward executed a difficult in-off red that made Rosamund call bravo again. Colonel Brecht raised his eyebrows. Rosamund looked at her feet, and Edward suddenly realised that for all her Edwardian majesty she had an impish streak. She was teasing Franz Brecht, and Franz was shuffling his feet.

Edward's score advanced to ninety-three. Colonel Brecht, with a break of twenty-three, advanced to ninety-seven. Edward collected two cannons, fluffed a third and left the German with an easy red to put down for the game. It lay only three inches from a corner pocket. But the Colonel's shot was a disaster. The red, limply struck, hit the corner of the pocket and gently rolled back in much the same position.

Edward, left with three balls in line, tried a cannon off the cushion, striking the Colonel's ball first. It failed. Again Colonel Brecht was left with an easy red to pocket. Again he missed. Rosamund emitted a delicate cough. Colonel Brecht, slightly flushed, stood back. Edward smiled. He was on to the German now. Franz Brecht was backing away from the prospect of taking on the intimidating Rosamund. The retired soldier was actually shy. Edward felt he must tell Celeste. He and Celeste enjoyed a good gossip.

He himself only needed to put the red down for the game. But his white was closed off from the red, as it had been before. He made his shot, striking the Colonel's ball just enough to send it so close to the red that it was simply not possible for the German to miss putting it down this time.

'*Himmel*,' breathed the Colonel, 'was that a shot, my friend?'

'Yes, a badly played one,' said Edward. 'It's left you with a sitter.'

With an air of resignation, Colonel Brecht pocketed the red.

'Well played,' said Rosamund. She rose coolly to her feet and selected a cue from the rack. 'I now have the honour, sir?' she said to the Colonel.

'Ah – you need not feel you must,' he said.

'In honour, sir, I'm committed,' said Rosamund.

Edward was fascinated. Damned if Celeste isn't right, he thought, damned if these two aren't actually taken with each other. The atmosphere between them was positively electric. Extraordinary.

'Well, it's worked out well enough for me,' he said. 'I need a rest.'

Colonel Brecht cleared his throat. Rosamund chalked her cue. Politely, the German offered her the choice of plain or spot white. Rosamund chose spot and broke off, handling her cue smoothly and leaving the red and white generously positioned for her opponent to open his account with a cannon. He bent stiffly to the task of consolidation, but lost himself with some uncertain cue work when his score was ten. Edward sensed he was a bundle of nerves. Poor old devil, there he was, a retired bachelor with a distinguished war record, and as sensitive as a wallflower in the presence of the composed Rosamund. Perhaps he had been glad to hide himself away from women in the Brandenburg Grenadiers. Up against an English war widow in a game of billiards, he was flushed and awkward, but full of glances.

Rosamund was obviously aware of it. From a civil, polite and distant attitude, she had advanced to the attack. She moved handsomely around the table, her green gown clasping her figure, and Edward saw that the Colonel hardly knew where to look as, bending over her cue, she displayed the deep valley of a most noble bosom. And she was no mean exponent of the game, specialising in dropping her ball in-off the red with smooth efficiency. And from time to time both balls disappeared into the corner pockets.

'Well played, madam.' The Colonel made the comment a little hoarsely as her score reached fifty, while his was only twenty-nine. Rosamund, finishing her break, left him well positioned. He gathered himself together and set about redeeming himself. Edward watched with glimmers of pleasure in his eyes. Rosamund was quite the coolest of women, the handsome Colonel tugging at his moustache between shots.

The scores advanced. When Rosamund was eighty-one, her opponent was seventy-two. She approached the table, bent over her cue, causing the Colonel to hastily lift his eyes elsewhere, and smoothly proceeded to reel off six in-offs in succession. That put her score on ninety-nine.

Now what? thought Edward. Is she going to demoralise him?

She missed her next shot.

'Good gracious,' she said.

'Bad luck,' said Edward. She glanced at him and caught the smile on his face.

'It's hardly a matter for levity, Edward,' she said.

'I agree. There's thunder and lightning in the air.'

'Thunder and lightning?' said Rosamund. 'It's only a game of billiards.' She caught the Colonel's eye. He was waiting politely for the conversation to finish. 'Pray proceed, sir,' she said.

'Thank you,' said Colonel Brecht. He ran up a break of twenty-one, bringing his total to ninety-three. But Rosamund only needed to score to win the game. The red ball was nicely placed for her to execute one of her fluent in-offs. Much to Edward's amusement, she elected to go for a cannon instead, a much more difficult shot. She played it well, however. Her ball struck the white firmly, and with topspin applied glided on, narrowly passing the red.

'Well played,' said Colonel Brecht, 'and thank you, madam, for an excellent game.'

'No, I missed the cannon,' said Rosamund.

She could, thought Edward, have easily pocketed her ball off the red. She might have got the cannon. Instead, she had missed it with beautiful finesse. Damn me, he thought, if she isn't going to let him beat her.

'Your ball just stroked the red,' said the Colonel.

'No, no,' said Rosamund, 'it missed.'

'I'm happy to concede the cannon,' he murmured.

'We'll refer to Mr Somers,' said Rosamund. 'Edward, was it a cannon or not?'

Edward, frankly keen to see how they would resolve it themselves, said, 'It may have been, it may not have been. It was all too much of a whisker for me, and I declare myself undecided.'

'Very well,' said Rosamund smoothly, 'I claim a miss. It's your shot, Colonel Beck.'

'Ah – I—'

'Please proceed,' said Rosamund.

The Colonel gave in and with the balls nicely set up rattled off three cannons. Edward sat rooted, for they were both on ninety-nine now. And damned if the Colonel didn't miss his next shot, a simple pot.

Rosamund gazed in haughty disbelief at him as he straightened up. He coughed. Edward laughed. The Colonel tugged his moustache. Rosamund's proud bosom quivered.

'You're laughing, Edward,' she said.

'I should think I am,' said Edward. 'Why not call it an honourable draw?'

'If Colonel Beck—'

'Now, Rosamund.' Edward's smile was reproving.

'Names confuse me,' said Rosamund, 'but very well, if Colonel Brecht is willing to call it a draw, so am I.'

'Yes, yes, of course,' said the Colonel, tugging his

moustache. 'Thank you for the game, madam. Ah – would you care – may I suggest a cognac for all of us in the lounge?'

'You're very kind,' said Rosamund, 'but if you'll excuse me, gentlemen, I shall now retire to my bed. Goodnight.' She picked up her evening bag and sailed in splendour from the room.

Colonel Brecht took his handkerchief out and dabbed his brow.

'Heavens,' he said.

'The ice is broken,' said Edward, 'do you realise that?'

'I realise it all too well, my friend, for I'm sinking beneath it. What an extraordinary woman.'

'Magnificent,' said Edward. 'Noble.'

'Ah, yes – quite so. Shall we enjoy a cognac, then?'

There were several other guests in the lounge, enjoying conversation. Edward and Colonel Brecht did not intrude on them. They found comfortable armchairs in the large, well-furnished room, and Celeste brought them their cognac. She slipped a note into Edward's hand. He read it. It was the little note from the Countess.

'I'm delighted, Celeste,' he said, 'please accept for me.'

'Oh, I will, m'sieur, and Mama is permitting me to go too. We aren't too busy, you see.'

There were ten guests in the hotel, a comfortable number for this time of the year.

Breakfast of rolls, croissants and coffee was served in the light and airy dining-room the following day, the tables covered with their morning cloths of white. Red tablecloths were used for dinner.

Not all guests were down yet. Present were Colonel Brecht, Edward, Rosamund, a retired American doctor, Martin K.Bush, an anonymous-looking silver-haired couple who spoke to nobody and rarely to each other, but smiled vaguely at all, and a slim, dapper man. A new guest, he was fair-haired and amiable, although his sharply-pointed nose was rather at odds with his agreeable air. Another guest entered the room, a lady in her thirties, whose silver-grey costume set off her brunette richness and put a neat, tidy outline on her figure. She glided past the dapper, eager-nosed gentleman rather as if he weren't there, but said a cheerful good-morning to everyone else. She eyed Edward with interest and selected a table next to his.

Edward gave her a smile, then returned to the notes he was scanning over his coffee. They were notes covering the first chapter of his assignment. It was time he began to seriously concentrate, to remember he was not exactly on holiday. Usually, he got down to work without difficulty. Things were a little different this year.

Celeste, coming to refill his cup, whispered to him, 'That lady is from Paris, m'sieur, and arrived last night. A designer of theatrical costumes. But I think she's looking for a little flirtation.'

'Who is?' he asked absently. 'Oh, yes.'

The lady in question, Estelle Dupont, once breakfast was served to her, consumed it with as much relish as she devoured the front page of the *Nice Gazette*. On the other side of the dining-room, Rosamund went through her meal with an air of aloof graciousness, like a woman who accepted the presence of other guests but hoped they would not spoil the moment by talking to her. She had no glances for Colonel Brecht, and for his part he too seemed solely interested in his food and coffee. Only the dapper gentleman, Monsieur Valery, appeared eager to communicate, smiling encouragingly whenever he managed to catch someone's eye.

Edward scanned on. Mademoiselle Dupont, finishing her breakfast, came to her feet and moved from her table. Edward looked up as she passed.

'Bonjour, m'sieur,' she said with a smile quite vivacious.

'Bonjour,' said Edward.

An attractive creature.

He stopped on his way back to his room five minutes later to speak to Celeste, catching her on her way from the kitchen with a fresh pot of coffee.

'Little angel and light of my life,' he said, 'you were right.'

'What about, m'sieur?'

'About Colonel Brecht and Madame Knight,' he whispered. 'She's begun a fencing match with him.'

'A fencing match?'

'Fascinating,' murmured Edward.

'You mean it's an opening engagement between two people not yet aware they're falling in love?' she whispered.

'Who knows, my infant, who knows?'

'Oh, by now I'm in a fever of interest,' she breathed.

'Let it be only a light fever,' said Edward, 'for I don't think developments are going to be too dramatic. A little delicious, perhaps, but nothing one could compare with an earthquake.'

'Oh, m'sieur,' she smiled, 'you are a lovely man.'

Edward was at work by the summerhouse twenty minutes later, the morning sunshine warm and mellow. His breathing was easy, his lungs appreciative of the clarity of the air. He concentrated successfully, perhaps because the knowledge that he had been invited to call on the Countess tomorrow had induced mental relaxation. His pencil raced over the paper. The silver-haired couple wandered out and did a quiet turn or two around the garden before disappearing. Then Rosamund emerged. She found a seat on the far edge of the lawn, where she sat reading, putting aside her hat and parasol to let the sun finger her chestnut hair.

Colonel Brecht appeared a few minutes later. Edward watched him eyeing Rosamund, deep in a book. He advanced casually in her direction. He paused midway, uncertainty taking hold of him. Rosamund looked up.

'Good morning, madam, good morning,' he said, and gazed hard at flowering shrubs.

'Good morning,' said Rosamund.

'Ah – yes,' said the Colonel, turned left and advanced on Edward. 'Another beautiful day, my friend.'

'Quite beautiful,' said Edward.

'You're writing, I see.'

'I think I should, you know. I have to earn my pay.'

'I won't interrupt,' said the Colonel. 'I'll take a brisk stroll.'

'Good idea,' said Edward. 'Ask Rosamund to go with you.'

'What? What? Heavens, you serious are?' In his agitation, Colonel Brecht fluffed the composition of his English. 'I am to be eaten alive this morning after last night making only the narrow escape?'

'Rosamund likes walking.'

'I am off,' said the Colonel and marched quickly away over the path that led around to the front of the hotel and the road. Rosamund, lifting her eyes from her book, smiled as she watched his retreat.

A wheelbarrow came into view on the path, the gardener pushing it. Edward got up and strolled over.

'Good morning, Gregory,' he said.

The gardener halted. His broad face, brown and weathered, broke into a friendly smile. His eyebrows hung bushily and his moustache needed trimming. His teeth showed pale nicotine stains.

'Good morning, m'sieur. A fine day.' His French was heavy, his voice a deep bass.

'You're new to me,' said Edward amicably.

'Yes, m'sieur.'

'You're a powerful runner,' said Edward.

'M'sieur?' Gregory did not shift his ground or lower his eyes. He merely looked puzzled.

'What happened two days ago that made you jump out in front of my car?' Edward's enquiry was friendly. 'I might have knocked you down, and that would have been very unhappy for both of us.'

'Ah, that was you, m'sieur?' Gregory shook his head. 'A close thing, yes.'

'Very. Did you go to the police, to the local gendarme?'

'M'sieur?'

'If someone fired a rifle at me, I'd certainly report it.'

'A madman, m'sieur,' said Gregory, 'but I wish for no trouble. I'm a Russian émigré, so better for me to live a quiet life, you understand. This is good work here with Madame Michel, work I like, so I keep from making trouble.'

'Yes, I see that, but why were you fired at, do you know?'

'M'sieur, on my way back from the village after ordering

potash, I entered the little wood there, just to look. A man came after me. For the sake of peace, m'sieur, I ran. Better for an émigré to run, not argue, yes?'

'You're probably right. But I wondered, of course.'

'A madman, m'sieur, that's what it was,' said Gregory.

'Then I should have run myself,' smiled Edward. 'I must say the lawn looks perfect for this time of the year.'

'Silver sand, m'sieur, that is what sharpens it and makes the grass stand up and breathe.'

'It doesn't always work like that for me at home,' said Edward amiably, as if his interest in the incident of two days ago had been superseded and dismissed.

'Ah, you must feed your grass first, m'sieur,' said Gregory.

'Generously, I suppose?'

'That is so, m'sieur.'

'Thank you, Gregory,' said Edward. 'What part of Russia do you come from?'

'Kiev, m'sieur. Russia is a sad country now, a sad and bitter country.'

'Yes, very sad. You don't like the Bolsheviks?'

Involuntarily, Gregory spat. Then he said, 'Your pardon, m'sieur.'

'No, I understand,' said Edward and returned to his table and his work. His breathing was a little painful. He sat back and let his body relax. The feeling of constriction often came on for no apparent reason at all. He had walked no farther than the length of a cricket pitch a few moments ago, and here he was feeling the pain in his lungs. He grimaced at the knowledge that it would be like this all his life. But he was luckier than others and could not complain. He even had a job, a fulfilling job. Some poor devils could not even rise from their chairs without going blue in the face. Poison gas. That was Satan's own brew.

'Coffee, yes, Edward?'

It was a soft whisper in his ear. He opened his eyes. Celeste was there, gently enquiring and solicitous.

'Great Scot,' he said, 'I fell asleep. In the middle of a perfect morning.'

'Only for a few minutes,' said Celeste. 'I was watching,

you see. I didn't want you to fall out of your chair. You'd like to order coffee?'

'Thank you, angel.' He looked across at Rosamund. The Frenchwoman in the silver-grey costume was sitting with her, and the two ladies were conversing loquaciously. 'Ask the ladies if they'd care to join me, Celeste.'

Celeste tripped across the lawn with the supple, rhythmic fluency of a girl destined to make heads turn in a few years' time, if not to some extent now. She spoke to the ladies, who turned their eyes on Edward.

'Thank you, dear man,' said Rosamund, 'we should love to join you.'

They drank coffee, the three of them, around the white-painted iron table. The Frenchwoman, Mademoiselle Dupont, was as vivacious as Rosamund was stately. Her conversation was about Paris and the theatre, and Edward's genuine interest was a stimulation to her. She had mobile features, her good looks a smooth ripple of activity, her teeth a repetitive flash of white between carmined lips. Rosamund made no attempt to intercede. She seemed amused by the Parisian woman's flowing monologues, all directed into Edward's ear. Everyone liked Edward. Everyone used him as a confidant. He was a kind listener. And he would have been a handsome man had his face not been so ravaged by strain and pain.

'The theatre,' said Mademoiselle Dupont, 'is more true to life than life itself, if you agree that life itself is people. In the theatre, all emotions play their part. In life, many emotions are repressed, for people generally behave not as they feel, but as they wish other people to see them. Calmness is used to hide rage, sweetness to hide malice, respectability to hide desire. Don't you agree, Monsieur Somers, that we all behave at times in a way that is a falsification of our true emotions? When one wants to scream with temper, one thinks of people regarding us in shock and horror, and so most of us, instead of screaming, go no further than looking offended.'

'It's an exercise in self-control, isn't it?' suggested Edward.

Mademoiselle Dupont's shapely round mouth opened,

and she laughed.

'Ah, you see, you are English, and use self-control to hide all your emotions.'

'One can't go around baring one's teeth and frightening little girls and small dogs,' said Edward.

'Without civilised self-control,' said Rosamund, 'we should create a jungle.'

'But it's strange, isn't it,' said Mademoiselle Dupont, 'that people go to the theatre to absorb themselves in Molière's gift for emotionalising life? Isn't it true that the English are passionately devoted to Shakespeare, whose plays are about treachery, murder, anger, revenge, love, hate and jealousy? Think of *Othello* and the sublimity of extreme, emotional jealousy.'

'I've never thought of extreme, emotional jealousy as being sublime,' said Rosamund. 'I'm sure jealousy should be repressed, not indulged. Didn't Shakespeare teach us the lesson of Iago's indulgence?'

'But how fascinating are people and their emotions,' said Mademoiselle Dupont, 'how fascinating that it is only the theatre which brings to life our darkest and most devious feelings.' She elaborated on the theme. Rosamund, sensing eyes on her back, looked round. Celeste stood at the open French windows of the lounge, and there was a perceptible frown on her face as she watched the lady from Paris monopolising Edward's ear.

The dear child is jealous, thought Rosamund. I must tactfully hint to Mademoiselle Dupont that Edward is regarded by Celeste as hers alone.

'If you two will excuse me,' she said, 'I shall go for a little walk, a short constitutional.' She rose to her feet and put up her parasol.

'Yes, do go, Rosamund,' said Edward. 'You may, with luck, bump into Franz Brecht.'

'I'm flushed with hope at the prospect,' said Rosamund. 'So nice to have talked with you, Mademoiselle Dupont. If you're here long enough, perhaps we may enjoy many conversations.'

'I'm not sure how long I shall stay,' smiled Mademoiselle

Dupont. 'A week, perhaps, or two. It will depend on Paris. But it's so enchanting here that I'm tempted to stay indefinitely.'

'How nice,' said Rosamund and sailed away, a blue dress gracing her handsome figure. She smiled as Celeste approached.

'Take care, my dear,' she murmured, 'Mademoiselle Dupont is already beginning to smother him.'

'Oh, what is she up to?' said Celeste, eyes flashing. 'All that energy and all those words. She's pouring herself all over him and will tire him into distressed frailty.'

'Distressed frailty? How imaginative,' said Rosamund and sailed on. She made her way to the road. She crossed it and took the winding path that led down to the beach. It was very narrow, and at one point there was simply no room to pass Colonel Brecht when he appeared on his way up. He halted, tall, broad and upright.

'Ah,' he said and fixed his blue eyes on her parasol.

'Ah?' enquired Rosamund.

'You are going down to the beach, madam?'

'I was,' said Rosamund. 'I'm at a full stop now.'

'*Himmel*,' breathed the Colonel, 'a fool I am.' He stood aside, pressing himself against the brown rocky outcrop. 'Your pardon, dear lady – dear madam – ah – madam.'

'The beach,' said Rosamund.

'A splendid tonic, madam. The air is like wine down there, the wine of the sea.'

'The wine of the sea?' Rosamund smiled. 'Are you referring, sir, to Homer's wine-dark sea?'

'Madam?' Colonel Brecht was cautious.

'You haven't read Homer? Your arm, sir, if you'll be so good, and you shall escort me down this trembling, dangerous path, and we'll breathe in the wine of the sea together.'

'Good God,' said the astonished Colonel. The path was a winding one, yes, but by no means dangerous.

'Sir, your arm,' said Rosamund with all the flair of a true Edwardian gentlewoman, although she was hard put to it to hide her amusement.

'A pleasure, madam, a pleasure.' What else could the floundering Colonel say?

'I trust so,' said Rosamund.

The path widened a little. They proceeded to negotiate it together, her hand light on his arm, her parasol shading them both. The sea was a shimmer of light, the air touched by the faintest of breezes.

'A beautiful day,' said Colonel Brecht.

'How fortunate we are,' murmured Rosamund, 'although privilege is an uncomfortable garment in a world of misery. But one must wear it bravely and without hypocrisy. What would happen if, driven by conscience, I cast mine off? A thousand shameless people would rush to pick it up.'

'True, madam, yes, true.' The Colonel guided her slowly round a corner, Rosamund in her white shoes picking her way carefully. 'One must, however, do what one can to raise the lot of the poor.'

'Your English is so good, sir, that we are actually holding a positive conversation.'

'The leg is being pulled, madam?' said the Colonel.

'I'm a little disgraceful at times,' murmured Rosamund.

'You are a very good billiards player.'

'I'm delighted to hear it, Colonel Brecht. What woman could wish for sweeter praise?'

'You use your cue most efficiently, most.'

'Oh, pray continue,' said Rosamund, 'I'm enthralled.'

The scent of wild shrubs and aromatic lavender, sharpened by the clean air and the light breeze, was a fragrance that invested the walk with enchantment. It made Colonel Brecht sigh, and his sigh made Rosamund smile.

They reached the beach. Its sand was golden. A man and a woman were disporting in the sea, their cotton bathing suits glistening.

'I must try that while the weather remains warm,' said the Colonel.

'I too am tempted,' said Rosamund.

'You have brought your costume, madam?'

'I always do. I've always managed to take a dip once or twice during October.'

'Ah,' said the Colonel, and emitted another sigh. The thought of Rosamund Knight clad in a bathing costume, her abundance at the mercy of clinging wet cotton—

'*Himmel*,' he breathed.

'Colonel Brecht?'

'One's imagination soars, madam.'

'Really? At what?'

'At such beauty,' he said, observing the laughing, splashing couple, the golden sands and the brilliant sea.

Rosamund smiled. She was ahead of the Colonel, for her imagination was far more comprehensive than his.

6

Lunch had been delicious. So much so that Edward felt he needed exercise.

'Celeste, I'm trying a walk to the village to get that pipe and tobacco for old Pierre.'

'Oh, you must wait,' said Celeste from behind her reception desk. 'I must ask Mama to let me go with you.'

'I think I can manage, my infant, and your mama has already given you time off for our visit to your Countess tomorrow.'

'Please wait, m'sieur,' said Celeste, quite set on the pleasure of walking with him. She flew to the little room which was her mother's hotel office, with its escritoire and its pen and ink. She rejoined Edward a few minutes later, wearing an outdoor frock and a straw hat. 'Mama has said everything must be done to accommodate you, even to the extent of parting with her valuable daughter for an hour.'

'Your mother is an institution of benevolence,' said Edward. 'We'll bring her back a box of nougat.'

'We're going to shower your money about?' said Celeste,

then spoke to Jacques, telling him she would be back in an hour and to refer any enquiries to her mother.

'No money will be wasted,' said Edward as he and Celeste left the hotel. 'I'm sure the pipe and tobacco are going to a deserving cause, and the box of nougat for your mother will be an investment. It will ensure favoured treatment for me. Favoured treatment from an hotel proprietor is a privilege much sought after by guests. More international crises have been caused by friction between hotel proprietors and guests than by the unsheathing of sabres.'

'That isn't true,' said Celeste. 'Come, m'sieur, let me take your arm and ensure you don't try to run.' She slipped her arm through his and they began a measured walk along the verge of the road. Edward used a walking stick to pace himself. The village was not far, no more than twelve minutes for a brisk walker, but twenty to twenty-five minutes for Edward. Celeste did not mind a leisurely progress at all. She was always happy to be with him.

From the window of her bedroom on the first floor, Rosamund saw them, Celeste in a pretty yellow frock arm in arm with him.

'The dear child,' murmured Rosamund, then turned and brought a bathing costume out of a drawer.

Colonel Brecht had actually brought himself to suggest a dip, though not without coughing a bit.

Edward took the ups and downs of the road in sensible style. He needed to stop only once, when he sat on a boulder and took a few deep breaths. Celeste was still concerned.

'We should have driven in your car,' she said.

'No, I must do some walking,' he said, 'and it's no great distance to the village.'

He did not look distressed, nor was his colour that of a man struggling to breathe. He had his own way of taking in air, slowly and evenly. They reached La Roche in twenty-five minutes. Its sunny, dusty triangle was surrounded by dry, dusty trees. Timber seats under the trees offered shade. Elderly men were playing boule on the triangle. On a seat sat old Pierre, the hotel's retired gardener, his shoulders bent and his face as wrinkled as a walnut. Celeste and Edward first went into the shop which, though small and almost as dark as a cave, sold a great variety of goods, including pipes and tobacco. And nougat from Montelimar. Edward bought a handsome box of nougat, which Celeste assured him would make her mother's eyes pop, then selected a briar pipe he knew Pierre would like. He also purchased 200 grammes of Pierre's favourite tobacco.

They took the modest gifts to the old man, and the wrinkles of his face disappeared inside a thousand new ones as he smiled in delight. They sat and talked to him.

'Oh, there's Gregory,' said Celeste. 'He's come to see if the potash has been made up.'

Edward saw the Russian gardener walk into the shop. From the opposite direction a swinging figure approached. It was Mademoiselle Dupont, vivid in the sunshine. Gregory came out of the shop, carrying a heavy sack. He deposited it in a little handcart, kept outside the shop for the convenience of customers, as long as they swore an oath to bring it back. The Russian went back into the shop for a second sack. That went into the handcart too. Mademoiselle Dupont stopped, smiled at Gregory and spoke to him. When he began to trundle the little cart, she walked with him, talking as vivaciously to him, it seemed, as she did to everyone. She saw Edward. She waved. He lifted his cap to her. She looked for a moment as if she would desert the gardener, but gave another wave and walked on with him. Celeste smiled.

'Do you think she's made her choice, Edward?'

'Choice?' said Edward, while Pierre peered at the sturdy figure of the man who had replaced him.

'She's a Parisienne,' said Celeste, 'she flirts.'

'You know her well?'

'No, this is the first time she's stayed at the hotel. You must avoid her, or she'll eat you.'

'She'll have to be very fond of bones if she wants me for her supper,' said Edward.

'Please, m'sieur,' said Celeste, 'you know I care deeply for you. You must not make me jealous.'

Edward laughed. Old Pierre, slightly deaf, was talking away, and the sounds of the game of boule interspersed his monologue like metallic thuds.

'A good man, a good man,' Pierre said, 'but not one to talk about himself.'

'You mean Gregory?' said Edward.

'Ah, he can make things grow,' said Pierre, 'but his tongue has little life to it.'

'Perhaps what he has to say he would rather keep to himself,' said Edward.

'Oh, Mademoiselle Dupont will find enough words for both of them,' said Celeste. 'Beware of her honey, Edward. You are so innocent.'

'Precocious girl,' said Edward, 'you're making a pretty little mistake if you think that.'

'When I was young,' said Pierre, 'things weren't like they are today. Precociousness, precociousness, yes, and everyone rushing and running. No one walks, no one walks, no one learns to walk. They all run before they can walk, and what is the consequence, the consequence? The world is full of people falling on their noses. Off you go, off you go.'

'Old Pierre, stop your grumbling,' said Celeste. 'I must get back to help Mama, and I've never fallen on my nose in my life.'

'It will come, it will come,' said the old man and grinned at her. Celeste, on her feet, stooped and kissed his cheek.

'There, old one, that's to show I love you,' she said.

'What? What?' said Pierre.

'She loves you,' said Edward, patting his shoulder.

'So she should, so she should. Who cut the flowers for her christening?' Pierre talked on as Celeste and Edward went on their way.

They walked at a very leisurely pace back to the hotel. Celeste did not, in any case, want to catch up with Gregory and Mademoiselle Dupont. She was sure the lady from Paris would take Edward over.

Rosamund and Colonel Brecht descended to the beach.

They were carrying their bathing costumes and towels.

'If the water is cold,' said Rosamund, 'I shall turn blue.'

'Blue is a pretty colour,' said the Colonel.

'I beg your pardon?'

'Blue – a pretty colour, madam.'

'I assure you, sir, that when I turn blue I don't look at all pretty.'

On the beach were two bathing huts, both owned by the hotel. Rosamund and the Colonel had been given the keys. Rosamund entered the hut reserved for ladies, and the Colonel disappeared into the other. Rosamund emerged a little later in a costume of navy blue, its skirt hemmed with white, and a bathing hat of matching blue and white. Her legs were long, handsome and bare. Colonel Brecht, in a sombre black costume, was awaiting her. His legs were even longer than hers, and strong and muscular. He averted his eyes at the appearance of Britain's Juno. Rosamund, at forty, did not consider herself the kind of bathing beauty newspaper photographers went clicking after at Brighton in the summer, but was quite confident about what her costume did for her well-preserved figure, and her smile came as Colonel Brecht cleared his throat.

'Are we to dash in and risk the temperature, or shall we dip our toes and try it first?' she asked.

'Allow me to advance and fall in,' said the Colonel, a German officer and therefore a gentleman, even though on the retired list. 'If you hear me cry out, it will mean, madam, that you should return to your bathing hut.'

'Advance, then, Colonel Brecht, and do me the favour of falling in.'

He approached the water resolutely, and she conceded he had a fine figure. He entered the sea without faltering, waded on and fell in when the level reached his thighs. He turned on his back. He emitted no cry. Rosamund hailed him from the water's edge.

'Well, sir?'

'Delightful, my dear lady, delightful.'

Rosamund went in. There was no one else about as she gently lowered herself and began an easy, steady breaststroke. The water, warmed by the Riviera sun during the long, hot summer, still retained that warmth. The Colonel floated and basked. Rosamund swam gracefully around. Yes, it really was delightful. One must snatch what one could of sea-bathing while the weather lasted. Sea-bathing was so good for one. Heavenly. Her active body revelled in the rhythm of swimming. Her cotton bathing dress clung in some places and ballooned in others.

The Colonel frisked about.

Binoculars glinted high above them, from just outside the little gate in the wall of the Villa d'Azur. It was one of the few ways in which Katerina Pyotrovna could participate in the activities of people. How happy they looked, the man and the woman, almost luxuriating in those warm blue waters. She saw the woman stand up, her bathing costume outlining her figure in wet, glistening blue. She saw the man swimming lazily in front of her. He turned to float on his back, the water waist-high around his companion. She saw him look up at the woman, who was not unlike a sea-goddess, so handsome was her figure, and she clearly saw him turn quickly over and swim away. And she saw a smile on the face of the woman.

She smiled herself. She put the glasses down. She sighed. She remembered the days when she too frolicked in warm seas and her bathing costume clung to her figure. Mama would come to wrap a towel around her, to modestly hide the shape of her blossoming breasts.

She entered her garden, closing the green gate behind her, and the high wall shut her off again from the world and its people. But she had received an answering note from Celeste to tell her that she was bringing Monsieur Edward Somers with her tomorrow.

A little pulse of pleasure beat.

'Remarkable,' said Rosamund after dinner that evening. She had just learned that Mademoiselle Dupont, like herself, was familiar with the game of billiards. 'Whist is usually the thing with the ladies here.'

'Whist?' Mademoiselle Dupont, brilliant in a deep red

gown, lowered her voice. 'I avoid all contact with such a dull game. I'm not treading on your toes by confessing that?'

'Not at all,' said Rosamund. She and Mademoiselle Dupont were taking coffee in the lounge, and other guests were drifting in. 'I've more of a liking for billiards than any card game.'

'Do they allow ladies to use the table here?'

'Why, of course,' said Rosamund. 'Madame Michel advances with the times, and would on no account allow the gentlemen to monopolise any of the amenities. That permits us to engage with the gentlemen, not spoil them. I'm not in favour of being left to twiddle my thumbs. If you're willing, mademoiselle, shall you and I challenge Monsieur Somers and Colonel Brecht to a game of billiards?'

'I'm very willing, madame,' said the Frenchwoman, quite animated. 'It's an excellent way of capturing two such personable gentlemen.'

'Capturing?'

'They are really the most interesting men here,' said Mademoiselle Dupont. 'Edward is extremely intriguing. He has a tired face, yet such fine eyes, and I feel some women could not look at him without wanting to kiss him.'

What an extraordinary statement, thought Rosamund. One must put it down to the woman being excessively French. And already she was using Edward's name.

'That's something which would do very well in a play,' she said, 'but might make Edward keep to his room if we all indulged our impulses. Do you wish to kiss him?'

'Don't you, madame?' asked Mademoiselle Dupont with an arch smile.

'Only in sympathy that so fine a man should be so physically reduced.'

'Ah, yes, gassed in that terrible and outrageous war,' said Mademoiselle Dupont indignantly, 'a war fought for gain by the imperialists.'

'Then they blundered, it seems,' said Rosamund, 'for there was no gain by any of them. Here is Edward now.'

'Edward?' It was Mademoiselle Dupont who rose to engage him. He crossed the room to join her.

She's taking him over, thought Rosamund. Celeste will fly into a sweet fury.

Celeste, indeed, entering a few moments later to pour coffee for guests awaiting it, stared at the spectacle of the Frenchwoman in flirtatious possession of Edward. She was outrageously close to him, her face lifted to his, her red-sheathed bosom breathing against his dinner jacket. She was exercising a winning smile and a sweet tongue.

Celeste served the coffee. Colonel Brecht entered. She served him too, then disappeared.

She *is* in a sweet fury, thought Rosamund. How enchanting. The French are very French at any age.

All ten guests were present. The spacious lounge, carpeted and restful, was a civilised retreat after dinner and very conducive to conversation, although in addition to the billiards room there was also a card room.

The dapper man, Monsieur Valery, hovered with an amiable smile on his face, obviously ready to take on either Rosamund or Mademoiselle Dupont at whatever social activity they cared to pursue with him. The two ladies, however, repaired to the billiards room with Edward and Colonel Brecht immediately they'd finished coffee. As they proceeded through the lobby, Celeste appeared. She detained Edward. The others went on, Rosamund with a little smile lurking.

'M'sieur,' said Celeste proudly, 'your affairs are none of my business, of course, but—'

'My affairs?' said Edward.

'But I beg you not to become inextricably involved with Mademoiselle Dupont.'

'I'm only going to play billiards with her, little angel.'

'I really don't care for her,' said Celeste.

'She's quite entertaining.'

'Oh, m'sieur, you are so naïve.'

'I was as a boy, before I found out how necessary it was to cope with terrible little girls. It was sink or swim.'

'It is not amusing, m'sieur,' said Celeste. 'Mademoiselle Dupont is not a woman who'd take care of you.'

'I haven't asked her to,' said Edward.

'I shouldn't like you to meet the Countess tomorrow if you

were covered with Mademoiselle Dupont's scent, as you are now.'

'Good heavens, am I?'

'How could you not be,' said Celeste, 'when you allow her to purr up against you like a cat?'

'Well, you must pray, sweet infant, that by tomorrow it will have worn off.'

'Play your billiards, m'sieur,' said Celeste, 'but beware of scented cats.'

'You delicious girl,' said Edward and patted her cheek.

He entered the billiards room. Colour glowed. The table was a deep green, Mademoiselle Dupont was a picturesque figure in red and Rosamund majestic in midnight blue.

The game was on. Rosamund exercised fluency with her cue. Mademoiselle Dupont was quick and exuberant. The Frenchwoman had played, she said, since girlhood. Rosamund had played during the nine years her marriage had lasted before her husband, a sapper, had been blown up by a German mine while tunnelling to lay a British one. She had been a widow now for twelve years, but did not live a lonely life. She had come to terms with the loss of a husband who had also been an ardent lover, and was not in desperate search for a new one. She enjoyed male company, however, and the discovery that Colonel Brecht was actually a shy man aroused the ineradicable tease in her. He had almost swallowed the best part of the Mediterranean when, on his back, he had looked up at her wet bathing costume clinging revealingly around her full breasts.

The two ladies ran the men close. Edward and the Colonel scored steadily, but Rosamund put together some excellent breaks, and if only Mademoiselle Dupont had been less flashy with her cue, they might have been in front. Certainly, they had the Colonel tugging at his moustache. Entirely a masculine man, he really did not want to be beaten by the ladies, and looked relieved when he and Edward clinched the close match.

'Thank you, mademoiselle.' He shook the Frenchwoman's hand. 'Thank you, madam.' He shook Rosamund's hand.

'Cognac as a nightcap for all?' suggested Edward.

'Thank you, but no,' said Rosamund. 'It's ten thirty and time for my bed.'

'Alas, I too am sleepy,' said Mademoiselle Dupont, 'but shall be alert and alive in the morning. Perhaps I can look forward to a few gentle walks with you during my stay, Edward.'

Dear me, thought Rosamund, she has no reticence at all.

Edward merely smiled, avoiding a commitment.

The door opened and Monsieur Valery put his head in, his pointed nose leading his enquiring look.

'Ah, the game is finished?' he said.

'Quite finished, m'sieur,' said Mademoiselle Dupont and, passing him by, flowed out of the room with a swish of silken red. Monsieur Valery's eyes sighingly followed her. Edward took pity on him by inviting him to join in the nightcap, and Monsieur Valery accepted with the gratitude of one longing for company.

Edward woke up just after midnight. He had been asleep for only an hour. His lungs felt congested. He got up and went to the casement windows, opening them wide. The night air was fresh, but not damp. He breathed it in. The moon was brilliant, flooding the land with light. He glimpsed movement close to the summerhouse, inside the shadow of the hedge. It came and it went, a movement in the shadow.

He thought about Gregory. The man seemed honest enough. He looked one in the eye and he answered questions. All the same, the Countess's doctor had obviously caught him prying. Whether the gardener had been there out of curiosity or for some other reason, he alone knew. Edward supposed it was Gregory who had flitted by in the garden a moment ago. The path behind the summerhouse led to the back of the hotel, and the man had a room in the basement.

Edward closed the windows and returned to his bed. Because he had been alerted, his ears picked up a little sound. He opened the door of his room and stepped quietly out. The hotel was invested with the silence of sleeping night. Except for little whispers of movement. Someone had entered through the back door, someone who was not treading the basement stairs, but the upper flight. There were no bolts used in the Corniche, no habitual locking of either the front or back doors, for crime was almost non-existent in this little area. Guests who liked to spend an evening in Nice or Cannes could return as late as they wished, and were only expected to enter the hotel quietly, front or back. The back stairs led to both upper floors.

Edward stood outside his bedroom, listening to the little sounds of someone cautiously ascending. A door opened on the first floor and a moment later the hotel was still and silent.

A guest had been out. A guest had returned. Edward went back to his bed.

7

The next day was again warm and sunny, the Riviera enjoying one of its extended summers. For her visit to the Countess, Celeste wore a dress of dark blue cotton with an open collar, and a loose white imitation silk tie. A straw hat sat on the back of her head. Celeste had never used the iron gates fronting the road, but turned into the wood right of them to skirt the walled drive and emerged from the trees a little way from the green wooden gate. She took Edward through on this same route. The wall gate was, as usual, open for her. She entered with Edward, closing the gate after her. The Countess was there, promenading the wide, extensive lawn, a blue-and-white parasol up.

Celeste thought how regal she looked. She did promenade, often, with Celeste beside her, and in the manner of a lady of grace superior. Celeste frequently felt, however, that a woman of spirited vitality dwelt within that elegant form, a woman longing to shed her cloak of constraint.

The Countess laughed when she saw Celeste in her dark blue, for she too had chosen blue. But hers was a blue as delicate as the azure sky. Hatless, her deep auburn hair was enriched by the light.

'Celeste, Celeste, your blue has outdone me, incorrigible girl,' she said, and planted a kiss on her cheek. 'Yes, how sweet you look. Monsieur Somers, is she not a picture?' She put the question lightly, smilingly, her eyes still on Celeste.

'I'm grateful for both pictures,' said Edward.

She lifted her clear grey eyes to his, and again he was held in mesmerised fascination. Reflections of life danced for him. And she, granted permission to receive a man she wished to make a friend, put out her hand to him, and the faint flush deepened her colour as he lifted her fingers to his lips. Edward could think of no other way of greeting her.

'Thank you, Countess, for inviting me,' he said.

'An arrangement isn't quite so startling as an unexpected collision, is it?' she said, her smile turning her vivid.

'Did we collide?' asked Edward.

'Almost,' she said. 'Thank you for coming today. I am Katerina Pyotrovna.'

'Of Bulgaria?'

'Yes, of Bulgaria.' There was only the slightest hesitation about her reply. 'It's a country now too unstable for many of us.'

'I'm sorry,' said Edward, who thought instability had been a characteristic of Bulgaria for more years than he cared to remember.

'Are you acquainted with Bulgaria?' she asked.

'Shamefully, no.'

'It has some virtues,' she said, and her smile was richly warm. Edward felt a sense of wonder that any woman could be so exquisitely beautiful when afflicted with such a fragile heart. Her hair was magnificent, her sky-blue dress a silken lightness that caressed her willowy figure. It was fashionably short, the hem flirting around her knees, her white silk stockings lending a gleam of enchantment to her shapely legs. Legs had become unveiled. That was because fashion had become inspired.

Celeste looked on. She was in a little wonder herself. The two of them seemed to have forgotten her already, and the delicate flush on Madame's face was surely because she was sensitively aware that the meeting was out of the ordinary.

Edward broke an electric silence.

'Celeste has told you I'm an insular man, I suppose,' he said.

'That you come from an insular country, England? Yes.' Katerina Pyotrovna's lashes flickered. 'I should call you Mr Somers, not Monsieur, of course.' Her warm voice became vibrant as she went on. 'You spoke of pictures. Life is never without pictures, is it? There are new ones every day, making yesterday's quickly out of date. But they're never forgotten, however old they become. They turn into our treasured memories.'

'One or two are hidden away,' said Edward.

'Yes, one or two,' she said, and shadows brought clouds to her eyes. 'Mr Somers, you and I have something in common, I believe.'

'If you mean neither of us is allowed to dash madly about, yes, we have that in common, Countess.'

'Yes. But you aren't parading gloom, and I refuse to.' She could have said that while his limiting factor was his poisoned lungs, hers was the compulsory restriction of the high walls.

'Well, there's still a great deal of pleasure to be had, isn't there?' said Edward. 'Invalids hang on to life with more determination than the healthy.'

'And our doctors are even more determined on our behalf than we are,' she said. 'Is your doctor full of do's and don'ts?'

'My doctor,' said Edward, 'rarely departs from don'ts.'

Celeste was positive now that they'd forgotten her. She did not mind. It was absorbing to watch them, to sense they were searching for words, the right words, the light and conversational words.

'Tea will be served at three thirty,' said the Countess. 'You will stay for that, Mr Somers, won't you?'

Celeste found a way into the proceedings then.

'Oh, I assure you, madame,' she said, 'Monsieur Somers won't go until he's had his tea. I'm afraid that's what comes of being incurably English.'

'Well, I am incurably—' Katerina Pyotrovna checked herself. 'Yes, I must admit to being incurably Bulgarian, and so I also enjoy tea.'

'The Bulgarians are tea-drinkers?' said Edward. Catching sight of hoops in the lawn, he asked, 'Countess, are you set up for croquet?'

'Croquet isn't forbidden in France, is it?' she said.

'I hope not,' said Edward.

'Mr Somers, do you mean you would like to play?' she asked, showing animation. 'You'd prefer croquet to a discussion on Bulgaria?'

'I am, of course, eager to hear why it's racked with instability.'

'I'm quite willing for us to defer to the importance of croquet,' she said.

'Well, I'll tell you, Countess, croquet is the one outdoor game I can manage, and I am, therefore, fanatical in my pursuance of it.'

She saw the humour in his eyes, the hint of laughter, and felt a responsiveness that quickened her. Of all things, she liked a sense of humour in a man. She liked it excessively in this man.

'Then away with Bulgaria,' she smiled, 'for I too can manage croquet and am probably even more fanatical than you are. We'll play, shall we, if Celeste will allow us? Will you, Celeste?'

'I shall be content to watch,' said Celeste, and meant it. She loved them both, and neither of them knew how much she wanted them to love each other. She was a born matchmaker.

'This is going to be delightful,' said the Countess. 'Celeste, there's lemonade on the terrace table.'

'Then I'll watch from the terrace table while swimming in lemonade,' said Celeste.

A few minutes later, the Countess and Edward were in earnest competition on the lawn. Edward, clad in a brown blazer, cream trousers and white cricket shirt, looked distinctively English. The Countess looked vitally involved. Amid the click and clack of struck croquet balls, she was alive with laughter and enthusiasm, and with alternating cries of triumph, anguish and protest.

'Mr Somers! Oh, shame on you!'

'All in the game, Countess.'

'No, no, I am Katerina Pyotrovna – and see where you've sent my ball, you dreadful man.'

'A rather well-struck thump, I thought.'

'A brutal croquet, sir – oh, I shall pay you back. Ah, now see what comes of your abominable thump. You're wired.'

'I see I've missed my shot, yes.'

'You have. Now I shall show you, with this ball.'

'Um – the other one, I think, Countess.'

'Never. I'm going to play this one.'

'Well, what are rules, Countess, when the game is so electric?'

'Stand back, sir. I'm going to roquet your blue ball.'

They were talking in English. Celeste spoke it well herself. It was a necessity in an hotel which received many English visitors. Celeste smiled as she listened to the repartee. Madame was sparkling, almost radiant in her enjoyment of her duel with Edward, who did not seem able to take his eyes off her except when he was making his shots.

A cry of triumph winged its way into the air.

'There, a roquet! Now I shall take my turn to thump.' Katerina Pyotrovna placed her red ball against his blue one, and put her foot on her own ball. Her lifted, silken-clad leg gleamed. Her eyes were intent, her mallet poised, her lips parted. Her mallet struck. Edward's blue ball sped yards over the lawn, far from the hoop he was attacking. Katerina laughed in delight.

'That's done it,' said Edward. 'No quarter will be given now, not an inch, no, by Jove, not an inch.'

Shaping to strike her red ball through the hoop, two yards away, Katerina lifted her head and smiled at him. The light poured over her face and burnished her hair. Everything to do with the joys of life was in her eyes.

'Oh, you are going to engage grimly?' she said.
'Ferociously,' said Edward.
'Good,' she said, 'I'm game.'
This little remark was so English that he said, 'Are you sure you're Bulgarian?' It was not a question, it was a comment, made with a smile and without seriousness, but Katerina's long lashes swept over her bright eyes and she bent her head again to her shot.
'We agreed to defer the Bulgarian question,' she said. She smote. The ball travelled smoothly and accurately, passing through the hoop. She looked up again, smiling in delight. 'There, what do you think of that for grim ferocity?'
'Intimidating. Play on, Countess.'
The game continued in its infinite variations. The mallets struck and smote, and Celeste watched the animated Countess battling against the measured deliberation of Edward. Croquet was a mystery to Celeste up to a month ago, when the Countess had begun to teach her. She knew enough about it now to follow the course of the duel, and to know when the Countess, claiming a lady's privilege, bent the rules to her own advantage. To Celeste, it seemed that croquet as played by the Countess and Edward produced definable vibrations of pleasure that had nothing to do with who was winning.
Edward, achieving a roquet, thumped Katerina's yellow ball a good twenty yards.
'Oh, you beast!' Katerina was not a woman then, but an indignant, anguished girl. 'You dreadful creature!'
'No quarter, not an inch,' said Edward.
'Oh, now my temper is up, sir.' But she was laughing, laughing, and from a window on the upper floor of the villa Dr Kandor observed her with a little frown. He had not seen her in such enjoyment since the Revolution. But he must not worry so much. This could do no harm. She had not a single streak of deviousness in her. She would do nothing and say nothing that was indiscreet. She wanted only a few friends, friends they could both trust, and the pleasure of occasionally seeing them. It could do no harm, making a friend of this man, who had been gassed in the war. She would be guilty of

no foolishness. He must allow her some contact with selected people. He and she, of course, had seen this man before. An Englishman. Harmless. Unless—

She had never been in love, never known a man.

Dr Kandor, observing her enraptured, drew his brows together.

Edward was increasingly fascinated. There she was, wholly exquisite, the essence of beauty and vitality, a slender but shapely delight. She had a weak heart? Impossible. There was no one else around apart from himself and Celeste, no servants, no doctor, no nurse, no companions. The pink-tinted villa, quite beautiful, was as quiet as if it held no living soul. No one came out to cast a solicitous eye over her, to suggest she must not overdo things. Overdo? She was a creature of vitality, as fluent as quicksilver, making him in his measured application feel very old.

'Mr Somers?' She had her eyes on him, the faint flush back on her face, and he realised he was staring at her. 'It's your strike – oh, I'm sorry, perhaps you've played enough – I'm afraid I forgot that you—'

'No, I'm fine.' He looked round as a little bell rang on the terrace. Someone had at last appeared, a broad-bodied woman in a servant's outfit.

'There, tea is served,' said Katerina, 'and I'm ready for it, aren't you?'

'After such a ferocious contest? Yes,' he said.

She put down her mallet.

'It isn't important, is it, that the game isn't finished? It's the participation, isn't it?'

'It's the fun,' said Edward.

'Oh, yes,' she said like a breathless girl. 'Thank you – I enjoyed it so much.'

'So did I,' he said.

They walked together over the lawn and up the steps to the terrace, where Celeste rose to greet them. With the enthusiasm of a young lady who had played her own self-satisfying part in bringing them together, she said, 'Oh, you had such a good game, didn't you?'

'Thumping,' said Edward.

'Celeste, did you see how belligerently he engaged every time he struck a roquet?' said Katerina. 'I'm exhausted from travelling first after one ball, then the other.' She sank into a chair. She did not look exhausted. She looked vividly alive. 'Tea,' she said. 'Now everything is perfect, isn't it?'

Anna had set out the tea things from the tray, and the table was laden with china, glasses, teapot, dish of lemon slices, sugar bowl, tea knives and a plate of cucumber sandwiches.

'Cucumber sandwiches?' said Edward, his face warm from the sun.

'Yes, that's right, isn't it?' said Katerina. 'Cucumber sandwiches are correct when the English take their tea at this time? I asked Anna to prepare some, and she's done so. She's also supplied you with a cup and saucer.'

'And she's bringing milk,' said Celeste. 'I asked her to, for Edward. Madame, you don't mind that I asked her?'

'No, child, I'm glad you did. Everything must be just right. Celeste, you may pour. Mr Somers has worn me out.'

Celeste looked worried.

'Madame, oh, you aren't faint? Should Dr Kandor be called?'

'No, no, sweet girl.' Katerina laughed. 'I'm exhilarated, not faint. It's Mr Somers we must concern ourselves with.'

'Not a bit of it,' said Edward. 'I shall devour the cucumber sandwiches with healthy relish.'

Celeste poured the tea the moment Anna came out with the milk. The servant took a good look at Edward, found nothing about him that offended her and went back into the villa.

Edward, drinking tea and consuming sandwiches, felt himself a man dwelling in the magic of a perfect afternoon. The sky was a deep blue, the sea full of lazy ripples, the terrace a haven of warmth. Celeste talked, winding her own spell around the day, and Katerina listened and smiled. Memories filled her eyes because of the girl's youth and innocence. And when Edward turned his smile on Celeste, Katerina cast fleeting glances at him. His thick hair was a little loose from activity and the sun had tinted him with brown. He reached his third cup of tea.

'Oh, you are like my family of loved ones,' she said. 'They drank oceans of tea at a sitting. Celeste has told you of the family my father served?'

'Celeste is always a library of information,' said Edward.

'She's exactly like the youngest of my family,' said Katerina.

'The family were noble Bulgarians?'

A little hesitation before Katerina said, 'Yes, of course. I call them my family because that's how I felt about them. The second eldest daughter was closest to me. She was my age. Each of us was a shadow of the other, you see. We shared every secret.'

'Madame, she was as beautiful as you?' enquired Celeste.

'Celeste, Celeste, how can I in all modesty answer that?' said Katerina. 'But it's true, of course, that one's shadow is identical. We all had such happy times, such rapturous years.'

'You and your shadow, Countess, and the rest of the family,' said Edward. 'What happened to them?'

'Happened?' The question seemed to startle Katerina.

'Well,' said Edward, 'I presume that at some time you and your parents left this household.'

'Yes. Yes.' She looked at her hands, studying them with care. 'It was the war. The war separated so many people. And it was never thought that Bulgaria would oppose Russia's cause.'

'That affected the fortunes of this family, Bulgaria joining the war on Germany's side?' said Edward.

'The war affected everyone and everything,' said Katerina. Her inspection of her hands coming to an end, she surveyed what was left of the cucumber sandwiches. Two remained on the plate. 'Celeste, another sandwich?' Celeste shook her head. 'They're not a success?' said Katerina.

'Oh, they're delicious,' said Celeste, 'but I've eaten all I can, madame.'

'Mr Somers?'

'One more, then,' said Edward, helping himself. 'You know, Countess, I don't think there was ever any declaration of war between Russia and Bulgaria.'

She thought about that. She said, 'We won't talk about the war and the sadness of separation. The day is far too nice. I'm unable to receive or entertain very much, as you probably know, and so this is an unusual pleasure for me, enjoying two visitors at once. And the game of croquet was an additional pleasure.'

Dr Kandor suddenly appeared. For a large man, he could move very quietly, and not until he was close to the group did Edward notice him.

'Good afternoon,' said the doctor civilly.

Katerina turned, giving him a smile.

'You must meet my new friend,' she said. 'Mr Somers, would you like to say hello to Dr Kandor?'

Edward came to his feet and shook hands with the physician.

'I think we met a few days ago,' he said.

'I am sure we did,' said Dr Kandor, 'and I hope you'll forgive me for not making you too welcome. I'll join you, if I may.' He drew up a chair. His expression bland, he said to Celeste, 'How are you today, Mademoiselle?'

'Oh, quite happy, Dr Kandor,' said Celeste.

'And do you see how good my game of croquet has been for me?' said Katerina.

'I can see it has given you a glow,' said the doctor. 'Now you must relax.'

'I am relaxing,' said Katerina. 'You must turn your attention on Mr Somers, who has been exerting himself playing a merciless game of croquet with me.'

'He has his own doctor, I'm sure,' said the physician. He regarded Edward with professional interest. 'Poison gas is pernicious. Are you still receiving treatment?'

'I'm looked at from time to time,' said Edward, 'but on the whole I merely follow my doctor's advice, which is to avoid strain, effort and fog.'

'You use a balloon? How often do you use it?'

'A balloon?' said Celeste.

'A balloon?' said Edward.

'You carry one, do you?' said Dr Kandor. 'A toy balloon which you blow up regularly?'

'Heavens, no,' said Edward. 'Should I?'

'It isn't an unknown therapeutic exercise for damaged lungs,' said the doctor. 'I've recommended it in certain cases, but it would not, of course, be correct for me to recommend it to you if your own doctor hasn't.'

'I'm interested,' said Edward, and fell into friendly conversation with the doctor.

In a little while, Katerina wondered why it was that, although Celeste was talking to her, it was Edward's voice she was listening to. It was a distraction of a disturbing kind. She looked at him. Engaged as he was with Dr Kandor, he caught her glance. He gave her a smile. She felt a warm, melting sensation. She had received a thousand smiles during her emergent years, from young and dashing officers, and from mature and polished men. She had teased them all and fallen in love with none. Then, when she had been at her most eligible, the Revolution had virtually cut her off from every man who might have been a suitor.

She was thirty-one now. Thirty-one. That was so old. Yet because of this man, hollow-cheeked and drawn, she felt like an uncertain and impressionable girl.

Celeste saw her watching Edward, with a strangely wondering expression on her face. Celeste smiled.

They had to leave at five o'clock. Celeste had to be back to help her mother, and five o'clock had always signalled the end of her visits. Today, however, the Countess seemed oblivious of time.

Celeste said, 'I must go, madame.'

'Celeste, but why?'

'It is five o'clock, madame.'

'Already? Already?'

Edward rose.

'I must totter along with you, Celeste,' he said. 'Countess, a lovely afternoon – thank you.'

'Oh, you will come again, won't you?' she said impulsively.

'With very much pleasure,' said Edward.

'For croquet and tea?' said Katerina.

'If the weather stays kind, yes, for croquet and tea. You're offering me an irresistible combination. Goodbye – and goodbye, Dr Kandor.'

She sat in silence after they had gone. Everything, suddenly, was so quiet, so empty. She felt a little ache, a little sad.

'You're satisfied with your afternoon?' said Dr Kandor.

'Boris Sergeyovich, thank you for the concession. There can be no danger, can there, from a man like Edward Somers? I should so like to have him for a friend while he's here.'

'We've found a gentleman, I think,' said the doctor gravely. 'In the world as it is, men of kindness and honour are few.'

'I know little of this world, Boris Sergeyovich,' said Katerina. 'I only know I should like to invite him many times, and not just every two weeks.'

'Here, in this garden, which is open to the sea, the air is at its purest,' said Dr Kandor. 'That is what his lungs need, air that is dry and pure. Katerina Pyotrovna, invite him as often as you wish.'

'Oh, thank you,' she said breathlessly, 'thank you.'

He took her hand and raised it to his lips.

'Only remember,' he said, 'that you are entrusted to me.'

Edward awoke in the night. No sound had disturbed him, nor was his chest troublesome. The activity of his mind had brought him out of his sleep. Her image filled it. She was all eyes, eyes full of laughter and life. He lay awake, thinking of her.

She too was awake, and out of her bed. Outside, the garden was ghostly-bright beneath the huge moon, the sea a vast shimmer of shining water.

No, she had never been loved by a man. No man had ever seen her as she was, as God had made her.

The croquet. The thumping.

She smiled, though her mood was not one of gaiety. It was one of longing.

What should she say in her note to him, a note that was to

ask him to visit her again?

'Please call, please bring me to life again.'

No, not quite those words. He would have to read between the lines of a far more formal invitation.

8

Edward was at work, pencil moving flowingly, abbreviating words as Dickens had when a court reporter. Would became wd, regiment became rgt, position became pn, artillery became aty, Ypres became Yp. His treatment was factual, entirely so, though he could not view the battle completely as an historian, for he had been there himself. Casualties evoked pictures of men blown to pieces by the power and ferocity of the German guns.

Rosamund was engrossed in her book a few yards away. On the other side of the lawn, Mademoiselle Dupont had Colonel Brecht by his ear. Edward, able to shut out extraneous sounds when his concentration was at its best, was patently not to be interrupted. Rosamund seemed equally unapproachable, such was her interest in her book, a biography of Queen Victoria. That left Colonel Brecht a helpless prisoner in the hands of Mademoiselle Dupont. From time to time he looked across at Rosamund, obviously in the hope that she would rescue him from the vivacious loquacity of the lady from Paris. Rosamund's conversation might have a teasing quality, but Mademoiselle Dupont's could be numbing. It reduced one to merely being a sounding-board.

Rosamund was quite aware that Colonel Brecht was in need of help. She let him suffer at length, however, on the perfectly reasonable assumption that she would be seen as an angel of mercy when she did finally exercise pity.

Monsieur Valery, as dapper as ever, made an appearance.

He strolled around the garden, calling an affable good-morning to everybody, saw that the attractive Mademoiselle Dupont was determinedly latched to Colonel Brecht, smiled a little disappointedly and wandered away.

Celeste came out, ready to take orders for morning coffee. She was pleased to see that Edward was by himself and that it was poor Colonel Brecht who was suffering the attentions of the flirtatious Frenchwoman.

'M'sieur?'

Edward looked up. Celeste smiled and placed a white envelope on his table.

'Celeste, how fresh you look,' he said.

'Oh, I am totally unspoiled, m'sieur. That has just come for you.'

He opened the letter, ordering coffee as he did so. Celeste went to collect other orders while he read the note.

Dear Mr Somers, I do hope you aren't suffering from yesterday's exertions, that you are well. Myself, I am very fit, and feel extraordinarily pleased with my powers of endurance.

I am at home tomorrow afternoon. For that matter, I am always at home, yes! Is it possible that I might have the pleasure of your company again, at the same time? I will understand if you are otherwise engaged, when I should like to suggest the following day. I am told the weather is set fair. I wish that it will bring the best of health to you. Katerina Pyotrovna.

PS My love to Celeste.

Edward refolded the note.

'You did say you wanted coffee, m'sieur?' Celeste was back.

'Yes, Celeste, a small pot, if I may.'

'With pleasure,' said Celeste, but refrained from despatching herself. She was in obvious expectation of information. Edward said nothing as he took up his pencil again. 'M'sieur, am I to stand here and die of curiosity?'

'I shouldn't like that to happen, no, not at all,' he said. 'Will it save your life if I tell you I've been invited to call on the Countess again, tomorrow afternoon?'

Celeste smiled happily.

'Oh, already, you see, you are in tender accord,' she said.

'In tender accord?'

'But yes, m'sieur, you and she. Already love is blossoming, already there are billets-doux. Write your answer and I'll have Jacques deliver it. You will send kisses?'

'Audacious girl, what's all this you're dreaming up?'

'But I'm not dreaming it up, m'sieur, never,' she said earnestly. 'You are made for each other. Even I can see that.'

'Even you? Only you, you mean. Off with your head, terrible infant.'

Celeste departed with a laugh.

Rosamund, finishing her coffee ten minutes later, closed her book and came to her feet. Colonel Brecht cast her a look of a drowning man. Rosamund gave him a little nod. Mademoiselle Dupont put a hand on the Colonel's arm to recall his attention. Mademoiselle Dupont, thought Rosamund, seemed a woman not disposed to let any man easily escape her. She also seemed set to have an affair either with Franz or Edward before she returned to Paris. How Edward would manage the vivacious lady in his state of health, only he knew. On the other hand, Rosamund doubted if he would fall for a woman so obviously a demi-monde. Poor Franz was a different kettle of fish. He would be netted while still clearing his throat.

'Colonel Brecht,' she called, 'I'll be down again in a few minutes to join you in our arranged walk. Will you meet me outside, on the steps?'

The Colonel came to life and sat up. Since no walk had been arranged, he knew Rosamund was putting out a lifeline.

'With pleasure, dear lady, with pleasure,' he said.

He was on the steps outside the hotel five minutes later, waiting for her as she emerged.

'Ah, there you are,' said Rosamund.

'Madam,' he said fervently, 'you are an angel of mercy.'

'Yes, I thought you'd think that,' she said. 'You find Mademoiselle Dupont a little tiring?'

'Charming lady, charming,' said the Colonel, 'but I've been crushed – yes, that is the word – crushed by the weight of words, madam.'

'An embarrassing position for a German officer to be in. Perhaps Mademoiselle Dupont is taking her revenge for your attempt to obliterate Verdun. Now,' she said, as they descended the steps, 'where shall we walk to?'

'To the village?' he suggested.

'Enchanting,' said Rosamund. 'I shall buy some pears for eating in the bath.'

'Madam?'

'That is the only place to eat a juicy pear, in the bath,' said Rosamund, the Colonel upright beside her as they walked along the verge. 'You may call me Rosamund, by the way. I'm no longer as sensitive about the war as Mademoiselle Dupont, who seems to think it was an imperialist plot. You and I must learn to live with its consequences. And you should tell her the theatre owes much to the patronage of kings, emperors and other imperialists. You must not sit and be crushed. You must strike back. Then she will fall into your arms. Women react lovingly to men who stand up to them. The day is delightful, isn't it?'

'Good God,' said the Colonel.

'Mademoiselle Dupont is extremely good-looking, and most men, I imagine, would like her to fall into their arms.'

'Ah – you have – madam, you have an incurable way of pulling the leg.'

'Oh, I'm quite serious,' said Rosamund, sailing along blithely in a cream dress and brimmed hat. 'You must take the initiative with the lady, and describe in exhausting detail the battles in which you were personally engaged during the war. You must make them full of shot and shell, ignoring all full stops in your narrative, as full stops will give her the chance to interrupt you. When she finally realises she has met her match, she may well be yours, Franz.'

'Stop,' said the Colonel hoarsely.

'That isn't the advice you want?' A bright figure of composure against the sunlit background of the Riviera, Rosamund pursed her lips thoughtfully. 'I've misinterpreted your feelings?'

'I am not a ladies' man – ah – Rosamund – as I am sure you realise, and to have Mademoiselle Dupont regard herself as mine is not the boot I want on my foot.'

'But you're an upright man, Franz, and could be just right for some feminine boots.'

Approaching the iron gates of the Villa d'Azur, they heard the sound of loose stones and chips slithering amid shrubs above them on their right. The Colonel briefly glanced and walked on. Rosamund came to a halt and looked upwards. She glimpsed a momentary flash of reflected sunlight.

The Colonel, stopping, looked back at her.

'A dog is up there, probably,' he said.

'No,' said Rosamund, frowning as the reflected glitter flashed again. 'Some beastly person has a spyglass on us. Whoever it is, what is he hoping to see? One would hardly canoodle on an open road, and in daylight.'

'Canoodle?' said the Colonel, retracing his steps to stand beside her. 'Canoodle?' He had a little difficulty in pronouncing the word. 'May I ask what that means?'

'It's the act of embracing with cuddlesome affection,' said Rosamund, eyes still on the shrubs above them.

'*Himmel!*' breathed the Colonel.

'Aren't you interested in that Peeping Tom up there?'

The Colonel seemed all of disinterested.

'No one is there, I'm sure,' he said. 'Perhaps a dog, scratching away at the earth. No one would want to look at me.'

Rosamund smiled. Used field-glasses, listed among secondhand war surplus, were fairly easy to come by these days, and one saw people carrying them about as casually as box cameras. The objects they observed were no doubt many and varied. It was not amusing to her to be considered an object. If people wanted to look at her, they could do so as she passed by. There was no need for the sick use of a telescope or binoculars, particularly as she was unlikely to take up any posture of a sensational kind.

She went on with Colonel Brecht. They enjoyed the walk in the sunshine, Rosamund inhaling heady draughts of an air laden with the scent of wild thyme, lavender and pine.

* * *

Monsieur Valery, apparently, was determined to cross the path of Mademoiselle Dupont with cheerful frequency. He believed, obviously, in the theory that to keep oneself in sight was more likely to pay dividends than sitting unnoticed in a corner. He intruded himself very affably into the billiards room that evening, taking a seat which enabled him to watch to advantage the svelte, red-gowned figure of the Frenchwoman at play. He was admiring of all her shots, whether good or not so good, and Rosamund thought it went without saying that he was also admiring of the lady's figure. All in all, in fact, he seemed to have every small man's infatuation for a woman taller than himself. Mademoiselle Dupont, however, appeared hardly aware of him. She was obviously far more interested in Edward. She was partnering him against Rosamund and Franz Brecht. The latter were well ahead, Rosamund a more consistent scorer of points than the Frenchwoman.

Mademoiselle Dupont maintained a possessive proximity to Edward whenever they were watching their opponents at the table. Her scent was delicate, her good looks enhanced by perfect make-up. Rosamund was her usual handsome self, and Colonel Brecht spent much time averting his eyes. Conscious, undoubtedly, of her valley of abundance and her off-shoulder gown, he gazed despairingly at the ceiling each time she made a shot.

She was in good form.

'You're going to run out,' Edward said to her when she needed only to add two to her break to win the game. 'Then I think I'll take a turn in the garden. Get a little fresh air, you know.'

Rosamund, however, failed to add to her score, and Mademoiselle went to the table. Rosamund, excusing herself for a moment, slipped out. She found Celeste.

'Celeste, my dear, Monsieur Somers is going to take a turn in the garden in a moment. Unless we're careful, Mademoiselle Dupont will endeavour to be on his arm. I rather thought you might help him avoid that.'

'Oh, yes. At once, madame. Immediately.'

Rosamund returned to the billiards room. She was just in

time to see Colonel Brecht score the two points that won the game for them. The Colonel was shaking hands all round when Celeste put her head in.

'M'sieur,' she said to Edward, 'there's a message for you. Could you come, please?'

'A message?' said Edward, and could think only of the Countess. He went after the quick-moving Celeste.

Monsieur Valery was suddenly beside Mademoiselle Dupont.

'Such an interesting game,' he said, 'and you were so unlucky to lose, mademoiselle. It would be a pleasure to have you all take cognac with me, or whatever else you might wish.'

Mademoiselle Dupont, looking slightly fretful at the disappearance of her partner, said that what she wished at the moment was to powder her nose.

Edward was taken by Celeste into the garden. The night was fresh, clean and silvery, the moon showing the first signs of its wane.

'There,' said Celeste, 'now you may breathe fine air instead of Mademoiselle Dupont's scent.'

'What about the message?' asked Edward.

'Oh, the message,' said Celeste, 'is that you're safer with me than her.' She put her arm through his and they strolled gently around the garden.

'I've a feeling,' said Edward, 'that my ability to resist Mademoiselle Dupont is being underrated.'

'Ah, but should you be overrating it, that could lead to disaster. You're so kind and trusting, m'sieur, that we must take no chances with a lady as hungry as she is.'

'Angel of thoughtfulness,' said Edward, 'I'm touched by your determination to save me, but I think Mademoiselle Dupont would herself assure you I'm in no danger. She merely likes an audience.'

'That's what you think,' said Celeste.

'Precocious girl, at sixteen you should be engaged in the innocent pursuits of the young, not advancing into the mysterious realms of worldliness. Hello, who's that?'

Someone came along the path between the hedge and the

summerhouse, emerging into the moonlight.

'Ah – Edward.' Colonel Brecht was a trifle taken aback. 'I thought you had gone to reception, to the telephone.'

'At the moment,' said Edward, 'I'm being perambulated around the garden by France's little mother. I thought you'd be having a cognac with Rosamund.'

'The dear lady has retired,' said the Colonel.

'And you're off for a brisk night walk?' said Edward. The Colonel was wearing a hat and a lightweight dark blue raincoat.

'Yes, quite so, my friend. A walk before bedtime usually puts me soundly to sleep. And it's a fine night. Ah, cheerio, then.' The Colonel's use of the English expression brought a smile to Celeste's face.

Off the German went, reaching the front steps from around the side of the hotel. Thoughtfully, he was wearing rubber-soled shoes, so that when he returned he would not disturb guests asleep.

'Breathe deeply, m'sieur,' said Celeste, as she and Edward resumed their gentle meandering, 'the night air is not too cold for you yet. You must be at your best when you visit the Countess tomorrow.'

'Did you get a good look at him?' asked the senior member of the investigative team.

'I was unable to see her,' said number two, 'but yes, I got a good look at him.'

'You agree it's Surgeon-General Boris Tchekov, once of the Imperial Army?'

'From the photographs we have, I'd swear it.'

'Good,' said number one. 'And where he is, she must be. He's had her under his wing for years. A tenacious man, but not a brilliant one. He has kept her out of sight, but not himself. He has unwisely forgotten that he's as recognisable as she is.'

'But we still need to get a look at her?'

'To fully satisfy ourselves, yes. One must consider he may be more cunning than he seems. In showing himself in the village, as he has done more than once, he might have been laying a false trail. The woman residing in the villa with him might not be the one we think she is. He might, perhaps, have sent her a thousand miles away months ago.'

'He might,' said number two, 'but I feel she's there.'

'Then make certain. Use your eyes. Discreetly and quietly. Clumsiness, comrade, could lead to our waking up one day to find the birds flown. That would be unfortunate. The villa now. We need to get into it some time. There'll be letters, papers and diaries, any of which could point us towards the others. You're aware of the uproar being caused by that wretched woman who's claiming to be Anastasia? They're dangerous, all of them. The villa is a difficult place to enter?'

'I examined the exterior thoroughly after getting over the wall the other night. The locks are formidable, and I suspect there'll be bolts as well. To effect entrance it'll be necessary to break a window.'

'Break a window?' said number one coldly. 'Break a window? Are you serious?'

'I withdraw that, comrade. We must use a glass-cutter.'

'And quietly. Tchekov has firearms. But first, lay your eyes on her. Identify her.'

'I will.'

9

Edward emerged from the pines adjacent the villa and walked up to the green gate in the high wall. The gate opened to his push. Katerina came down from the terrace as he entered, closing the gate behind him. She was hatless, her hair a deep-fired brilliance in the sunlight, her eyes warmly bright, her white dress summery.

'Thank you so much for coming,' she said.

'I'm not late?'

'Oh, no,' she said, but she had been down a few minutes ago to look for him.

He laid fascinated eyes on her. She was not a shy or diffident woman, but his survey brought the colour to her face. Her blood was flowing a little fast.

'You look remarkable,' he said.

'Healthy, you mean?'

'Yes, that as well, Countess.'

Her colour deepened.

'I am Katerina Pyotrovna. Will you call me Katerina, please? And I may call you Edward?'

'I shan't object.'

'Then come, Edward,' she said, 'and we'll play croquet and later have tea. Yes? That's agreeable to you?'

'Very,' he said. 'It sounds perfect.'

'Yes? It isn't dull? You would really like to play again and then have tea?'

'If you'll allow me to play at my slow pace, Katerina.'

'Oh, you may play as slowly as you wish,' she said, 'and I, of course, will remember not to over-exert myself. Dr Kandor has commanded restraint.'

'I'm sure he has,' said Edward. As before, there were no other people to be seen. Dr Kandor did not appear, nor were there any signs of servants. 'Who keeps your garden so well, and your lawn so perfect?' he asked as they advanced to the croquet area. The mallets and balls were out.

'Oh, Sandro is our gardener. He works on it each morning. He's also a house servant with Anna. That's all, just Anna and Sandro. They see to everything, except that I look after my own room and a few other things. Edward, I'm not simply a player of croquet. I'm in the garden only in the afternoons mostly.'

'I assure you, I'd never think of you simply as an exponent of croquet,' said Edward. With his back to the sea, he surveyed the villa. Beyond it was the wall, and beyond that were the pines and the road. And beyond the road was the rising incline covered with maquis scrub, desultory pines and wild olives. Somewhere up there, Rosamund had told him, a person had been using a spyglass yesterday morning. The garden of the villa was visible from way up. He wondered a little, remembering the original incident, and feeling certain it was Dr Kandor who had fired that shot over the head of the man Gregory.

'Edward, what is that you have?'

He turned to her. She was looking at the leather case he was carrying.

'My camera,' he said. 'If you don't mind, I'd very much like to take a photograph of you.'

Katerina stiffened.

'But why?' There were little vibrations in her voice.

'It worries you, that I'd like a photograph of you?' he said, curious because she seemed so reluctant.

'No, of course not, but—' She stopped as Dr Kandor emerged from the villa and walked down the terrace steps towards them.

'Mr Somers, welcome,' he said and shook hands with Edward. His eyes picked up the meaning of the leather case. 'You've been taking photographs?'

'No, none so far,' smiled Edward. 'But I've asked the Countess if I might take one of her.'

'And she's expressing modesty?' Dr Kandor's smile did not disguise his tendency to take the world seriously. A smile was merely a momentary lightening of his inbuilt gravity. 'The Countess is convinced she photographs badly.'

'A rose may hang its head,' said Edward, 'but can never look anything but beautiful.'

Katerina laughed, but still did not give him permission to use his camera.

'Well, Countess Katerina?' said the doctor. 'Are you able to refuse him one photograph after that?'

'Dr Kandor?' she said, regarding him uncertainly.

'Be generous,' said the doctor.

'I really don't wish to press her if she'd rather not,' said Edward, a little surprised that the taking of a snapshot should become something of an issue.

'I'm sure you'll take an admirable photograph,' said Dr Kandor, and smiled again, this time at Katerina.

'Oh, I will sit for you, Edward,' she said, 'but first must get my hat.'

'I'd like you without your hat,' said Edward. He did not want her to hide her magnificent hair.

'I agree,' said Dr Kandor. 'Let him take the photograph while I get your hat, for you should wear it while you're playing croquet.'

He made his way back to the terrace. Katerina's hat lay on the table there. Edward took out his camera and his subject stood with the sun on her face, her expression a little tense.

'No smile?' said Edward. 'I'm not taking a tooth out, you know – there'll only be a click and hardly any pain.'

She laughed then and he caught her in close-up, her face vivid and animated, and her hair a shining, burnished crown.

'It was all right?' she said.

'All right?' Edward laughed. 'That doesn't cover it at all. You may rely on it, Katerina, that if the photograph is no more than all right I'll throw the camera away. I'm expecting nothing less than exceptional.'

He would have liked to take several of her, but since she did not offer, he let it go. Dr Kandor returned with her hat. Edward removed his jacket for the game, the sun being hot, and very kindly the doctor took the garment and the camera up to the terrace. He hung the jacket over the back of a chair. He looked over his shoulder and saw the two of them preparing for the first strike. He re-entered the villa, taking the camera with him. He opened it up and exposed the film to the bright light of the window for long seconds. One had to accept the probable, the showing of the photograph to friends, to fellow ex-officers, perhaps, and it was not difficult to imagine someone saying, 'She reminds me of – let me see, who does she remind me of?' And then the guesses and perhaps a reference to a newspaper or a book.

He returned the camera to its leather case and placed it on the chair. He sat down, took out a pipe, filled it, and sat quietly smoking and watching.

Katerina was alive, as alive as an exuberant girl.

'Edward – oh! You're cheating!'

'Never.'

'But you are – you're taking a croquet without making a hit.'

'I glanced your ball, I thought.'

'No, no.'

'Are you sure?'

'Well, I'm not precisely sure. Are you precisely sure?'

'No, hopeful that you'll concede.'

Her laugh was rich, her eyes dancing.

'Oh, I concede, then. Take your croquet, but if you thump my ball – oh, you beast – that's fiendish. You've sent me into the shrubs. Off with your head!'

'You've read *Alice in Wonderland*?'

'Of course. English literature was Mama's favourite reading.'

'Bulgarian families seem commendably well educated.'

'Oh, my family was exceptionally so. I am exceptional beyond praise.'

'Very true,' said Edward, smiting for a hoop and failing.

'I am joking,' she said.

'I'm not. I'll get your ball, Katerina.'

'No, no, I will go.' Her face was a little warm. 'You must not run about.'

'Neither must you.'

'But we're doing very well together, aren't we?' she said, and he watched her as she glided over the lawn to retrieve her ball from the bed of bright-flowering shrubs. It was impossible to believe that a woman so rich with life should have a weak heart.

He watched her make her shot from the edge. She struck her ball with a smooth crack. It travelled in a rush over the mown grass, and a laugh of sheer delight broke from her as it cannoned into his red ball.

'Now that *is* exceptional beyond praise,' said Edward.

'Oh, did you see it, Edward?' She came up, warm, quick and glowing. 'I've never played quite such a good shot as that, never. That's because—' She broke off, bending to place her ball against his red one. She looked up from under her hat. 'Oh, it's because I'm enjoying it so much. Is it foolish, even childish, to find so much pleasure in a little game of croquet? Is it the silly, aimless pleasure of people who have nothing else to do while others work?'

'Perhaps it is for some,' said Edward. 'I don't think it is for you.'

'I'd like to be able to work, to be useful,' she said. 'I'd like to do many things.' She might have said she would like to go out into the world and be as much a part of life as other women were. She bent to her ball again, and Edward wondered why there were apparently no friends, no caring friends, and, most of all, why there was no caring man who loved her and wanted her as his wife. Could any man have found a lovelier or warmer one? What did her weak heart matter? Her presence alone would bring light and joy to a home.

He looked up, at the silent Dr Kandor sitting at the terrace table, and at the climbing vista beyond. A little flash of light caught his eye. The reflection, he thought, of the sun on the polished brass of a telescope. It came and went. It came again.

'There,' said Katerina, sending his ball running.

'Katerina, were you playing croquet yesterday morning?' he asked.

'No. I'm busy in the house in the mornings. I said so, didn't I? I'm in the garden only during the afternoons. There, go – go—' She watched her struck ball. It passed through the hoop. 'Oh, do you see, I'm at the top of my form, Edward.'

She was a delight to him. They played on, he pacing himself and she in exhilaration. He had the oddest feeling that she was trying to cram the vitality of a lifetime into a single hour. There was no word of caution from Dr Kandor. He seemed not at all concerned about her physical extravagance. When she finally won the game, she appeared to think victory was marred by the conclusion of play.

'Oh, how sad,' she said. 'I'm afraid it's all over.'

'Much to my mortification, it is,' said Edward.

'You're really mortified?'

'Not really. I enjoyed every moment.'

'Oh, that's everything, isn't it, enjoying each moment?'

'With you, yes, that's everything, Katerina.'

'You really are—' She paused, she smiled.

'Yes?'

'Very nice,' she said. 'Shall we have tea now?'

He climbed the terrace steps very slowly. He always climbed steps slowly. But in an instinctive gesture of concern, Katerina put a hand under his elbow. It made him wish for a return to vigour and health, so that he could stand before her with as much to offer her as any normal man.

Dr Kandor shared tea with them, and they talked, all three of them. Edward asked questions about Bulgaria. The replies from both Katerina and the doctor were lightly informative. Edward thought, not for the first time, what an extraordinary aura of grace and regality she had. And her latent love of activity was in her eyes. They were quick, expressive and as clear as mirrors. She had, he discovered, little teasing moments, as if she could not wholly put aside the years of her youth. Yet she was, quite completely, an enchanting woman.

When it was time for Edward to go, Katerina glanced at Dr Kandor, who reached for her wrist and felt her pulse. He pronounced it excellent.

'That means I can offer you revenge, Edward,' she said, and she accompanied him to the gate. 'I'm not being too demanding, asking if you'll come again?'

'You're being very gracious,' he said, 'but I think it's my turn to do the honours. I've a car at the hotel. Would you care to take a ride with me – a morning or afternoon spin? I handle it very soberly, and you won't be subjected to anything hair-raising. A gentle hour's ride out and a gentle return? Would you like to?'

He saw how the prospect tempted her, even fascinated her.

'Oh, how lovely,' she said, 'Edward, how marvellous. I – oh, I'm not sure.' Her lashes dropped. 'Dr Kandor, perhaps, would think – no, I'll speak to him and write you a little note. If he thinks it would be unwise, you won't mind spending the time here instead?'

'A car ride with you, or croquet with you, either would be a pleasure.'

When he had gone, Katerina approached her doctor in such a beguiling way that his little alarm bell began to ring.

'Boris Sergeyovich, you consider Edward a splendid gentleman?'

'Have I said that, Katerina Pyotrovna?'

'Oh, I think so, and I agree with you. He's perfect as a friend, isn't he?'

'Is he?' murmured the doctor.

'Suddenly, how fortunate I am. I have sweet Celeste and Edward as my friends, and you to protect me. You also see to my health, so that I don't have to call in strange doctors.'

'I've little work to do as a medical man,' said Dr Kandor. 'I've no wounded soldiers in my care, and you are never ill.'

'Well, perhaps I'll develop a little chill this winter or sprain my ankle,' she smiled. 'Oh, by the way, Edward would like to take me for a drive in his car. I'd enjoy that very much. I can hardly say no, can I? Especially as he assured me he'd drive very carefully.'

Dr Kandor sat up.

'Madness indisputable,' he said. 'I've seen his car. You'll be open to every pair of eyes he passes. And who can say he'll return with you? Who is to say it won't be the most specious way of abducting you and delivering you into the hands of your enemies? Edward Somers seems an honourable man, yes, but you and I could both be deceived.'

'How could we be? He's been staying at the hotel every winter for years, and we've been here not quite two years. Boris Sergeyovich, you aren't thinking. Had he been a new visitor, had he suddenly appeared, then it would be reasonable to have suspicions. As it is – oh, you only have to look at him and speak with him to know you could trust him. I could trust him with my last breath.'

'With your life, Katerina Pyotrovna?'

'Yes, with my life.' She was unhesitating. 'As I trust you. Oh, you must consider him a genuine friend, or you wouldn't have encouraged him to take that photograph of me.'

'To be cautious, to be careful, doesn't necessarily mean one is distrustful. The photograph will not come out. I opened up the camera and exposed the film.'

'Oh, how could you do such a thing!' Katerina flushed in distress. 'That was unworthy.'

'Nothing I do in your interests is unworthy to me,' he said. 'I did not spoil his film because I distrust him, but because it's wiser for no one to have photographs of you.'

'You let Edward take the photograph so that he wouldn't think our refusal strange?'

'I think you understood that at the time, Katerina Pyotrovna.'

'I did not think you intended to ruin it.'

'To want him to have a photograph of you is not the wisest thing.'

'He's my friend,' said Katerina, 'my only friend apart from Celeste. I'm even denied contact with the Grand Dukes—'

'The Grand Dukes who live in Nice are of the kind who'd make the most dangerous friends of all. One or two of them would sell you to the Bolsheviks for less than the price of a necklace.'

'Boris Sergeyovich, your protection of me is very precious.' Katerina gently pressed his hand. 'I know you are right about the Grand Dukes. But please let me go with Edward. See, I'll wear a veil and ensure we don't drive to Nice. There, that's a splendid idea, isn't it?'

'I'm uneasy,' said the doctor.

'You needn't be.'

'I'm uneasy about your feelings. I did not anticipate there was a danger you might fall in love. I've this moment realised the danger is very real. He is in your eyes, Katerina Pyotrovna.'

The colour rushed to her face. She stood up and gazed fixedly at the sea.

'I will not discuss that.' She was quite imperious. 'You've no right to ask me to.'

'I'm not asking you to. I'm concerned about what it might lead to.'

'I am not falling in love,' she said fiercely, but he heard the vibrations in her voice, always a sign of emotion in her. 'I've only seen Edward twice.'

'Three times. Perhaps the first time was enough. You

began to dream that day.'

'Boris Sergeyovich!' She turned. She stamped her foot. 'I will not discuss it, no!'

She swept away, into the villa, to hide what was in her eyes.

He sighed.

Edward woke up again that night. He was used to broken nights, to the hours when his suffering lungs brought him out of sleep and induced him to take one of the tablets prescribed by his doctor. He was not used to being woken up by a disturbed mind.

Who was she, besides being Countess Katerina Pyotrovna of Varna? Who was so interested in her, but so unwanted, that Dr Kandor not only kept a rifle to hand but was ready to use it? Who was using a telescope to observe her?

Why had she been so hesitant to let him photograph her?

10

Close to lunchtime the following morning, Celeste arrived at Edward's elbow. He was at work in the garden, detached as usual from the activities of other guests. Celeste had a letter for him. It had just arrived from the Villa d'Azur.

'M'sieur,' she murmured, 'look – another billet-doux.'

She stood by while he read it, for she wished to miss nothing of a developing relationship that was touching her romantic soul deeply.

Dear Edward my friend, I am in such pleasure in informing you that Dr Kandor, having given your suggestion generous consideration, has said a drive in your car will do me no harm whatever, providing you are not a madman behind a wheel. I have assured him that you have assured me you aren't. Will you let me know, please, when I am to expect you to call for me, with the car? I am, in friendship, Katerina.

He read it twice, then smiled up at the hovering French girl.

'Thank you, Celeste,' he said. 'This is from the Countess.'

'I already know that,' said Celeste.

'Then you're not burning with unsatisfied curiosity? Good.'

'Oh, m'sieur, you're merciless in your secrecy.'

'Shame on me. Well, if you must know, I'll be taking her for a drive in my car tomorrow afternoon.'

'Oh, such an achievement,' breathed Celeste rapturously. 'She never goes out, she has to be so careful.'

'Yes, very careful,' said Edward.

'Isn't it sad, her fragile heart?' said Celeste. 'You must take the greatest care of her. But only think, m'sieur, how sweet her thoughts of you must be for her to risk a drive in your car.'

'Your imagination, young lady, is running away with you.'

'Write your answer,' smiled Celeste, bobbed hair springing, 'and Jacques will take it immediately after lunch. We mustn't keep the Countess in suspense.'

'Oh, we're all in this, are we?' said Edward.

'No, no,' protested Celeste, 'it's just between you and me.'

'I think that covers everybody here and in La Roche,' said Edward.

'It does not,' said Celeste proudly. 'I'm true to you and Madame.'

'Yes, little one, but you're not to assume she and I are anything except friends.'

'No, m'sieur, of course not. I'll go away now and let you compose your loving answer to her.' She went off, humming a song.

Edward retired to his room to write his reply to Katerina. He was delighted, he said, to know the car drive was on, and would pick her up tomorrow afternoon at two thirty, if that was convenient to her. He sent her his regards and best wishes.

When Katerina received his note, she read it with care and then put it away with the previous one he had sent. It was a family tradition, never to destroy any correspondence. Tradition aside, she wished to keep his little notes in any case.

Mademoiselle Dupont, meeting Edward as she descended the stairs on her way to lunch, detained him with a smile and a few words.

'Edward, I do wish you would spare some time from your writing in order to save me from being bored to death by Monsieur Valery.'

'Is he a bore? He seems a quite affable gentleman.'

'Oh, he's affable enough, yes, but he has no conversation.'

'I don't shine myself, mademoiselle. At least, no one has ever said I do.'

'But you are such a good listener. I implore your sweet consideration of my woe.'

'Your woe?' Edward smiled. 'Well, I'm listening. Or, if you wish, join me for tea on the lawn this afternoon. It's lunchtime now.'

'You can offer no more?' Mademoiselle Dupont sighed theatrically.

'I must get on with my writing.'

'Tomorrow I should like to escape, to go to Nice, perhaps,' she said. It seemed an obvious invitation for him to drive her there.

'A taxi can be hired, mademoiselle. Myself, I'm taking a friend for a drive.'

'Ah, Rosamund, no doubt.'

'No, another friend of mine.'

'Alas,' sighed Mademoiselle Dupont, 'this is a most depressing day.'

'I think you'll find lunch will set you up again,' said Edward.

'May I join you, Edward? Thank you. Marie will set a place for me at your table. How nice. Lunch at least will be a congenial hour.'

Celeste, who shared the dining-room duties with Marie out of season, was so disenchanted with the sight of Mademoiselle Dupont lunching with Edward that the looks she cast him were singularly pointed. Mademoiselle Dupont, however, enjoyed her lunch very much, for her captive audience had a more intelligent ear than certain other gentlemen. Or so she assured Edward. Monsieur Valery, sitting alone, seemed resigned to the fact that the lady from Paris had no preference for him. His ready smile was more soulful than cheerful.

Rosamund and Colonel Brecht, also sharing a table now that their compatibility had advanced, provided Edward with glances of sympathy, but truth to tell he was able to absorb Mademoiselle Dupont's monologues quite painlessly. She had his ear, certainly, but his mind was on Katerina.

Someone else was also interested in her. Someone with a telescope.

Edward began to worry. He must talk to her tomorrow afternoon.

They had not been going for more than five minutes before she was patently exhilarated.

She was out. She had left her high walls behind. She was actually out, and with a man considerate and kind, a man of gentle humour who belonged to the world she had not known for years. The open car was a creation of engineering magic, pursuing a steady course in the direction of Monte Carlo. She had wanted to go that way, she had told him, not Nice. Well, they could get to within sight of Monte Carlo in an hour, Edward had said.

She was a picture, he thought. From her securely fitted hat depended a veil, a full veil. To keep the dust out, she said. Veils no longer being a fashionable accessory to any kind of outfit, except mourning black, hers gave her an outmoded Edwardian look that to him was neither incongruous nor unsuitable. It turned her into an enchanting picture of a bygone age of grace. She wore an oatmeal-coloured costume, and on her lap was a folded coat to wear if the weather became fresh.

But it was balmy at the moment. The warm breeze flirted

around them, and the Bentley took the winding road unhurriedly.

'Oh, this is lovely,' said Katerina.

'The pace suits you?'

'Yes. I shouldn't want you to drive fast. Not because I don't think you could be as dashing with a car as men like to be, but because at this speed I can observe everything at my leisure. Edward, how kind you are to me, helping me to forget my sadness.'

'Sadness?' he said.

Under the veil, her eyes clouded.

'Oh, because of my heart,' she said lightly.

'Are you sure it's only your heart condition, Katerina?'

'Yes. Of course. Yes.'

A car, coming up at speed, closed on them, and Edward, as soon as a straight stretch occurred, pulled well over to allow the driver to overtake. The car passed them with a roar, a closed black French car, and so near them that metal almost touched.

'Clown,' muttered Edward.

'A wild one,' said Katerina, watching the car pull away from them.

'We could catch him up and eat him,' said Edward.

'Could we?' Katerina sounded as if the idea excited her, as it did.

'You'd like us to?'

'Oh, yes – but—'

'Yes, but we won't,' said Edward. 'Once the challenge would have fired both of us, and we should have charged headlong after the idiot, but we must run at a walking pace now, you and I.'

'Oh, I don't mind at what pace we pursue this outing,' said Katerina. 'You've no idea how I'm enjoying it. I feel as if the whole world is opening up to me. I'm actually seeing it come to life.'

What she was seeing were the changing views of the coastal drive, which in truth were all very similar, and no grander than the vista she saw each day from her villa. It was what she was feeling that mostly affected her. She was exhilarated with a sense of freedom, and the sweet pleasure of being with Edward. The sea on her right came to her eyes like gently swirling pools of blue, lapping at sandy coves far below. The rocky coastline, with its varying levels, was filled with the flora of the Mediterranean. Pines, myrtles and wild olives sprouted amid maquis and garigue scrub. Broom, gorse, lavender and rosemary proliferated, and the aromatic scents were carried on the breeze in extravagant abandon.

Edward drove as he had promised to, carefully. In any case, it was impossible to attain any consistent speed on this winding, hilly road, with frequent hairpin bends to negotiate and a dizzy drop on their nearside. The French drove on the right, not on the left. Further, it was necessary for him to avoid any situation in which his physical control of the car would be subjected to sudden effort and stress. That could bring on the kind of attack that would lay him low. And since the main purpose of the drive was to give Katerina a leisurely outing, there was no reason to hurry. The little principality of Monte Carlo lay ahead, and they might just have time to drive around it before returning.

There was little traffic now that the summer season was over. A car was still a luxury to most people.

'Would you like us to park the car in Monte Carlo and look at the shops?' he asked.

'Thank you, Edward, but no,' she said. Dearly she would have liked that, but definitely she could not risk it, even with her veil. There were exiles in Monte Carlo, as well as Nice, and some exiles had eyes sharp and inquisitive.

Motoring around a long bend, with a rocky, shrub-covered descent on their right, the sea far below, they heard a car behind them. It was approaching fast. There was nothing else visible on the road, nothing coming towards them, but even so Edward did not intend to signal the car to overtake. The bend made it far too risky. So he gave no signal, nor did he draw the Bentley closer to the edge. But he heard the car accelerate, and he knew it was going to chance the manoeuvre.

'The idiot – if anything is on its way round the bend—'

The car, a black saloon, roared alongside them, powering

hard. Edward sustained shock and Katerina drew a hissing breath, for the car was dangerously close. Worse, it was angling, cutting in on them. It happened so fast, the powerful burst of speed, the violent assault on the Bentley and the angled thrust, that catastrophe loomed. The black saloon was a hideous menace, threatening to batter them off the road, over the edge and down to the rocks and the sea below.

But Edward, holding his line, although his offside fender was being mangled, pulled sharply on his handbrake. The Bentley shuddered to a crash stop. The black car, deprived of its prey, shot towards the edge in front of the Bentley and was brought back from the brink of suicide by a lightning spin of the wheel which sent it careering to the other side of the road. It straightened up, harshly scraping rock, and roared away. It was the same car that had overtaken them fifteen minutes previously. It showed no number plate, not now. It had obviously stopped some way back in a side road, and the driver, who had since shown his intentions to be murderous, had waited there for them to pass and then got on to their tail again.

Edward sat, breathing painfully.

'That was not very friendly,' said Katerina, and if her body was still stiff with tension, her voice was remarkably calm.

'Not very friendly? My God,' said Edward, 'it was murderous. Katerina, are you all right?'

'Thank you, yes, Edward. I've known other unfriendly people – during the – during the war. I think you saved us by stopping as quickly as you did.'

'The only thing I could do.' He drooped over the wheel, fighting to pull air into his lungs, which seemed in tortured rejection of it. She put a hand on his arm.

'Edward, are you in pain?'

'No.' He wheezed. He felt like an old man, ancient and bronchial. 'A little—' He coughed. 'A little short of breath, that's all. Give me a moment.' He wheezed again, his lungs fiery.

She looked at him, at his bent head and his open mouth. She felt in pain for him, a pain that came from knowing there was nothing she could do to ease him.

'Rest as long as you like,' she said softly. 'You are a dear friend, I think, and when you feel better, perhaps we should turn round and go back.'

He was racked, suddenly, by a fit of coughing. When it subsided, he lifted his head, and his thin face looked ravaged.

'You think, Katerina,' he said with an effort, 'that farther on he may be waiting for us, whoever he is?'

'We should go back, don't you think so?' she said, her expression unreadable behind her veil.

His lungs began to take in air.

'Katerina, who are you?' he asked. Only by the grace of God was she still alive instead of lying smashed and dead on the rocks below.

'I am Katerina Pyotrovna of Varna,' she said quietly, 'but the best of my years were spent with the family my father served.'

'No, Katerina, that's not the reason why you're shut up in your villa.' A car passed them. The driver glanced at them, but did not stop to ask why their offside fender was mangled. 'Why are you shut up?'

'Because the peace and quietness of the villa are good for my condition.'

'Did you feel, a few moments ago, that you were near to heart failure?'

'Yes, Edward, I did.'

'Katerina—'

'Please,' she said, touching his arm, 'you must always believe what I say, and you must not ask questions. I am still alive—'

'Still?'

Behind the veil there was a ghost of a smile.

'Yes, I'm still alive. Because of you. You were so quick. Your beautiful car became a great heavy weight, quite immovable. I am glad and grateful you are my friend. But let us go back.'

'I'm worried about you, and very concerned. Someone with a telescope has been watching you in your garden.'

Katerina stiffened.

'You've seen him?'

'No, but I'm sure he's been up there, up amid the trees on the other side of the road. I must ask questions. Why would anyone want to train a telescope on you?'

'People can't always be understood, Edward. People do very odd things. I would like—' She hesitated.

'What would you like?' he asked, his breathing easier by far now.

Again there was a glimpse of a faint smile.

'I would like you to call tomorrow and play a peaceful game of croquet with me. Edward, is that a little demanding of me, to ask more of your time from you?'

'There must be no more outings?' he said.

'Oh, yes, I would so like that,' she said, 'but for the moment – Edward, will you think about tomorrow and send me a note if you can come?'

'I can promise you now that I'll come.' Another car passed. Its swish made them both jump a little.

'Edward, I'd like to have a note from you.'

'Sometimes, you know,' smiled Edward, 'you're no older than Celeste.'

'Well, Celeste is very sweet,' she said.

'We'll go back,' he said, 'though we can't turn here.'

He restarted the car and they went slowly along the road until they found a place where he was able to turn and begin the drive back. They were both quiet. Edward was thinking about the driver of that black saloon. Had he simply been a maniac? If not, why had he done what he had? His deadly action had been aimed at Katerina, almost certainly. Edward's thoughts raced. How could the man have known it was Katerina in the Bentley? No one knew he'd been taking her for a drive, except Celeste. And Rosamund. He had mentioned it to Rosamund, his outing with the Countess who lived at the Villa d'Azur, and Rosamund had been a little teasing.

He felt a gloved hand on his arm, and a warm pressure.

'Thank you, Edward, for everything,' said Katerina.

A strange sadness afflicted him. He loved her.

* * *

She knew she must tell Dr Kandor, and did. They sat in a room that looked out on to the terrace and garden, and the doctor, frowning, tugged at his beard.

'You're going to tell me I must never go out again, aren't you?' she said.

'You were close to death, and you've been watched by someone with a telescope? That's what you're saying?'

'Someone with a telescope – that's what Edward has said.'

'Then I'm going to tell you, because I must,' said Dr Kandor, 'that we can stay here no longer. Another place, another country, must be found.'

Katerina paled.

'No! No!'

'Someone has discovered us, Katerina Pyotrovna.'

'You can't know that,' she said in distress. 'This afternoon it may have only been some crazy madman, and all kinds of people use telescopes for all kinds of reasons.'

'Do you believe that?' he asked in his grave way.

'Yes. Yes.'

'No, it's what you wish to believe,' he said.

'Boris Sergeyovich,' she said desperately, 'we aren't going to run again, we aren't.'

'We must.'

'No!'

He sighed.

'I've made certain promises and accepted certain responsibilities,' he said. 'I've done so willingly, out of loyalty and love. In keeping my promises and discharging my responsibilities, I have to discount your emotions, and you know I must. You too must pursue a path of obedience, for the sake of all. Undoubtedly, we've been discovered, and therefore we must go, taking Anna and Sandro with us, as soon as I've decided where we shall go and when.'

'Oh, Boris Sergeyovich, you're breaking my heart,' she said.

'One day, perhaps, when the world is less cruel and more forgiving, you may all be together again. Edward Somers is only a part of one more episode in your long journey towards that day.'

'I'm to give up Celeste and Edward, the only real friends I've had in many years?'

'Yes, Katerina Pyotrovna,' he said.

'But I'm a nobody,' she said, 'I'll never be a somebody again. It's an absurdly romantic notion to imagine we can know high station again. Might I not be allowed to live as a nobody, to have friends, to have a – a—'

'A lover? A husband?'

'Yes, Boris Sergeyovich, yes. Soon I'll be too old.'

'There are people who'll never recognise you as a nobody,' said the doctor. 'I think you've just had an encounter with one of them. So, I must make plans.'

'In making plans,' she said palely, 'you will reduce me to misery.'

'I think not,' he said, 'you aren't the kind to yield to self-pity. You are the best of them, Katerina Pyotrovna, the bravest. Meanwhile, we've acquired a dog. We have no bodyguards, because bodyguards attract long noses and curiosity. But because lately we've suffered an intruder, I've bought a dog which will prevent anyone getting in. Come, I'll show you.'

He took her through to the rear of the villa, and there introduced her to a large Alsatian. The animal, deep-chested, its pointed ears stiff and erect, bristled as the doctor brought Katerina close.

'Oh, I once had a dog, sweet and affectionate,' she said, 'and this creature is ten times its size.'

But she was unafraid and stooped to the animal. The doctor caressed its nose. It sniffed in suspicion at Katerina.

'This is your mistress,' said the doctor, and Katerina laid a hand on its head, between its ears.

'Oh, you are magnificent,' she said.

'He's met Anna and Sandro, and now you,' said Dr Kandor.

'He must also meet Celeste and Edward,' said Katerina, 'and I shall call him Prince. That's a proud name for a proud dog. Boris, while we're still here, I may continue to see my friends? I've invited Edward to call tomorrow afternoon.'

'While we're still here, I've no objection to this,' said the doctor, 'and Edward Somers has proved himself a courageous friend. But you must say nothing about going.'

'I must tell him.'

'You must not. There will be too many questions. We shall simply disappear, Anna and Sandro one day, you and I next, at night. I will arrange it.'

'How long will you give me before you break my heart?' she said sadly.

'It will have to be as short a time as possible,' he said. 'But your heart will mend. You have the pride and resilience of an empress. You were born to be an empress.'

Katerina walked slowly away. Prince, the Alsatian, followed her, tail wagging.

11

Edward, fresh from a bath, sat wondering why a beautiful woman with a weak heart had not had an attack at a moment that had been horrifying. He penned the note she had asked for.

> *Dear Katerina, I'd like, if I may, to accept your invitation to see you tomorrow. The pain of being on a hiding to nothing at croquet will be indistinguishable from pleasure. I hope very much you're suffering no delayed shock from this afternoon's unpleasantness. No one could have been calmer or braver. I salute you. Sincerely, Edward.*

He was in the hotel garden a little later, regarding the flushed evening sky and the onset of twilight. Anxiety beset him. He knew himself totally committed to Katerina's well-being, and he was certain other people weren't. He himself could not have been the target of that murder attempt. It had to be Katerina. Mystery encompassed her existence.

The evening was autumnal. Celeste arrived. He had ordered a Pernod.

'M'sieur – Edward? I've served your aperitif in the lounge. It's too cold for you out here.'

'Is it?'

'It will be, in just a few minutes,' she said. 'What has happened to your car? Jacques said it was damaged, so I looked. Such a mess. I'm worried that you had an accident while you were out with Madame.'

'I brushed a wall. Another car took up too much of the road. But it's only the fender. I'll take it into Nice tomorrow to get it fixed. If your kind mama will allow, would you like to come with me? We'll leave after breakfast and be back by lunchtime.'

'A ride to Nice?' Celeste's eyes sparkled. 'Oh, how good you are to me. I'm enchanted.'

'If your mama can spare you, be enchanted,' said Edward.

'To Mama,' said Celeste proudly, 'you're as irresistible as you are to me.'

'I don't think that can be strictly true. By the way, I've a note.' He handed it to her. 'Can you get Jacques to deliver it this evening?'

'Oh, but yes,' said Celeste, seeing to whom it was addressed. 'Heavens, the profusion of billets-doux – I'm overwhelmed.'

'Do try, my little chicken, not to be overwhelmed to the point of expiring,' said Edward. 'I must go and find my Pernod. I think I need it, Celeste. Did you, incidentally, mention to anyone that I was taking the Countess for a drive this afternoon?'

'Certainly not,' said Celeste, 'I'd never disclose details of your trysts with Madame.'

'Let's go in,' said Edward.

Rosamund and Colonel Brecht came out to meet them as they approached the French windows of the lounge.

'You're so often together, you two,' smiled Rosamund.

'Oh, we are devoted, madame,' said Celeste with her air of ingenuousness. 'Tomorrow morning we are driving into Nice.'

'Nice? How tantalising,' said Rosamund.

'Ah – would you like a visit to Nice some time, Rosamund?' asked Colonel Brecht in his diffident way.

'Join us tomorrow morning,' said Edward, 'and I'll drop you both at the shops and pick you up later.'

'You really are a dear man,' said Rosamund, 'thank you. Did you enjoy your outing today? Franz and I are both curious to know what your mysterious Countess is like.'

'Oh, you scattered the news around that I was taking her for a drive, did you?' said Edward lightly.

'I mentioned it to Franz, since it was rather an event,' said Rosamund. 'Do tell, Edward, what is she like? You and Celeste seem to be the only people who have met her.'

'She's very good at croquet,' said Edward.

'Croquet? Croquet?' Rosamund arched her eyebrows.

'She is charming, madame,' said Celeste, 'and very beautiful.'

'Charming, beautiful and also mysterious?' said Rosamund. 'Then you must have had an exciting outing, Edward.'

'Momentous,' said Edward.

They entered the lounge, the meeting-place of guests who liked to enjoy an aperitif or two before dinner. Celeste closed the French windows and drew the velvet curtains.

'M'sieur,' she said to Edward, 'there is your Pernod, on the corner table.'

'Celeste, may I have a dry Vermouth, please?' said Rosamund.

'Ah, yes, and for me,' said Colonel Brecht.

Celeste departed. Rosamund looked around. There were three other guests present, the silver-haired couple and Dr Bush, the American.

'Where's the voluble Mademoiselle Dupont?' asked Rosamund.

'My information,' said Colonel Brecht, 'was that she had gone into hiding to escape Monsieur Valery.'

'Such is life,' said Rosamund, 'and such are its perversities, that a woman who can't do without the company of men finds herself pursued by the one man she has no interest in. I shall recommend to Monsieur Valery that he continues his pursuit. Doggedness and persistence may yet bring him victory.'

'I have a feeling that too close a pursuit is more likely to bring him a thick ear and a black eye,' said Edward.

Celeste brought the drinks, mixed by Jacques. There was no bar in the Corniche. Hotel bars were an innovation, imported from America, and known only to the grander establishments so far. Madame Michel saw to it, however, that drinks were always available to her guests.

Edward sat quietly thinking.

'Shall we – ah – take dinner together for once, Rosamund?' suggested Colonel Brecht, no doubt encouraged by the fact that yesterday they had shared a table for lunch.

'For once – ah – I'm agreeable,' said Rosamund gravely, 'but it must be understood, as is the way at this charming place, that the custom of individual tables shall remain generally inviolate.'

'No, it would not do to find oneself taking breakfast every morning with a talkative person,' said the Colonel.

'I don't consider myself talkative,' said Rosamund, 'especially at breakfast.'

'I wasn't thinking of you, no, no,' said the Colonel. 'You are entertaining, not talkative.'

'I've a soft spot for men who are quick to make amends,' said Rosamund.

Edward smiled. Rosamund and Franz Brecht had achieved rapport.

The night was still. The moon, fading but still huge, cast its silvery light. The dog's pointed nose lifted, its ears pricked. It came to its feet. It did not bark, but trotted silently around the side of the villa from its kennel. It padded over the lawn. It stopped, hackles rising. It moved again, fast, bounding towards the little gate in the high wall.

It barked ferociously as it hurled itself at the gate.

On the other side of the wall, feet retreated in haste. The ground, strewn with pine needles, whispered as someone began to run fast.

Katerina awoke.

So did Dr Kandor. He put on a dressing-gown and went out to quieten the dog, and to stand and listen.

He heard nothing. But he knew someone had been there.

Nice was always at its best in autumn. The heat of summer could sometimes be trying. The warmth of a friendly autumn could be mellow, and that, combined with the sea air, provided perfect conditions for anyone with affected lungs. Edward could never be persuaded, however, that Nice was preferable to La Roche.

He put Rosamund and Colonel Brecht down in the Promenade des Anglais at a little after ten o'clock, and promised to pick them up at noon. Rosamund looked distinctly picturesque in a powder-blue costume and blue cloche hat. The Colonel looked handsome in a light grey suit and Panama hat. Rosamund intended to take him round the shops, and the Colonel appeared uneasy, as if he thought he would be expected to gaze at window displays of French lingerie. It was quite possible that Rosamund meant to ensure he would do precisely that.

Indeed, he soon found himself sharing her observation of an exquisite French corset, black and trimmed with lace.

'Enchanting,' said Rosamund, 'and so kind to one's figure.'

'My dear lady, I am of the ignorance total about such things.'

'Then it's time you were educated, Franz.'

'We aren't going in?' he said a little hoarsely.

'You don't care to?' Rosamund regarded him thoughtfully. 'The assistants, you know, are always so much more interested when a lady is accompanied by a gentleman. You're expected, when in France, to do as Frenchmen do – give your advice and opinions on a prospective purchase.'

'I'd almost prefer to find myself accidentally locked up with Mademoiselle Dupont.'

'I'm sure you would,' said Rosamund sweetly. 'She has

such a good figure and such ravishing ways.'

'*Himmel*,' breathed the Colonel.

'I'm only teasing,' said Rosamund.

'I am relieved.'

'Good gracious,' exclaimed Rosamund as they turned to walk on.

'You've forgotten something?' said the Colonel.

'I've just seen something,' said Rosamund. 'On the other side of the street. Look.'

The Colonel looked. On the opposite side of the wide boulevard Mademoiselle Dupont was sauntering and window-gazing. In a white dress patterned with black polka dots and a white hat, she was attractively symbolic of the graciousness of Nice.

'One can't fault her appearance,' said Colonel Brecht, 'or complain about her being here.'

'No, I don't mean that,' said Rosamund. 'Look there.'

He followed her eyes. Coming along the pavement was Monsieur Valery, his slight figure nattily clad in a cream suit and a brown trilby hat on his head. His walk was brisk, his air perky and inquisitive, as if he was looking for someone. He saw Mademoiselle Dupont and darted quickly up to her. She turned. Distinctly, her reaction at seeing him was cold. He spoke to her. She drew herself up and made an angry gesture. She walked away. He followed her, catching her up and persisting with his importunities.

'There, he's anchored himself to her,' said Rosamund, 'and she so prefers Edward, and Edward so prefers Celeste and the mysterious Countess of the Villa d'Azur. Come along, Franz.'

The Colonel still had his eyes on Monsieur Valery. He was frowning.

'Idiot,' he muttered.

'Come along,' said Rosamund, 'there's a shop ahead which specialises in the most delightful creations.'

'Not – ah – dear lady, not – ah—'

'No. Men's clothes. We'll see if there's anything there which will suit you. A dashing spotted bow tie, perhaps.'

'Bow tie? Bow tie of the spots? Rosamund—'

'Come along, Franz,' said Rosamund yet again, and was laughing as they went on their way.

'M'sieur, yes,' said the works foreman, 'a new fender.'

'Fitted by twelve o'clock?' said Edward.

'Certainly, m'sieur, certainly,' said the foreman of the comprehensive motor garage which specialised, among other things, in attending to the needs of the various British cars that found their way into Nice.

'Thank you,' said Edward, and dropped a French banknote into the man's hand. He was accorded a smile of Gallic appreciation. 'I wonder if you could help me with another matter? I'm interested in the car which damaged mine and didn't stop.'

'The scoundrel, m'sieur, should be reported to the police.'

Celeste opened her eyes wide. Edward had told her he brushed a wall.

'The car in question was a black Citroën saloon,' said Edward, 'and suffered a damaged bonnet and wing. It hasn't been brought here for repairs?'

'No, m'sieur, I can assure you it hasn't.'

'I'd like to trace it, without the help of the police.'

'Ah,' said the understanding foreman, 'to come face to face with the miscreant, m'sieur?'

'Precisely.'

'M'sieur, I'll make telephone calls, to other garages. When you return for your car, perhaps I'll have some information for you.'

'It's possible, of course, that the driver may not have brought it to Nice for repairs.'

'I'll make some calls, m'sieur.'

'Thank you,' said Edward.

'Oh, this is disgraceful,' said Celeste as they left the garage, 'you did have an accident when you were out with Madame. It's deplorable of you not to have told me.'

'We all have our regrettable moments, my infant.'

They strolled in the sunshine, Celeste in a pale yellow frock and straw hat. She looked young, buoyant and pretty.

She also looked indignant.

'Edward, I'm ashamed of you,' she said. 'Such a terrible shock for my Madame, to find herself in a car accident. Her heart, did you think of her heart?'

'I'm always thinking of her heart, Celeste. Fortunately, she remained calm and unshocked. Celeste, has it occurred to you that she may not be confined to her villa because of her heart? Has it occurred to you that she isn't being protected from physical stress, but something else? The accident was no accident. The other car tried to batter us over the edge of the road and over the cliffs.'

'Oh, it can't be true!' Celeste was appalled.

'It is true, I'm afraid. But keep it to yourself, my sweet little friend. Promise?'

'Yes, of course,' said Celeste, 'but how can anyone want to harm the Countess? She's so sweet, so gracious, so kind.'

'I wonder where her husband is?' said Edward thoughtfully. 'Or is there a husband? She wears no ring. What became of the Count of Varna, if there is a Count of Varna?'

'Stop,' gasped Celeste, 'it's too much for me.'

'Shall we walk a little more slowly, angel?'

'Oh, a thousand pardons, m'sieur, I'm going too fast – but I'm agitated, you see.'

'Let's continue on to the Imperial. Then we can sit and drink coffee in the sunshine until it's time to go back to the garage. That will be enough exercise for me, since I'm due to play croquet this afternoon.'

'Oh, you are going to visit her again?' said Celeste. 'Again? Then how happy I am for you, and will pray that rose petals will fall around you both.'

'Rose petals?' he said as they entered the broad tree-lined promenade.

'Always at weddings there should be rose petals,' said Celeste.

'Was there ever such precociousness?' said Edward. 'There'll be no wedding, you terrible child.'

'But where there is love—'

'Where there's a very fertile imagination, you mean. I'm no man to make a husband, Celeste.'

'Oh, such gloom,' vowed Celeste, shaking her head. 'How can you be so poor in spirit? That isn't like you at all.'

They turned into the spacious forecourt of the Imperial and found themselves a table. A waiter hastened up, pulling out a chair for Celeste, into which she sank with the feline grace of a girl young and free-limbed. Edward ordered coffee. The sun poured brightness over the face of Celeste and warmed his lined features. Celeste thought she would like to kiss him. He was not to know that her precociousness hid her love for him. She spent the busy summer months looking forward to autumn and winter, when she knew he'd be there. Sometimes frost nipped the ears early in the morning, and sometimes he spent hours writing in the quiet of his room. She had fervent hopes for him, but she viewed the long slender talons of Mademoiselle Dupont with jealousy and horror. It was the Countess she had her eye on for Edward, because she could not think of two people who would look after each other better.

'I've just thought,' she said, leaning forward to whisper. 'If that other car tried to push you off the road and to send Madame to a fearful death, the person driving it must have known she was going out with you.'

'Yes, Celeste, that's quite a thought.'

'Ah, m'sieur.' The works foreman greeted Edward cordially. 'All is ready.'

'Thank you,' said Edward, and inspected the new fender. 'Excellent. Anything else?'

'Yes, m'sieur. The car you spoke of was returned to Heriot's this morning. It was hired from them by a gentleman who signed himself Henri Lascalle of Lyons. He left money to pay for the damage.'

'I'm greatly obliged,' said Edward and handed over another banknote.

'A pleasure, m'sieur.'

Edward settled the bill. On the way to pick up Rosamund and Colonel Brecht, he said, 'Celeste, when we get back to the hotel, could you find out if there's an Henri Lascalle of

Lyons listed in the telephone directory?'

'You're very optimistic, Edward. I don't think there'll be any Henri Lascalle of Lyons, or a telephone number or an address.'

'How shrewd you are, young lady. But we'll check, shall we?'

They picked up their friends. Rosamund and the Colonel seemed satisfied with the time they had spent in Nice. The Colonel was carrying a small packet and a dainty striped box tied with ribbon.

'I've bought a delicious négligé,' said Rosamund, when the car was under way, 'and Franz has bought a tie. I helped him select the tie, but he refused me any help at all with my purchase.'

'So should I have done,' said Edward.

'We aren't living in the time of Victoria,' said Rosamund, 'and we are, after all, in France.'

'I have suffered the ordeal frightening,' said Colonel Brecht.

Celeste smiled. Mama had said that Madame Knight was leading Colonel Brecht by the nose, and that his nose was having the time of its life.

But although some things were amusing, it wasn't anything but deadly serious to know that someone had tried to kill Edward and the Countess. Edward could not possibly have imagined it, unless he was over-sensitive about Madame.

There was no Henri Lascalle in the Lyons telephone directory. Edward thought it might, therefore, be a good idea to go into Nice again as soon as he could and ask someone at Heriot's for a description of the man.

'You're still satisfied about having taken the car back?' asked the senior member of the mission.

'I've assured you I am,' said number two.

'I think now that you should have abandoned it, not

presented yourself again.'

'I must point out you gave no instructions to that effect, comrade.'

'I agree, but it was something that might have reasonably occurred to you.'

'When?'

'At any time between the moment when you failed and when you returned the car.'

'I thought it was agreed that the hire and return of the car was to be a completely straightforward operation.'

'Yes, it was. It was also agreed the car might sustain a little damage, but not as much as it did. Further, their escape enabled them to report the incident.'

'With all respect, comrade,' said number two, 'it's a little late for these second thoughts. But I've insured against answers to questions, as I told you.'

'We must hope there are no questions. Insurance can't be guaranteed. However, it's done now. Unfortunately, I doubt if we can catch her in the open again. It will be trickier now. Concerning the dog – it must be dealt with.'

'Poisoned meat?'

'Arrange it – after you've attended to Tchekov.'

'That won't be easy.'

'I'm confident, comrade, that you'll make up for yesterday's failure.'

Katerina received Edward at two thirty in a spirit of over-bright gaiety. Dr Kandor was out, she said, attending to a little business in Nice. She was, therefore, entirely under Edward's protection for the afternoon, or until the doctor returned.

'Protection?' said Edward.

'Yes,' she smiled. 'You're to protect me from any tendency I might have to rush excitedly about.'

'You feel a little recklessness coming on?' he asked.

'Not really. I feel only a wish for a peaceful game of croquet with you. So there must be no thumping or whacking. We'll be friendly to each other and only make little taps. You would like to play?'

There was no question of his being unwilling. Croquet, whatever other people thought about it, was a game of magical enjoyment when played in this garden. Katerina invested it with laughter, anguish, triumph and pleasure.

As they picked up the mallets the Alsatian appeared. It advanced, bristling, head thrust forward and teeth showing. It began to bark at Edward, and to circle around him.

'Prince!' Katerina called to the dog. 'Come here.' She put out a hand. The Alsatian, still bristling, still keeping its eyes on Edward, approached her. She put her hand on its head. 'Edward, come and let Prince meet you.'

'That's a brute of a dog to say hello to,' said Edward.

'Prince, this is my friend Edward. Edward, give him your hand.'

'To eat?'

'No, no, silly.' Katerina laughed. 'Stroke his nose.'

'He'll swallow my arm as well.' But Edward stroked the long nose, while Katerina held the collar. The dog was stiff and suspicious, and its legs were rigid.

'A friend, Prince, a friend,' said Katerina soothingly, and the Alsatian's head came up and its nose nuzzled Edward's hand in acceptance.

'You're a beauty, old boy, aren't you?' said Edward.

'There, now he knows you, now you're friends,' said Katerina.

'My relief is immeasurable. Where'd you get him?'

'Dr Kandor bought him for me.'

'To guard you, Katerina?'

'To keep me company,' she said.

'Well, he's a wise acquisition,' said Edward, 'whatever the reason.'

The Alsatian sat and watched the game, tail thumping. Katerina applied herself with her usual zest, quickly becoming involved in the many quirks and facets of the kind of game she liked to play when competing against Edward. Yet little silences not at all usual began to emanate from her. Edward, striking for a hoop and missing, glanced up with a rueful smile. She was not looking at the play, but at him, and her eyes were like deep grey pools of sadness.

He felt an intense longing to bestow laughter on her.

'Katerina, it's your play.'

'Yes? Yes?' She did not seem fully aware of what she was about as she advanced. She was not even looking at the ball she was to play. She caught her foot in a hoop. She tumbled. Edward caught her. She turned in his arms and lifted her face, wide eyes strangely clouded. She was so close that her vitality seemed to effect an electric transference from her body to his. It poured into him, and he felt the impossible was happening, that he was vigorous and healthy again. It was the essence of wishful dreams. Her lips were parted, her breathing quick and her body full of tremors. Her sadness was gone, and she was in as much wonder as he was. 'Edward?'

But the Alsatian was there, pushing its nose between them and rumbling nervously and sensitively, and the sweetness of the contact was broken.

Edward released her. His arms fell away. She did not move, she still looked up at him, wonderingly and giddily, her face deeply flushed.

'Katerina, are you all right?' It was the most prosaic of questions after the most dreamlike of moments.

She came to. She turned, bent her head and gazed blindly at her ball.

'Is it my shot, Edward?'

'It's your shot, Katerina.'

She struck. Her ball glanced his.

'A roquet, Edward.'

'Agreed.'

She stooped to reach down for the ball, then straightened up without touching it. She put her mallet down.

'I think – I think a little rest,' she said. 'No, a little walk, through the gate and to the cliff top. Will you give me your arm, please?'

'If you'd prefer to rest—?' He was not sure at any time just how much her weak heart troubled her, and whether or not it occasionally put her in pain. He thought she was in some discomfort now, that her blood was struggling to reach her heart, for she was so subdued. But her face showed no greyness, no spasms of pain. He gave her his arm. She took it and they walked to the gate. He opened it and they passed through into the little open space fringed by the pines that stretched almost to the cliff top. There was a bench made of French oak just beyond the front wall, where one could sit to look down over the rocky cliff to the beach on the left and the expanse of sea all round. Just to the left of the seat was a stepped descent for the use of the villa's residents. It brought one down to the beach, the beach also used by the hotel guests. A handrail gave support, for the steps, cut out of the rock, were steep. Other people could not climb them from the beach, however, for there was a locked gate at the bottom.

As they walked to the bench, Katerina's arm encircled his warmly, and she said, 'You're very sweet to me, Edward.'

'I'm worried about you,' he said as they sat down.

'No, no, I'm quite all right,' she said. 'I'd simply like to sit here with you for a little while. Look – people on the beach.' She smiled. 'The weather is still so kind.'

He saw three people down below. Two were entering the sea, and the third stood watching them.

'It must be very kind,' he said.

'Are they from your hotel?' she asked.

'Probably, but from this distance I'm not sure.'

'You can use these, if you like.' Katerina reached under the bench and drew out a case containing binoculars. She smiled again. 'I use them so that I can feel in contact with people. Is it rather an intrusion on their privacy?'

'Not if they're behaving themselves.'

She laughed softly, watching him as he took the binoculars out and trained them on the figures far below. He picked out the swimmers. Rosamund and Franz Brecht. She was Junoesque in her bathing costume and he was strong-chested and brown. On the beach, watching them and calling out to them, was Mademoiselle Dupont, her green dress lightly fluttering.

Edward lowered the glasses and looked around. He turned. The high wall hid the villa and the climbing heights behind it.

'Excuse me a moment,' he said, and went back to the open gate. From just inside it, he used the binoculars to observe the slopes covered with pines and shrubs. He fanned the glasses. There was no one to be seen. If someone had already had a good look at Katerina, a further study of her was unnecessary.

'What have you been doing?' she asked when he returned to her.

'Taking a look at the view from your garden.'

'But why?' she asked.

'Just as a matter of interest.'

'You are becoming curious?'

'Yes, Katerina, I am.'

'You must not worry about me.' Katerina gazed at the shimmering sea. 'Edward, why is it you've never married?'

'Oh, circumstances, I suppose. And I'd make a very unsatisfactory husband, you know, always having to sit down when the situation demanded activity.'

'You can't expect me to agree with that,' she said. 'I'm sure there are many women who would never consider you unsatisfactory. What does it matter that you can't run or hurry about? Edward, you can't really think that if you proposed to a woman who loved you, she would only say yes on your assurance that you could run up a mountain.'

'But a few little hills have to be climbed in a marriage, don't they?'

'Not by yourself,' said Katerina. 'The two of you would climb them together. Has there been no one you would like to have married?'

'During the war there was my fiancée, Emily,' said Edward reminiscently. 'I wrote to her from hospital some months after I'd been gassed. We agreed to break the engagement. It was the fairest thing for both.'

'I refuse to believe that Emily thought that.'

'She protested quite vigorously, true,' said Edward, 'but it would have been asking too much of her to be more of a nurse than a wife.'

'That's ridiculous,' said Katerina. 'Look at you – you are out, you drive a car, you play croquet, you take little walks –

no, no, you weren't fair at all to her, or yourself.'

'Emily was a very active young lady, pursuing healthy outdoor interests.'

'Perhaps, if you had let her decide for herself, she would have surprised you,' said Katerina.

Edward thought how perfect her English was. It contained not the slightest accent. There were never any faults in either pronunciation or grammar. If there was anything particularly her own about it, it was the absence of colloquialisms or fashionable slang. She did not use words or phrases like spiffing, jolly good, old thing, cheerio, ghastly, darling or flapper, all currently in vogue. Hers was a very correct, even dated, English. She must either have lived among perfect linguists or been carefully taught by – an English governess?

'Emily is very happily married,' he said, 'to a small landowner.'

'A small landowner?' said Katerina. 'A little man, Edward?'

He laughed.

'No, Katerina, a quite tall man with a modest amount of land.'

'Oh, a kulak,' she said.

'A kulak?'

'Yes, that's—' Katerina bit her lip. 'Yes,' she said lightly, 'in my country an owner of a small amount of land is called a kulak.'

'In Bulgaria?'

'Bulgaria does have its own language,' she said, and Edward made a mental note of the fact that that answer did not necessarily mean yes. 'Edward, do you have regrets that you let Emily marry someone else?'

'I think I was a little sorry for myself at the time,' he said, 'but no, I can't say I feel regrets now. I suppose that means we weren't inconsolable soulmates. I see her now and again, and we're good friends.'

'Edward, is it bad sometimes, your chest and your breathing?' she asked.

'Sometimes.' He felt singularly well at the moment, and also peaceful and relaxed. He was aware of the tranquil effect she had on him. In her company, one asked for no more than to look at her and listen to her. Her grey eyes reflected wandering and wondering thoughts now, as if her mind was gently chasing things unknown. 'That's why I spend the winters at the Corniche,' he said. 'I'm lucky that I'm able to.'

'And you're an historian, you're writing about the war?' she said.

'I'm one of the team of British soldiers and civilians engaged in the task.'

'Isn't it wonderful, then, that you can do that, that you don't have to live in a hospital but are able to do something so interesting and satisfying?'

'Yes, I'm a lot more fortunate than others, Katerina.'

'Celeste, however, is very concerned that you live alone, that you have no wife,' said Katerina.

'I think she's been looking for someone suitable,' said Edward. 'And why do you have no one to care for you, except your doctor?'

She turned her eyes to the sunlit figures down on the beach.

'Dr Kandor would tell you why,' she said quietly.

'He'd talk about your weak heart? You're to have no husband to give you love and care? Who has decided that for you?'

'You must not ask such questions,' she said.

'Then may I at least ask what happened to the Count of Varna? I presume he exists, or did exist, that you were married—'

'I am not married. I am a countess in my own right.' Katerina looked up as the little bell rang on the terrace. 'There, tea is ready. Please don't frown, Edward. I have no dearer friend than you. It's a happiness to me, to have you visit me so often. So come, let's see what Anna has brought out for our tea.'

Over tea she was very bright again, and the time ran away from them. Dr Kandor did not return until Edward was on his feet, about to say goodbye to Katerina for the time being. He took the opportunity to express his concern at what had happened yesterday, and to offer the opinion that the man in the other car was drunk. He thanked Edward for his clear-headed action that had reduced the seriousness of the incident to merely something unpleasant. It was he who saw Edward out through the green gate, saying a cordial goodbye to him.

Katerina smiled sadly at him when he returned to the terrace.

'Boris Sergeyovich, you've spent the day making arrangements to hasten my separation from my friends?'

'Nothing has happened during my absence?' enquired Dr Kandor. 'Sandro and the dog took good care of you?'

'Nothing happened,' said Katerina.

'I've made enquiries,' said the doctor, 'and considered certain avenues. America, I feel, would be best.'

'America? America?' Despair showed. 'No. I refuse. I should never see my friends again.'

'It's a fact of our present existence that neither of us can have permanent friends,' he said. 'I shall try to arrange the acquisition of a property in one of the New England states. There, I'm told, properties can be found which would be very suitable, with spacious grounds to ensure the privacy we need.'

'Such privacy will mean something very close to solitary confinement,' said Katerina bitterly.

'Anna and Sandro will be there. So will I. We shall enjoy our pleasant times, our music and our chess.'

'Music and chess? That is all I'm to have?'

'You'll take the treasures you hold dear, Katerina Pyotrovna,' he said.

'A few trinkets, a few letters, some other little things – must it be America? That's so far away, so very far.'

'Distance is advisable at the moment. We shall come back one day, one better day.'

'Oh, Boris Sergeyovich, for us there will never be a better day, there will never be a restoration,' said Katerina sadly.

'We shall return,' he insisted.

'Yes, when I'm old and grey and withered, when I've lived seventy years without knowing a single lover, or even a kiss – yes, even a kiss. Do you realise that never, not once in all my life, has a man kissed me?'

Dr Kandor regarded her sombrely.

'Katerina Pyotrovna, you've always had a fine sense of what was right,' he said. 'You've always been able to draw a firm line between the permissible and the indiscreet. I think you've enjoyed the permissible.'

'Oh, flirtations with young officers – those did not lead to the kind of kisses I mean,' said Katerina. 'Those were only butterflies in a meadow and raindrops on windows, and as instantly forgettable as giggles.'

'You are what you are,' said Dr Kandor, 'and therefore not a woman to collect lovers.'

'I don't want to collect lovers,' she said emotionally. 'Women who collect lovers experience excitement, but know little of happiness. One lover, Boris Sergeyovich, that is all I ask.'

'Not so long ago, it was just one friend. A week ago, it was just one more friend. Now it's just one lover you want.'

'Boris Sergeyovich, you know how old I am. Thirty-one. And I am still a virgin. Look at me, and tell me, am I to be denied for ever?'

'I look at you every day, Katerina Pyotrovna,' he said, 'and I see you always as the woman you are. You were not entrusted to me so that I could approve a lover for you.'

'I won't go to America,' she said.

'You'll be safer there than anywhere in Europe. With luck, we can arrange a sea passage in seven days.'

'Seven days?' Katerina looked stricken.

'I'll hire a car that will collect us here at midnight. I've already placed the villa in the hands of selling agents.'

'Seven days?' she said again. 'That is all I have?'

'You also have life,' said the doctor.

'I breathe. I walk about. I have no life.'

12

Edward, returning to his room after breakfast, let his eyes take in the aspect of the garden while he reflected on the fact that it was now three days since he had last seen Katerina. It seemed like three weeks. She had said nothing about a further meeting. Nor had she sent him one of her written invitations. He had thought she would. If their afternoons had come to an end, perhaps that was all to the good. If it was, it did not feel so.

He looked at himself in the mirror. He knew he could not be called handsome or vigorous-looking.

He left the hotel, started his car and began to motor to Nice. It was still very much on his mind, that incident on the road. In Nice, he found his way to Heriot's, the car dealers. He went to the office of their hire department. The manager was extremely helpful, giving him a description of the man who had hired a saloon car, a black Citroën, four days ago, and brought it back damaged. It had struck a wall, apparently. The description was of a man of medium height, in a grey suit and hat, clean-shaven and aged perhaps thirty, perhaps a little more. That could have been anybody. No, there were no distinguishing features.

Edward wondered if he had been expecting details of someone he knew. Such an expectation had to be absurd. Did he, in the back of his mind, have a vague image of Dr Kandor, the impassive, unreadable Bulgarian? That had to be impossible. Yet the doctor had passed the incident over lightly, with a suggestion that the driver of the other car must have been drunk. He had given the impression that it was worth neither discussing nor enquiring into.

Edward thanked the car hire manager and left. He called

in at the municipal library and asked to see some dictionaries.

He was very thoughtful when he came out.

The word kulak was Russian. It meant a peasant more affluent than others. It meant a peasant who was the proprietor of a small amount of land.

He motored back to the Corniche, arriving in good time for lunch. Celeste, catching sight of him on his way to his room, went to the reception desk to get the letter that awaited him in its pigeon-hole. She took it to him.

'M'sieur, another one,' she said, 'another billet-doux. It was delivered two hours ago, so I've brought it at once, even immediately. Shall I wait while you write your reply?'

'Thank you, little angel, but if an answer is required I'll see you later.'

'Oh, of course,' said Celeste, 'you must have a few minutes to yourself while you count the kisses Madame has sent.'

'Terrible girl, be off with you.'

Celeste laughed as she departed. Edward read the note.

Dear Edward, I am distressed. Why have you not called? What have I done? Are we no longer friends? Have I taken up too much of your time? If so, you must forgive me, but do please let me hear from you. Are you unwell? I pray not. I am ever and always your friend. Please remain my friend too. Katerina.

What an idiot he was. Perhaps any man who was still a bachelor at thirty-five was unimaginative about women and their feelings. She had had to spell out the obvious, that she was entitled to expect some initiative from him. He sat down and wrote in profuse apology for his shortcomings, and declared he would call on her this afternoon. He hoped, he said, that she would not set her dog on him for his thoughtlessness. He gave the letter to Celeste, who asked him if he would like Jacques to take it now, before lunch.

'I'd be very grateful,' he said. She called Jacques, gave him the letter and the porter went at once to deliver it. Edward expressed pleasure at such service.

'There's lobster for lunch, m'sieur,' smiled Celeste.

'Lobster as well as service invaluable?' said Edward.

'For you, yes. Oh, Mademoiselle Dupont asked for her place to be laid at your table. I told her that could only be arranged with your permission.'

'Well, I don't mind. Let her share my table.'

Celeste, ignoring that, said, 'Why did you go into Nice this morning.'

'To ask a few questions.'

'M'sieur,' she whispered, 'no one could really wish to harm Madame. It must have been an accident the other day.'

A thought struck him. The unhelpful description from the helpful manager related to a man who had called twice, once to hire the car and then to bring it back. It would not have been a brief meeting on either occasion. Something better than a vague description should have been possible. Had there been collusion for a financial consideration? A further visit to Nice was called for.

'Where did you get to this morning, Franz?' asked Rosamund over lunch.

'Ah, yes,' said Colonel Brecht, studying his lobster salad with keen interest. 'A long walk. Very satisfying.'

'Are you related to Houdini?' asked Rosamund.

'Houdini?'

'I've noticed your disappearing acts lately.'

Colonel Brecht swallowed lobster, then cleared his throat.

'Ah – I enjoy walking,' he said, 'and I wish to take care.'

'Take care? Of what?' Rosamund was amused.

'That I do not come to bore you. You are a charming lady, a kind and interesting companion, while I am a man of limited social graces. I am – ah – what would be the word?'

'You're thinking of stodgy, perhaps?' said Rosamund.

'What is stodgy?' asked the Colonel.

'Indigestible,' said Rosamund.

'*Himmel* – it's as bad as that? I am indigestible?'

'I don't think so, no. Nor should you. Next time you go walking, ask me to go with you. I also enjoy it – more so with an escort.'

'You really are most kind, most charming,' said the Colonel warmly.

'Oh, I'm always at my most gracious when there's lobster in front of me,' said Rosamund.

'Edward – oh, how nice.' Katerina put out both hands in glad welcome, and Edward took them. 'Your little note was such a relief to me – I thought you simply must be unwell. But here you are, and quite yourself, and getting very brown.' Her eyes were warm, her hands pressing his.

'And how are you, Katerina?' he asked, wishing himself equipped to be much more than a friend to her.

'How am I?' She smiled very brightly. 'Oh, much better now that I know you haven't set me aside.'

'Set you aside? Katerina, that's preposterous.'

'Oh, I can be very preposterous when I'm upset,' she said.

Edward saw Dr Kandor on the terrace, the Alsatian beside him. The dog, ears pricked at the advent of Edward, came down the steps and trotted up to him. Edward stroked its ears.

'Try biting me, old boy,' he said, 'I've upset your mistress.'

Katerina smiled, hiding emotions critically sensitive. He was not to know how little time she had left here. Despite the doctor's presence, she put her arm through Edward's and walked to the terrace steps with him. Boris had warned her not to show herself in the garden, not to make herself a target for anyone on that ascent beyond the road. Someone capable of trying to murder her in a car was just as capable of shooting her.

'Edward, shall we sit and talk?' she asked.

'That shouldn't be too painful,' he said.

She laughed, but emotionally. She wanted the afternoon to be endless, she wanted a looming midnight flight put off for ever. They sat at the terrace table, while Dr Kandor strolled thoughtfully around the garden, hands behind his back and pipe between his teeth. The Alsatian lay beside Katerina's chair, nose between its front paws and tail lazily thumping.

They talked lightly, of inconsequential things. Edward went along with her smiling mood, but sensed it hid a seriousness. Although Dr Kandor did not come up from the garden, his presence seemed to Edward to have an inhibiting effect on Katerina. She did not mention croquet, and since he was quite content to sit with her and observe her, he said nothing himself about a game.

But she did suddenly say, 'Perhaps we can play croquet next time you come – perhaps tomorrow? That's not too soon? You could come again tomorrow?'

'Indeed I could,' he said. 'I've yet to chalk up a win.'

'But, Edward,' she said, 'who will remember which games were won, which were lost and which were unfinished? I shan't. I shall only remember how well we were matched, and how the afternoons never lasted long enough.'

He thought again how faultless her English was, and, in its way, how oddly dated. Most other English-speaking women would have said, 'Darling, who cares about points? Points are so boring, so utterly tedious, don't you know. Do get me a drink, sweetie.' What he did not think about was what her words implied, that soon there would be no more croquet, only the memories.

Anna brought out the tea tray. Dr Kandor came up to the terrace.

'May I join you?' he asked in his grave way.

Over tea, he took up the conversation, interesting himself in Edward's work. His questions were keen and Edward was responsive. His answers led to a discussion on the events that had brought the war about. His own view was that it was due to Austro-Hungary's mistaken belief that she could go to war with Serbia and treat as a bluff the Russian Tsar's declaration to side with the Serbians.

'It might have been a war exclusively between Austria and Serbia, if the Tsar had kept out. His intervention brought Germany in to support Austria, and that brought France in because of her treaty with Russia.'

'Is it your opinion, then,' said Dr Kandor, 'that Tsar Nicholas was responsible for making the war such an extensive and calamitous one?'

Katerina sat tense and silent, her eyes on Edward.

'No, that's not my opinion at all,' he said. 'Austria must take most of the blame because of misguided recklessness. Germany must take some for her invasion of Belgium. The Tsar's armies were the least well equipped to fight a full-scale war. The Tsar was decisive in his loyalty to the Slav nations, but indecisive in all else, it seems. He was a homely man, not a warrior.'

'You will excuse me, please,' said Katerina in a shaking voice. She rose to her feet and disappeared into the villa.

'I must apologise,' said Edward. 'I've either bored her or distressed her.'

'The war, Mr Somers, was unkind to all of us,' said the doctor. 'Please allow the Countess her distress, and make no mention of it when she returns.'

'I'd like to talk about the incident on the road,' said Edward. 'I'm sure it—'

'It was frightening, of course,' said Dr Kandor, 'but an accident, undoubtedly. I'm sure you have no enemies who'd wish to kill you, and who would want to harm the Countess? Some of the wild people who live in Nice or Monte Carlo were almost certainly responsible. Many of them fill themselves with wine, then climb into their cars and make lethal weapons of them. You and the Countess were fortunate. No more need be said of an incident she'd like to forget. She won't wish to hear us talking about it when she rejoins us.'

'Do you know your villa's been watched by someone with a telescope?'

'The Countess told me you'd mentioned that,' said Dr Kandor imperturbably. 'Did you see the person?'

'I'm certain I glimpsed the telescope. So did another guest at the hotel.'

'Mr Somers, who would be interested in us, except some unfortunate individual with a sick curiosity?' said the doctor.

'Or someone with a murderous intent?' said Edward. 'That was no accident on the road, Dr Kandor. The driver was no drunken idiot, far from it.'

'I appreciate your concern, Mr Somers,' said Dr Kandor, 'but you are worrying unnecessarily. Hostile intent is out of the question. I am an innocuous man, the Countess the most inoffensive of ladies. Ah, here she is.'

Katerina, reappearing, approached the table, and not for the first time Edward was fascinated by her almost regal elegance and grace.

'I'm so sorry,' she said as she sat down. But she did not explain why she had absented herself. 'What are you talking about now?'

'Little nonsenses,' said the doctor.

'Then continue, please,' said Katerina, 'for I'm addicted to little nonsenses. Intellectual discussion is all very well, but put four intellectuals together for a whole week and you wouldn't hear a single laugh from any of them, from the time they begin their learned conversation until the time they finish – if they could finish. Do you agree, Edward?'

'Among intellectuals,' said Edward, 'I'm so out of place I creep away to look for someone like Celeste.'

'Oh, yes,' said Katerina warmly.

'One acknowledges the infectiousness of the young,' said Dr Kandor.

'One acknowledges that professors spread wisdom,' said Katerina, 'but it's people like Celeste who spread joy and light.'

Dr Kandor demurred.

'One cannot compare the high spirits of youth with the wisdom of the learned,' he said.

'I can,' said Katerina. 'Love is far more precious than wisdom.'

They talked on for a while, then Dr Kandor consulted his watch.

'It's after five,' he said.

'You mean it's time for Edward to go,' said Katerina.

'I mean it's time for you to take a little rest,' said the doctor. He did not object when she walked down to the gate with Edward.

'Edward, you will call again tomorrow, please?' she said. 'You can spare the time from your writing?'

'Without any effort at all,' he said, hiding with a smile the longing he had for her, just as she was hiding all she felt about the moment when she would know she would never see him again. 'We're to play croquet?'

'We shall play croquet, yes,' she said, 'and enjoy another memorable game.'

Tense, she gave him her hand. He pressed her warm fingers. Hers clung tightly for a brief moment. He wondered if he was wrong in thinking her eyes misty.

'Katerina—'

'Yes?' She was very emotional.

'Take care,' he said.

They had known each other such a short time. There were all the years before, all the years of the future, and what they had given each other was invested in the fleeting moments between.

'Tomorrow,' said Katerina.

'Tomorrow,' said Edward.

When he had gone, she rejoined Dr Kandor.

'You told him nothing, I hope,' said the doctor.

'About our leaving? No,' she said. 'But, oh, Boris Sergeyovich, anywhere except America. America is on the other side of the world. It's too far. Switzerland, perhaps, or Italy – why not?'

'Too close,' he said. 'I must decide and you must accept.'

'And if I refuse?' she said.

'You can't refuse, Katerina Pyotrovna, you know you can't.'

'Take care in how you regard me,' she said, 'for I'm becoming desperate.'

'Are you in love?' he asked, perturbed for once.

'That is nothing to do with it.'

'It's everything to do with it. Katerina Pyotrovna, you shouldn't have left the table, you shouldn't have shown such agitation. Your friend is an intelligent man. He will think about what he was saying when you rushed away. He will find a connection. You were very agitated.'

'You may have grown a suit of armour, Boris Sergeyovich,' she said, 'but I have not.'

* * *

'Nothing has been accomplished, comrade,' said number one.

'I beg to differ,' said number two. 'We've at least identified them, both of them. There can be no mistake about her, you agree?'

'I agree.'

'As to further action,' said number two, 'you must concede there are difficulties. Especially as we have strict orders not to lay ourselves open to arrest.'

'I'll make my own concessions, comrade, and do my own thinking. Let me point out we're risking security by making contact as much as we do with each other.'

'We must exchange notes,' protested number two.

'The birds are to be disposed of, comrade, or they'll fly away.'

'I've looked for opportunities every day.'

'Look again.'

13

Rosamund, entering the village the next morning to go to the shop, smiled as she saw the upright figure of Colonel Brecht outside its door. He was talking to someone, a man in a dark suit and hat.

'May I get to the door, Franz?' she said as she came up.

Colonel Brecht, startled, spun round. Rosamund's smile was sweet.

'Ah – I had no idea,' he began, then tugged his moustache and said: 'But you are just in time to help this gentleman, perhaps. He's trying to find his way to a village called Le Maqui.' He turned to the man, whose face was square and dour. In French he said, 'It's correct, you wish to know the way to Le Maqui?'

The man lifted his hat to Rosamund.

'If you please,' he said in accented French.

'Can you help, Rosamund?' asked Colonel Brecht. 'You know this part of France better than I do.'

'Le Maqui is only a few kilometres,' said Rosamund. 'Continue through this village, m'sieur, and when you reach a little road on the right you'll find it will lead you to Le Maqui.'

'Thank you,' said the dour-faced man and strode purposefully away.

'The villagers could have helped you, Franz,' said Rosamund, indicating the elderly inhabitants playing their habitual boule on the triangle.

'I was about to recommend that,' said the Colonel, 'just at the moment when you arrived. You're shopping?'

'If I can get through the door, yes,' smiled Rosamund.

'Ah, your pardon, dear lady,' said the Colonel and moved aside. 'Ah – have you come to buy handkerchiefs?'

'I think I mentioned I was in need, and they have the prettiest lace ones here.'

'Then permit me, please,' said Colonel Brecht, and fished out a small wrapped box from his pocket. 'I could not resist hastening down to buy them for you. The gift you will accept, I beg?'

'So that is why you disappeared again.' Rosamund accepted the box very graciously. 'How could I say no to such charming generosity? I'm overwhelmed. Dear me, how nice you are. I shall now give you the pleasure of escorting me back to the hotel, where I left Mademoiselle Dupont trying to seduce Edward from his work. If you care to accompany me, we may be able to take her off his hands.'

'Delighted,' said the Colonel fervently.

Katerina, walking slowly down the terrace steps, stopped as Dr Kandor called to her.

'No, you should not wander around the garden,' he said. 'Please stay on the terrace.'

'I wished just for five minutes out here,' she said.

'Keep to the terrace, won't you?' he said kindly.

Katerina came back up the steps. She looked big-eyed, as if she had not slept well. The Alsatian moved around her. Dr Kandor nodded. He liked her always to have the dog close to her when she was outside. He went down the steps himself, lighting his pipe as he made his way to the little gate. Katerina, standing on the terrace, watched him as he went through the gate. He too occasionally liked to wander out there, beyond the wall, and look at any people who were on the beach. He would stand there, she knew, lost in his own thoughts, reflecting on his more active years when he had been the Surgeon-General of the Imperial Army.

Katerina picked up the dog's leash from a chair and clipped it to the collar. She stooped and fixed the leash to a leg of the table.

The dog pricked up its ears after a while, bristled, barked and strained at the leash.

Edward was preoccupied during lunch. Katerina was beginning to haunt him, a very disturbing thing to a man who felt ill equipped to take care of a woman. His emotions were playing the very devil with his work.

The dining-room wore a leisurely air. Only six guests were present, and the voluble Mademoiselle Dupont was among the absent ones. Monsieur Valery, her *bête noire*, was consuming his meal fairly cheerfully, but would obviously have enjoyed it more had she been there to enchant his infatuated eyes.

She appeared eventually, but looked wildly agitated. She swept up to Edward, who was drinking his coffee.

'Edward – please come outside – quickly, quickly.'

Rosamund and Colonel Brecht looked up as Edward followed the Frenchwoman out of the room. Celeste, in the kitchen, was spared the sight of Mademoiselle Dupont taking him into the empty lounge.

She turned to him, wringing her hands.

'What's wrong?' asked Edward.

'Something terrible. At the Villa d'Azur. Someone fell

from the top of its cliff – dead, Edward, dead!' She wrung her hands distractedly.

'Oh, my God, no.' The shock induced a violent constriction in his chest. He fought for breath.

In the lobby, Madame Michel was suddenly confronted by a dark, wiry man as he burst in through the front doors. He thrust a letter into her hands. It was addressed to Edward. The man turned and left without a word, running down the steps to the road. Madame Michel took the letter into the dining-room, where Rosamund informed her that Edward was elsewhere, with Mademoiselle Dupont. Madame Michel found them in the lounge, where the Frenchwoman was spilling distracted words.

'For you, m'sieur,' said Madame Michel, giving the letter to Edward. She saw his face, darkening as he fought for breath. 'Sit down, m'sieur, sit down – what is wrong? What has happened, mademoiselle?'

'Oh, it's terrible, madame, terrible,' gasped Mademoiselle Dupont, 'a man has fallen to his death from the Villa d'Azur. I came to tell Monsieur Somers first, because he's acquainted with them there.'

More words tumbled from her lips as Edward, wheezing, opened the letter.

Edward – please come – please help me – Dr Kandor is dead – I need you. Katerina.

Mademoiselle Dupont, strolling on the beach, had seen it happen fifty minutes ago, she said. She had heard a cry and seen the man falling from the cliff top, twisting and bouncing down over the rocky incline, and landing dead and broken on the rocks at the foot. She had run to him and seen he was dead. There was a boy at the other end of the beach, a boy from the village, and she had sent him back there to get a doctor and a gendarme. They were there now.

Mademoiselle Dupont collapsed into a chair. Madame Michel put her hand on Edward's shoulder.

'I'll send Celeste to comfort the Countess,' she said.

'We'll go together,' said Edward, 'I can manage.'

'You are sure, m'sieur?'

'Yes. Give me a moment.'

'If you are very sure,' said Madame Michel gently, 'then go by yourself. Celeste will be too emotional for a while.'

It was not far, the villa, but Edward's chest was tight and painful, breathing an effort, and for all his sense of urgency he had to walk slowly. He heard running footsteps behind him as he approached the villa. Celeste was flying to catch him up.

'Oh, Edward,' she gasped as she arrived beside him, 'Mama told me – oh, of course I must come too – I shan't be hysterical. It's dreadful, dreadful – Madame's good doctor, who took such care of her – what can we do?'

'Comfort her?' said Edward wheezily.

'How could he have fallen like that?' Celeste was pale with shock. 'He was such a careful man in all he did.'

Yes, thought Edward, Dr Kandor was the last man likely to fall carelessly off the top of a cliff.

The body had been brought up. The doctor now lay dead on his bed, with a sheet over him. The gendarme was questioning Anna. Sandro, the other servant, the dark, wiry man, was on the terrace, eyes glittering as he stared at the view of the sea. At the rear of the villa, the Alsatian was barking. The doctor from La Roche was talking to Katerina. She, white and numb, was seated at the table. As Edward and Celeste entered through the green gate, she came to her feet.

'Thank you, doctor,' she said quietly, 'my friends are here now.'

'But is there nothing I can do for you, Countess? You're in shock—'

'Yes, I am, but I'm not ill.'

Since he knew what others had heard about her, that she had a weak heart, Dr Bruge was reluctant to leave it at that.

'Allow me to prescribe—'

'A little sedative of some kind, Dr Bruge, that's all I need, thank you,' said Katerina.

'I'll make it up here,' he said, and went into the villa with his bag.

Edward and Celeste came up the steps and Katerina put her hands out to them.

'Thank you, thank you for coming,' she whispered.

'Oh, madame,' said Celeste, and took one hand between hers and pressed it.

Katerina's eyes were on Edward. In hers, tragedy was darkly reflected.

'Say nothing for the moment, Katerina,' he said. He knew she must have had to talk at length to the gendarme and the doctor. 'Sit down with us quietly for a while, won't you?'

They sat down. Celeste, eyes huge and sorrowful, glanced from one to the other. In their silence they were one, Madame with her head bowed, her hand tightly clasping Edward's.

Anna said protestingly to the gendarme in her heavy French, 'But I saw nothing, nothing, and have told you so. I am in the kitchen, doing lunch. I am not knowing what is happening or where the Countess was. Sandro, he is in the village then.'

'I'm not trying to alarm you,' said the gendarme, making notes, 'only trying to find out if anyone, besides the lady on the beach, saw him fall.'

He came across to Katerina. He bowed. He was the village policeman, and a friendly man. He advised Katerina that he must telephone the prefect of police at Nice to report the tragedy. There was no telephone at the villa, and Edward supposed this was because Dr Kandor had wanted an extra touch of peace and quiet for Katerina.

The gendarme departed. Dr Bruge came out with a glass in which he had mixed the sedative. Katerina drank it. The doctor, assuring her he could be called on if required, that he would issue the certificate, contact the coroner and the undertakers, made a sympathetic exit.

Quietness descended.

'No one saw it happen, no one,' whispered Katerina, 'except the woman on the beach.'

'No one could have expected to see it from inside the garden or from here,' said Edward, 'the wall hides the area outside. Someone might have heard something, perhaps.

Sandro wasn't in the garden? I believe he usually does garden in the mornings.'

'Sandro was in the village,' said Katerina. 'I sent him to buy a few things. He bought all our supplies, food and so on, and isn't a man who would ever talk.'

Why, thought Edward, should he have to be a man who would never talk?

'You and Anna were in the house?' Edward's chest was slowly freeing itself of constriction.

'Anna was in the kitchen,' said Katerina tonelessly, 'I was in my room. I heard Prince barking. I had tied him up. He runs about and digs up the beds unless someone is giving him attention. It upsets Sandro. I came down to see why Prince was barking. There was no one about. I went down to the gate and heard a woman calling up to us from the beach. Her voice wasn't loud from that distance, but it seemed clearly frantic, and going to the top of the cliff I saw her. I also saw someone lying on the rocks. I went down the steps to the beach.'

'Those steep steps?' said Edward. 'And up again? Could anything have put more of a strain on you, or anyone else with a heart condition?'

'I did not think about that,' said Katerina, quietly grieving. 'I went down, Edward, and there he was, his neck broken, his head broken and his hair wet with blood. Oh, poor Boris Sergeyovich, so loyal, so caring, so dead.' She closed her eyes and compressed trembling lips. A little shudder shook her body. Celeste pressed her arm.

'You must rest, madame, you mustn't sit and think about it. Edward will stay with you. Yes, Edward?'

'I'll stay,' said Edward.

Celeste rose. She was quite sure these two should be together. She stooped and kissed Katerina's cheek.

'Dearest madame,' she whispered, and she left, to return to the hotel.

'Katerina, do you want to rest, to lie down?' asked Edward.

'No, not yet.' She sat, looking at the sea, her grief visible and unashamed.

Edward thought.

'A pity about the dog,' he said.

'Edward, you are saying that the dog could have prevented Boris falling?'

Edward was saying things might have worked out differently if the dog had not been tied up, and if Dr Kandor had had the animal with him. But he could not put it as plainly as that.

'There have to be ifs, Katerina.'

'Yes, I know. If only – if only.' She was pale, but her sadness was touched by resolution, as if fate's darker familiars were old antagonists of hers, as if she had fought them before and would again. Her back was straight. 'But all the ifs are only straws that have disappeared before the wind. My doctor and guardian is very dead. Without him, I'm alone. They will now try—' She broke off.

'They? They, Katerina? Who are they, and what is it they'll try?'

'No, it doesn't matter,' she said.

'It matters very much,' said Edward. 'I'm not going to insist you tell me anything you don't wish to, and this is hardly the time to make myself a nuisance. But I don't believe Dr Kandor would be careless enough to fall off that cliff any more than I believe the driver of that car was drunk. What I do believe is that someone wanted Dr Kandor out of the way, so that you were deprived not only of your physician but your protector as well. Am I near the mark?'

'I can't answer questions, Edward.' Katerina was very resolute. 'Please don't ask me to.'

'Well, instead of questions I'm going to tell you one or two things. Again, you need not say anything unless you wish to. I care a great deal about you—'

'Edward?' She turned her eyes from the sea at last and looked at him like a woman willing him to lift the worst of her grief from her.

'You're a very cherished friend, Katerina,' he said, 'and I'm going to tell you you're not Bulgarian. I think you're Russian. I think the family you often talk about was your own family, and that your father was perhaps high up in the service of the Tsar.'

Katerina sat rigid, hands clasped in her lap and knuckles white. Again her eyes were on the sea, and her teeth were biting her bottom lip.

'No questions, no questions,' she whispered.

'No, no questions, Katerina. I'm also going to tell you, however, that you must move out of this villa. I know your servants are here, and the dog, but you'll be safer elsewhere.'

Katerina drew a deep breath.

'Edward, I can't go looking for a place in Nice or Cannes.'

'That's the last thing I'd want you to do,' said Edward. 'You must move to the Corniche. I know Madame Michel will gladly give you a room. I know, if you want to, that you can keep to it and have your meals served to you. You'd rather people did not stare at you. The veil you wore that day told me you preferred not to show your face. There's no other woman of beauty who'd want to do that. At the Corniche, Madame Michel will let you have all the privacy you want. She won't ask questions, either. But I'm not going to let you stay here.'

Katerina's eyes swam.

'You'll be there, won't you, Edward?'

'Yes, close to you and keeping an eye on you, though I shouldn't make the most vigorous of bodyguards.'

'But you'll be there,' she said. 'I will come. But, oh, poor Boris Sergeyovich. I'm so sad, Edward, so sad.'

'Yes,' he said, remembering with a deep twinge of regret his suspicions of the doctor's part in Katerina's life. 'I feel so sure, Katerina, that someone was always close, always in a position to observe something of your routine here. Did Dr Kandor make a practice of going out to the cliff?'

'He went out sometimes. Not in a routine way. Just sometimes.'

'Sometimes was enough to mean once too often.'

Katerina's eyes registered plain, unhappy understanding.

'You really believe someone pushed him, don't you?' she said.

'Pushed him or hit him from behind. Someone who was watching from those pine trees and came very quietly out of them. Yes, the opportunity was there. It was a very expedient way of disposing of the doctor. To have shot him would have meant a murder hunt. Now there's only an accident to investigate, a fall from the top of the cliff, and the coroner might only have to decide whether it was misadventure or suicide. Do you realise, Katerina, that had we gone over the cliff several days ago, no alternative verdict would have been considered – it would almost certainly have been recorded as death by accident.'

'I have put you in danger too, haven't I?' she said.

'I shouldn't want to back away,' said Edward, 'and don't intend to.'

'I think I'm a little fatigued,' she said.

It was more than that, thought Edward. It was shock and incredulity that Dr Kandor was dead, and her mantle of mourning was heavy.

'Go and rest,' he said.

'You'll wait here for me, you won't go?'

'I shan't go, Katerina.'

'Thank you.' She pressed his hand gratefully and went into the villa.

The servant, Sandro, was down near the green gate, with the Alsatian. He turned as Edward called to him. He came up to the terrace, his wiry frame energetic, his dark face sombre.

'M'sieur?' he said.

'I shall be taking the Countess to the hotel,' said Edward. 'She'll stay there for a while. You understand?'

'I understand, m'sieur,' said Sandro in good French.

'Are you from Bulgaria, Sandro?'

'Excuse, m'sieur?'

'I wondered if you came from the Countess's country,' said Edward.

'Of course, m'sieur,' said Sandro, but his eyes were blank.

Edward thought it necessary to say, 'I'm a friend, Sandro.'

'I know, m'sieur. Anna also knows. Thank you, m'sieur.'

'You're a gardener,' said Edward.

'That is so.'

'Do you know the hotel gardener?'

'I have seen him, m'sieur. I could not say I know him.'

'He's a White Russian,' said Edward.

'So I've heard, m'sieur.'

'He's an excellent gardener.'

'Then he's an honest man,' said Sandro.

'Thank you,' said Edward.

Sandro nodded and left the terrace. The Alsatian stayed with Edward. Edward sat, willing to wait as long as necessary for Katerina to reappear. He must go into Nice again and make further enquiries at Heriot's. He could, of course, report the incident on the road to the police. But however wise that might be, he knew Katerina would be quite against it. And her secrets were her own until she decided otherwise.

The autumn days, which had been so serene, had lost their aura of enchantment. Peace and beauty were receding before the advance of murder and malice. A very fatal accident had happened to Dr Kandor. With him out of the way, an accident equally fatal was no doubt awaiting Katerina.

Why? Who was she? A deposed aristocrat with high connections?

Anna came out to say the Countess was quietly resting.

'Good,' said Edward.

'Ah, but so terrible – the doctor – terrible,' said Anna mournfully, her eyes red. 'Now what will happen?'

'Nothing, I hope,' said Edward. 'I'm going to take the Countess to the hotel for a few days, to give her time to think and to make decisions.'

Anna's broad face looked troubled.

'There is so much more to her life than a few days in an hotel,' she said.

'Is there, Anna?'

Her eyes became as blank as Sandro's.

'She has said she will go with you?'

'Yes,' said Edward.

'Perhaps – yes – perhaps for a few days.'

'I think so, Anna.'

'Yes – yes – thank you,' said Anna and went back into the villa.

Edward wondered when the police would arrive. He was

sure they would come. They would not leave the matter in the hands of the local gendarme. He winced at the thought of Katerina enduring their questions and going through everything again with them.

An inspector and a gendarme arrived from Nice an hour and a half after Katerina had gone to rest. They came by car and Sandro let them in, opening up the rarely-used front gates. The inspector had a paternal look and bright, shrewd eyes. Edward introduced himself, while Sandro went to ask Anna to inform the Countess.

'I'm Edward Somers, staying at the Corniche. I'm a friend of the Countess.'

'You're a friend, m'sieur,' said the inspector, 'but not here when it happened?'

'No, I was at the hotel, having lunch,' said Edward.

'Do you know who was here?' asked the inspector.

'The Countess and her servant, Anna, and both were in the house.'

'Yes?' said the inspector, which was to tell Edward he could not possibly have known who was in the house and who was not.

'Yes,' said Edward, which was to tell the inspector not to start off on the wrong foot.

'Is he also a servant?' asked the inspector, indicating Sandro, who was calming the bristling Alsatian.

'Yes. That's Sandro. He and Anna are the only servants. Sandro, by the way, was in the village at the time.'

'Thank you, m'sieur,' said the inspector, showing a slight smile of gratitude for this piece of unrequested information. 'Pardon me.' He descended to the lawn to engage Sandro in a lengthy dialogue, the gendarme accompanying him.

Katerina reappeared. She had changed into a lemon-coloured costume with a matching little hat and veil. The veil was up. Edward could think of no woman more exquisite. Her eyes were dark with mourning for Boris Sergeyovich, but she held herself upright. Her glance at the little group on the lawn was one of sad regret that there had to be more formalities. She turned to Edward.

'I thought perhaps I should have dressed in black for my

doctor,' she said, 'but felt he wouldn't want that. Thank you for waiting. I have packed a case and shall be ready to go with you as soon as the police have left.'

'I'm very pleased,' said Edward.

The inspector and the gendarme came up to the terrace.

'Countess Varna?' enquired the inspector of Katerina.

'Yes, I am Countess Varna.'

'I am Inspector Cartier from Nice.' The inspector made a little bow. 'Allow me to express my sympathy for this tragedy. I regret the formalities necessary, but I hope I shall cause you no distress. First, I'd like to see Dr Kandor.'

Katerina closed her eyes for a moment.

'Anna will take you up to his room,' she said.

The inspector and the gendarme were taken up. Katerina remained on the terrace with Edward.

'It's unavoidable, I'm afraid,' said Edward gently.

'I know, and there'll be an inquest, of course, which I shall have to attend.'

'I'll go with you.'

'Will there be many people?' she asked.

'A few, I imagine.' He smiled faintly. 'You can wear black then, with a veil.'

'Edward,' she said emotionally, 'I'm so grateful – I'm in need of someone close, someone very kind and understanding – I should feel very alone without you.'

'I feel very inadequate,' said Edward.

'No, you are my tower of strength, my very dear friend,' she said, 'and I'm so glad you're here.'

He wanted to take her into his arms. Instead he said, 'Celeste will be very happy to have you at the hotel. She'll give you love and care.'

'Love is precious, isn't it?' said Katerina. 'I—' She was interrupted by the reappearance of the inspector and gendarme.

'Thank you, Countess,' said the inspector. 'I'm now able to advise you that the body can be placed in the care of the undertakers. I regret very much so terrible an accident. He was your own doctor?'

'Yes. For many years.'

'I'd like to see the place he fell from. Would you be so kind as to show me?'

'I can't show you the exact spot,' said Katerina, 'only the cliff top.'

'Of course.' Inspector Cartier's sympathy was sincere. Edward was aware of the effect Katerina could have on people. She walked down the terrace steps. She turned and looked up.

'Please come, Edward.'

He walked beside her over the lawn, the policemen following. They went through the gate and to the bench seat. Beyond the seat was a level area of hard ground, the cliff top. The stepped descent lay on the left.

'Yes,' said the inspector, standing close to the edge and viewing the rocky fall to the beach, 'I see. A formidable and cruel drop.' He examined the hard ground. It bore no footmarks. 'A man might become giddy and fall, or he might jump.'

'Jump?' said Edward.

'Do you know, Countess, if Dr Kandor was in good health?'

'I've never known a healthier man,' said Katerina in a suppressed voice.

'Nor I,' said Edward.

'But all the same, he fell,' murmured Inspector Cartier. 'Or jumped. We must consider that, Countess. Did he have any unusual worries?'

He had many worries, but Katerina did not say so. They were not, in any case, the kind of worries to make him jump to his death.

'He did not inform me of any,' she said. Edward, close to her, felt her trembling.

'There was a lady, I believe, who saw him fall,' said the inspector.

'Yes,' said Edward, 'Mademoiselle Dupont, also staying at the Corniche. And there was a boy on the beach, whom Mademoiselle Dupont sent to the village for help.'

'Thank you, m'sieur,' said the inspector. 'I'd like to talk to the lady. I'm sorry, Countess, about all the formalities, but it's necessary in such cases to try to establish what facts we can.'

'I understand,' said Katerina quietly.

'An accident or suicide?' said Edward, who was sure it was neither.

'Exactly, m'sieur,' said the inspector. 'It's an unhappy thing for friends or relatives to be faced with the possibility that suicide was committed, for they naturally think they have in some way failed the dead. It's a consideration, however, we can't set aside. Countess, it's over, our conduct of formalities with you. Thank you for your patience with us. I must go to the hotel now and find Mademoiselle Dupont.'

'Inspector,' said Edward on an impulse, 'would you be so kind as to take the Countess with you? She's transferring to the hotel for a few days.'

'With pleasure,' smiled the inspector, 'with great pleasure.'

Katerina said, 'Edward, you—'

'Please go with them, and get Sandro to load your case in,' said Edward. 'I'll follow in a few minutes.'

In the closed police car she would not be seen. She could transfer to the hotel in an invisible way. If there were eyes around, looking for her, they would not spot her in the police car. They would not even look for her in that. And for him to follow on, walking, that was advisable too. It would look as if he had just left her, as if she was still in residence at the villa.

He spoke to Sandro. Sandro's eyes glittered and he promised to keep a close watch. He would sleep in the garden, he said, not far from the dog.

14

The inspector was asking questions of Mademoiselle Dupont in Madame Michel's private sitting-room. Celeste was seeing to the establishment of Katerina in a ground floor room next to Edward's, an arrangement which the French girl thought entirely sympathetic and suitable. Edward, having arrived after a slow walk, was talking to Madame Michel in the lounge, which they had to themselves. He was emphasising the need to take great care of the Countess.

'But of course,' said Madame Michel, 'her bereavement and her weak heart will command the best care we can give her.'

'No visitors, I think,' said Edward, and the proprietress looked at him with a slight lift of her brows. 'Or if anyone does call to see her, I'd be grateful if you'd first refer to me. Failing that, ask the Countess herself whether she wishes to receive the caller. Would you do that, madame?'

'Very well, m'sieur,' said Madame Michel.

'She'll stay in her room most of the time. You can serve her meals there?'

'Gladly. I've never seen her until today, do you realise? One can imagine grace in a countess, but I had no idea the Countess of Varna was quite so superb and beautiful, although Celeste has said so a hundred times. She has wonderful eyes, but so haunting.'

Yes, thought Edward, they are.

'Madame, might I ask a particular favour of you?' he said. 'Would you please have the hotel doors locked at night?'

'Locked?' said Madame Michel. 'But that has never been necessary, and if guests are out – why do you ask such a thing?'

'I do ask it, madame, without explaining it.'

'You've a very special reason for not explaining?' she said.

Edward smiled.

'Isn't it true, madame,' he said, 'that in France it's the reason which is important, not the explanation?'

Madame Michel returned his smile.

'One likes to think so, without quite believing it is so,' she said. 'Very well, I'll see what I can do about the doors at night, though I shouldn't want to provoke patrons into deserting us. M'sieur, I feel I must mention it – you're looking ill.'

Edward, grimacing, said, 'Well, that's the devil of it, feeling only half a man every time the lifeboats are launched.'

'That is quite wrong,' said Madame Michel reprovingly, 'and is certainly not the most intelligent thing you've ever said.'

'Oh, I'm guilty at times of feeling sorry for myself,' said Edward.

'The cure now is a large cognac,' said the proprietress on a practical note. She turned at a knock on the door. 'Enter, please.'

Inspector Cartier came in. He gave Edward a friendly nod and thanked Madame Michel for the use of her sitting-room.

Edward said, 'May I ask if Mademoiselle Dupont was informative?'

'She was most helpful,' said the inspector. 'She's quite sure that Dr Kandor jumped. She felt he came off the cliff as a man might after suddenly making up his mind to go to his death.'

Edward thought that a man who was violently pushed might just as easily look as if he had jumped.

'How dreadful,' said Madame Michel. 'Oh, the sorrow there is in the world.'

'Bulgarians, I believe, are emotionally impulsive,' said Inspector Cartier.

'You've spoken to the Countess?' said Edward.

'No. I thought it unnecessary to add to her distress at this moment. I must return to Nice.' And the inspector shook hands and departed.

Mademoiselle Dupont came in, looking sad.

'Edward, how tragic,' she said. 'The poor Countess was so stricken when she saw him, lying there on the rocks. She said not a word, not one. She couldn't. The shock must have been dreadful for her, with her weak heart. She climbed back up the steps so slowly, so unhappily. I wanted to go with her, to comfort her, but she refused. So I stayed until the doctor and the gendarme arrived from the village. There was nothing, of course, the doctor could do, except help the gendarme carry the body up. The Countess is a good friend of yours, isn't she? I'm so sorry, but it will at least be a comfort for her to stay here a while.'

'Yes, it's something,' said Edward. 'The inspector said you felt that Dr Kandor jumped.'

'Yes, it was so sudden and quick,' said the Frenchwoman, 'such a startling movement. I assumed at first that he fell, but thinking about it made me feel he leapt. The inspector advised me I'll be called to attend the inquest, so I shall stay until it's over.'

Edward rather wished only Celeste and her mother knew about the arrival of Katerina, but that had not been possible.

'It's been an ordeal for you, mademoiselle,' he said.

'It has,' said Mademoiselle Dupont tiredly, 'and I shall never be able to forget the sight of that poor man falling. And I've had no lunch and am going to get a headache.'

'Would you like some coffee, mademoiselle, or a headache powder?' asked Madame Michel. 'And a salad can be made up— '

'No,' said Mademoiselle, 'what I would like to order is a large cognac.'

Edward gave her a smile of sympathy and made his way to his room. Celeste appeared.

'The Countess?' he said.

'Oh, her room is a harvest of comfort to her,' said Celeste. 'She's very quiet, sitting in a chair beside her window.'

'I'll let her rest,' said Edward.

'Yes, but she will want to see you later, m'sieur, I'm sure.'

* * *

He lay on his bed and let the tension drain out of him. His breathing was wheezy, and there was a feeling familiar to him, that of painful, abrasive lungs combined with physical weakness. Wryly, he conceded he was entitled to feel sorry for himself. He needed at this moment to be capable of exceptional endeavours, to create peace and security for Katerina, who spoke such fascinating English but was no more English than Pavlova. And as much as any threatened woman, she was in desperate need of a strong right arm and a haven. That need was obvious, although she would answer no questions and had disclosed nothing.

Through the open shutters of the Venetian blind that covered the casement doors, he caught a glimpse of Rosamund and Colonel Brecht in the garden, their continued rapport apparent.

His eyes closed. He had long since discovered that, much as he disliked being inert, the only cure for an attack was rest. His mental activity slowed, his mind blanked and he slept.

'Edward?' The voice was soft and warm.

He awoke. Faintly, he was aware of a delicate scent. He turned his head and there she was, sitting on the bedside chair. The light was magnificent, the dipping sun bathing the room with fire. Her hair was aflame, her face lambent with russet.

Edward indulged himself in the extravagance of a quotation.

' "The Assyrians came down like wolves from the fold, their cohorts were gleaming in purple and gold." Are you their Queen?'

Katerina smiled and gently shook her head.

'I am nobody, only Katerina Pyotrovna. Celeste said you looked unwell. So I came to sit with you. I've been here twenty minutes. You've been fast asleep. Are you better?'

'I took a little rest.' He sat up. 'I'm fine now.'

'I'm sorry to have been such a worry to you.' Her eyes were melting in the fire. 'You are sure you're better? I feel so guilty, Edward, making such demands on you.'

'Do friends make demands on each other? Not really. I get

little attacks for no apparent reason, but a rest always does the trick.'

'Edward, would you like some tea?' Katerina brightened at the idea. 'Perhaps Madame Michel will serve it to us both. It will be all right to have tea in here with you?'

'I can't think of anything nicer,' said Edward. 'I'll go and order it.'

'No, I will. I'll find Celeste.' She swept out in an enthusiastic rush. She returned a minute later. 'There, Celeste is seeing to it herself. When I asked her she said, "Oh, at once, madame, if not immediately." She's irrepressibly sweet, isn't she? I've such a comfortable room, next to yours. Celeste said it was advisable to have you close enough to look after me.'

'In between my coughing and wheezing?' smiled Edward.

'Was it Achilles who was the Greeks' greatest warrior?'

'Yes.'

'Well, in a crisis,' said Katerina, 'I would rather have you than Achilles. Edward, I'm full of grief. It's been such an unhappy day. But you've helped me bear it better than anyone else could.' She sat down again. He lay back and relaxed, immersing himself in the atmosphere of magic she created for him. Her lashes flickered, and her eyes travelled uncertainly. She saw two people in the garden. 'They are guests, those two?'

'Yes, but you won't be compelled to meet anyone you don't wish to. The lady is English, Mrs Rosamund Knight. The gentleman is Colonel Franz Brecht, a German. As a widow whose husband lost his life fighting the Germans, she was very cool towards him at first— '

'So should I have been,' said Katerina quite fiercely. 'The Germans were responsible for sending that ice-cold monster, Lenin, to destroy Russia by revolution.'

'That was a blow at your heart, Katerina?'

'Revolution feeds on hatred and cruelty.' Katerina was stiff, her hands tightly clasped. 'It doesn't build, it destroys. Perhaps that German out there was one of those responsible for sending Lenin to Russia.'

'Perhaps,' said Edward, watching her profile. 'But he and Mrs Knight are the most agreeable of friends now. I think they'll remain friends.'

'They are your friends too?' Katerina managed a faint smile.

'Yes, but not as you are.'

'I am special?' she said lightly.

'Yes,' he said. He knew her as a woman of secrets and griefs. He knew Dr Kandor had been her mainstay, her sure-minded guide, a man of strength and decision. He slipped from the bed, wanting to dispel the suggestion of being the invalid. He ran his hand through his tousled hair, and Katerina watched him as he took a brush to it.

His body was as slender as her own, and she supposed the illness of poisoned lungs had robbed him of flesh. But he had such fine eyes, such a good, firm mouth. She wondered what it would be like to kiss him.

Celeste knocked and brought in the tray. She smiled, and set the tea things out on the little table. There was a glass in a chased metal container for Katerina, a china cup and saucer for Edward. There was lemon for Katerina and milk for Edward.

'Shall I pour, madame?' asked Celeste.

'Thank you, Celeste,' said Katerina.

Celeste poured. She did not talk, she did not scatter effusions of lightness or sympathy. It was not the moment for too much talk of any kind. It was a day of tragedy, its only sweetness, perhaps, in that it was drawing Edward and Madame closer together. Celeste was willing to surrender her most cherished guest to her most cherished friend. To no one else.

She left them to their tea and they drank it in an unusual and sensitive silence, Edward because his every emotion was committed to her well-being and words were hard to come by, and Katerina because she could say nothing of what she wanted to unless he spoke first. She was basically an extrovert, but not a woman to discount conventions or modesty. It was impossible for her to tell a man she loved him, unless he declared himself first. And Edward, although not particularly conventional, believed it would be totally unfair to ask any woman to marry a wreck. Katerina did not even think about that herself, except to instinctively regard him as a man whom a woman would take particular care of. She was quite unable to understand why some lady called Emily had allowed him to make a decision unfair to both of them. They could not have been truly in love. To Katerina, love was life's most precious gift, to be nurtured, cherished and enjoyed, to help forgive and be forgiven. Loved ones departed in body, never in spirit. They remained in one's mind and heart, irrespective of the human imperfections common to all people.

'I think it's cooling outside,' said Edward, seeing Rosamund and Franz leaving the garden.

'Yes,' said Katerina in her quieter way. 'And Boris Sergeyovich will have been taken away now, do you think?'

'Yes, I'm sure he will,' said Edward. She looked so sad that he wondered if they had loved each other, she and Dr Kandor. 'Will he be given a Bulgarian or Russian funeral, Katerina?'

Katerina sighed.

'Does poor Boris Sergeyovich make you think of Russia, then?' she asked.

'Russia, somehow, keeps creeping up on me.'

Katerina rose and turned her back.

'Do you know any Russians?' she asked.

'I've come across one or two Russian émigrés in London,' said Edward.

Her voice vibrating, Katerina said, 'If Russia is ever on your doorstep, Edward, you must bolt your door. What do they say about Russia, the one or two émigrés you know?'

'That Russia has always walked hand in hand with tragedy, that Russians enjoy sorrow more than laughter, and prefer funerals to weddings.'

'Perhaps that's right, even if a little cynical, although I've known— ' Katerina made one of her pauses. 'I must go back to my room or Madame Michel will begin to disapprove of me. I shall take dinner privately.'

'Yes, I understand,' said Edward, 'but later on, when you feel safely installed here— '

'Installed?' Katerina turned and smiled. 'I am sad, yes,

but I'm not a piano or a telephone.'

'No. That was badly put. But when you feel less sad and much safer, you may like to show yourself and dine at my table.'

'No, no,' she said, 'if I show myself and people talk about me, others may discover me.'

'Others, Katerina?'

'Those responsible for sending Boris Sergeyovich to his death,' she said.

'You believe what I believe, then?' said Edward.

'I knew it, Edward, before you did.' She glided out, closing the door behind her.

Katerina retired early to her bed, but sleep was elusive, and Celeste, peeping in at ten thirty, found her awake. The girl sat with her for a while, then sought Edward, about to retire himself.

'M'sieur, she's still grieving and I think would so like to see you.'

'She's not asleep yet?' Edward had sat up talking with Rosamund and Franz. He was unwilling to go to his own bed until he was sure Katerina was sleeping and the hotel secure. Two guests who had been out had returned, and Madame Michel had been able to bolt the front and back doors.

'She's in need of a little love,' whispered Celeste. 'I'm going to take a camp bed into her room and sleep there, and while I'm seeing to it, I think she would like it if you'd go and say goodnight to her. I wonder if Dr Bush has any medicine for making a sleeping draught?'

'Ask him, you precious girl,' said Edward. He went to Katerina's room, knocked lightly and entered to the sound of her voice. He did not put the light on. The moon, though waning fast, filtered its own light through the shutters. Katerina lay in her bed, her hair a mass of darkness against the white pillows. 'Katerina, why aren't you asleep?'

'Edward?' Her hand reached out and curled around his. 'How silly I am. I'm so tired, yet I can't sleep.'

'Well, I'm going to say goodnight to you and watch you

close your eyes. And Celeste is going to be here with you.'

'That sweet child. I'm ashamed, needing the comfort of her presence.'

He brought her hand to his lips.

'Goodnight, Katerina.'

'Edward, I— ' Her voice was a nervous vibrating murmur. 'Edward, would you kiss me, please?'

He bent low to kiss her cheek. She turned her face and her warm lips unashamedly received the pressure of his own. His were firm, engaging in a moment of ardour, and hers were quivering, questing and enquiring, seeking a knowledge of love. Her vitality communicated itself to him, as it had once before, and his blood coursed and quickened.

'That was very sweet,' he said, and was not to know it was the first time she had experienced a kiss like that.

'Now I shall sleep,' she breathed. 'Thank you, Edward.'

She looked up at him, waiting perhaps for him to say he loved her. He gave her a smile, seeing her eyes like pools of darkness. A long sigh escaped her, and her lashes fell. He thought again how like a girl she could be, for all her poise and elegance. It was as if she could not put her years of joyous youth behind her.

At the door, he said, 'I'm going into Nice in the morning. I'll see you when I get back. Sleep well, Katerina.'

'Goodnight, dear Edward.' Her voice was a dreamy, floating murmur.

The villa slumbered. The dog was asleep in its kennel. The quietness of the night seemed undisturbable, even when something was thrown high over the wall to hit the ground close to the kennel. It made only a slight plop as it landed. The dog, however, instinctively alerted, woke up. It came out of the kennel, ears stiff and hackles up, rumbling in its throat. It smelled meat, and padded forward, sniffing.

It reached the meat, which was impregnated with strychnine.

A boot came down hard on the juicy slab. The dog, interested but uneasy, found itself deprived. It barked, it snapped at the boot.

Sandro said nothing. He listened. He slapped the dog's nose. The Alsatian whined. Sandro stayed still, listening. He heard the faintest of sounds. Someone outside the wall was in cautious retreat.

Sandro's teeth glimmered, his booted foot crushing the meat. He had once been a Cossack cavalryman. Badly wounded in the stomach during a battle against the Austrians, his life had been saved by an Imperial Army surgeon, subsequently the Surgeon-General.

He stroked the dog's ears.

'They're after you now,' he whispered, 'so be as quiet as the dead. They think she's still here. They'll come back – tomorrow, perhaps, or the next night. We'll wait for them, my hungry one, and you shall have them. Boris Sergeyovich will expect it of us. Until they come, you shall stay out of sight, in the kitchen, and, as I say, be as quiet as the dead.'

He slung his rifle, picked up the poisoned meat and walked quietly away to dispose of it.

'The dog, then?'

'It took the meat, comrade. I heard it come from its kennel. I heard it whine in its hunger for it.'

'Good. Tomorrow, then, break in. Search her room for every paper, letter and diary you can find. There will be some information that will point us to the others.'

'The two servants— '

'Quietly, comrade, you will do it quietly, without waking them. And remember to take a few valuables. It must look like a common burglary. Is the dog dead?'

'One can't see through a wall, and I made no attempt to climb it. The animal was noisy before it took the meat. That would have alerted the servants. I left immediately.'

'I see. Well, you can go now.'

'Comrade— '

'Don't harass me. Go.'

* * *

Edward, waking up early, found himself fighting for breath. Bitterly and fiercely, he got up to do his fighting on his feet. He stood at the casement doors, sucking air into his compressed lungs. The sun was up, covering the hotel garden with warm morning light. Gregory, the gardener, was already at work. An honest man, Sandro had said, and Edward believed him.

Over breakfast, his breathing still crippled him. He postponed his trip to Nice. Celeste was concerned. Clouds of autumn came to turn the morning cool, and Edward went to his room to work. Katerina slept late, for Celeste had managed to get Dr Bush to mix a sleeping draught. The retired American practitioner used them himself from time to time.

Katerina knocked on Edward's door at mid-morning. She saw he was working. She asked if she might just sit by his windows, promising to keep him silent company. Edward, although he knew her presence would be a distraction, pulled up a chair for her. She sat down. She kept her promise. She did not say a word. She watched him at his writing. He coughed frequently. It made her bite her lip. Celeste brought them coffee at eleven o'clock. Katerina got up and followed the girl out, closing the door and detaining her.

'Celeste, is there nothing we can do for Edward's cough? Or is there nothing he should be doing for it himself?'

'Nothing, madame,' said Celeste. 'It's not the cough of a chest cold, it's the cough of a man with poisoned lungs. The attack will pass – it always does.'

'He has to live with such attacks?'

'Yes, madame. He does. You must take no notice. You see, he's very aware of his disability as it is. It's one thing to keep an eye on him, it's a different thing to worry and fuss. Ask him to play dominoes. We French like to play dominoes, and it's a favourite game with Edward.'

'But he's working, Celeste, he's writing.'

'Madame, you aren't too sad to play dominoes?'

'Dominoes is a game strange to me,' said Katerina, 'but no, I'm not too sad.'

'If you'll let Edward teach you, he'll soon forget he needs to cough. He'll be enchanted.'

'Will he?' said Katerina with a little smile.

'Madame, can you doubt it?' protested Celeste.

'Oh, yes, I can doubt it. He looks very dark and unsociable.'

'That's because you are very beautiful and desirable— '

'Celeste?' Katerina was gently restraining.

'A hundred pardons, madame, for being so personal, but it's true. And he, you see, in his own eyes, is a lesser man than many others.'

'Celeste, that isn't how he should think of himself. I've been sitting with him, and he's been so silent, and I've been mourning Dr Kandor and thinking about him being so dead – and, oh, I need light and air and warmth and love. Celeste, dear child, I am a miserable creature, am I not?'

Celeste smiled.

'Madame, ask him to teach you how to play dominoes,' she said.

'Very well, I will.' Katerina went back into the room. Edward was just tearing up a sheet of paper. 'Please, Edward,' she said, 'I should like to learn how to play dominoes.'

Edward looked at her in astonishment.

'Dominoes?' he said. He put a hand to his mouth and coughed. 'Dominoes?'

'Only if you can spare a little time from your writing.'

'Willingly,' said Edward. He thought her composed, her quietness the badge of her grief for her doctor. She had given in to no noisy tears, but her sadness was there, he felt. 'You really wish to play dominoes?' he said.

Katerina, aware that neither of them had been able to relax, said, 'If you would like to, then so would I.'

Edward got up to fetch a box of dominoes that lay on the mantelshelf. He placed it on the table, clearing away his papers. Katerina brought up her chair and her coffee, and they sat down together. An extraordinary sensation of pleasure invested Katerina. It was extraordinary, for it came of such a little thing – simply the act of sitting down with Edward to play dominoes.

Edward, afflicted by a coughing bout, put his hand to his

mouth. When it was over, he said, 'I'll go back to my writing after lunch.'

He showed her how to play threes and fives. The principle was so simple that she picked the game up at once. Little comments were exchanged, and Edward also offered advice on tactics. He stopped coughing and began to breathe more freely. Katerina, noting this, noting how his involvement with the simple game removed from him his awareness of his ailment, felt a warm glow of pleasure. They played for over an hour, she as competitive as he was, if less experienced.

'How many games did I win?' she asked at the end.

Edward, referring to the score sheet, said, 'Three.'

'As many as that? Already I'm so proficient? What is your score?'

'I won seven games,' said Edward.

'Edward, are you sure?' she asked.

Checking the figures, he said, 'A miscalculation – we each won five.'

'How gallant,' said Katerina, and put her hand over his. 'Edward, you are very good for me.'

'Since I feel so much better, Katerina, I'd say you're extremely good for me.'

'Thank you, Edward.'

Celeste served lunch to them in Edward's room, and the day passed quietly and companionably.

The man, slim and agile, came noiselessly over the wall, his jacket protectively covering the cemented ridge of broken glass. Pulling the garment after him, he dropped lightly to the ground. The night was dark, clouds smothering the moon. He put his jacket on and stood with his ears straining. Not a sound came from the unlighted villa. He made a slow, cautious advance over the lawn and ascended the steps to the terrace. He paused and listened again. There was neither sight nor sound of the dog. He walked silently up to the curtained French windows, and from his pocket took a glass-cutter and a rubber sucker. Carefully, he drew the glass-cutter down a side of a pane. A little frictional rasp resulted.

In the kitchen, the Alsatian's ears stood up and it came to its feet. At the sound of an uneasy, rumbling growl, Sandro put his hand tightly around the dog's jaws.

'Quiet, little swine. Come with me, come silently.'

But when the dog reached the large room that opened out on to the terrace by its French windows, it broke free of Sandro's restraining hand and barked ferociously. It leapt savagely towards the curtained windows.

Outside, the intruder froze, then turned and ran, taking the terrace steps recklessly. Sandro drew back the curtains and opened the doors.

'Go, my hungry one. Pull him down. Go.'

The Alsatian leapt out. At the green gate, in the darkness, the man was tugging the bolt back. Hearing the rushing, snarling animal, he pushed the gate open in frenzied fear and went through, slamming it shut after him. The dog was there, its leap pushing the gate open again. The man fled. The dog caught him in his flight along the top of the cliff, jaws closing around his sleeved right arm and pulling him down. The man screamed.

Sandro arrived, gun in his hands. The Alsatian, teeth clamped around an arm, had the man grounded and palsied.

'Get up,' said Sandro in his mother-tongue. He prodded the dog. 'Leave him, my beauty.'

The Alsatian released the arm. The man, white-faced in the darkness, came to his feet.

'No harm – I was doing no harm,' he said in French.

Sandro's teeth glittered.

'You are a liar, a pig, a murderer,' he said in Russian.

'No – no—'

The dog was a bristling threat, and Sandro's smile was icy. The man had understood Russian.

'Walk,' said Sandro.

'I—'

'Walk.'

The man, prodded by the rifle, obeyed. With Sandro at his back, he walked along the edge of the cliff in the darkness, the growling Alsatian a frightening escort. He tried to explain he was no more than a modest burglar. Sandro poked him with the rifle butt and told him to shut up. He made him walk four hundred metres from the villa, passing the Corniche that was a pale edifice on the left.

'Stop,' said Sandro. The man halted. 'Turn,' said Sandro.

'Wait, let me—'

'Turn. This is where we shall leave you.'

The man turned, facing the edge of the cliff and the dark sea. Sandro hit him violently between his shoulder blades. He screamed as he pitched forward and tumbled over the cliff top. Sandro heard the faint sounds of body striking the rocky, inclining cliff face. He did not hear the sound the man made as he struck the rocks below in bone-breaking finality.

'One for one, my hungry wolf,' said Sandro to the dog, 'that is something to help Boris Sergeyovich rest in peace. Come.'

15

Edward was able to motor into Nice the next morning. He went through his breakfast healthily, making up his mind he was fit for the trip. Mademoiselle Dupont smiled at him from her table, though she looked as if her witnessing of Dr Kandor's plunge to death had affected her sleep. But she was at least spared the unwanted smiles and importunities of Monsieur Valery, who had not yet appeared for breakfast.

Celeste wanted to go to Nice with Edward, but her mother could not do without her this time. Four guests were leaving and three winter guests were arriving. It meant busy work for the small staff, and Celeste must do her share.

'But, Mama—'

'Yes, yes, I know, you think Monsieur Somers shouldn't drive to Nice by himself. You forget he drives all the way here from England. I know you like to be with him, but he'll be here until April.'

'Oh, but, Mama—'

'But, but? Come, come, you mustn't attach yourself to him so possessively. People will talk. Look how you've grown lately.'

'Why should people talk about that?' protested Celeste. 'One does grow, Mama. It isn't at all unusual. However, if you're sure you can't do without me, I'll stay, of course.'

'I'm gratified,' said Madame Michel drily.

'I just hope Monsieur Somers experiences no difficulties,' said Celeste. 'If calamity strikes, think of the remorse you'll feel.'

'Well, before he goes, have a brief word with him, child, and tell him, for my sake, that in no circumstances is he to let calamity strike.'

'Yes, Mama.'

'Has Monsieur Valery still not taken breakfast?'

'No, Mama. I think he must have gone out early for some trip he forgot to tell us about. Oh, I must go and get the Countess's breakfast tray.'

'Try not to let it take you more than half an hour,' said Madame Michel.

In Nice, Edward drove towards Heriot's amid the morning traffic. He stopped first, however, to go into the municipal library again. He scanned the pages of a weighty tome entitled *The Last Tsar of Russia*. His reading began to absorb him. The portrait woven by the biographer of Nicholas and Alexandra produced an impression of autocrats entirely devoid of autocratic character or political insight. They were husband and wife, and they were parents, and as such they were faultless in their love, devotion and care. In all else, they were inadequate, it seemed. Nicholas was indecisive, Alexandra a dreamer.

Edward turned to a long chapter describing the looks, the attributes and the characters of the children.

The youngest, the Tsarevich Alexis, the heir to the throne, was, apparently, an engaging boy, with all a boy's aptitude for mischief and pranks. He was also a figure of heartbreak to his parents, especially to Alexandra, who had transmitted to him the disease of haemophilia. His frequent illnesses had been critical, and Alexandra, in her mysticism, believed that only the charlatan monk, Rasputin, had the power to heal him.

There were four daughters.

Olga, Tatiana, Marie and Anastasia. Olga was the eldest, Anastasia the youngest. They were, according to the biographer, girls of great charm, all endearing in their different ways. The descriptions were detailed. Edward absorbed every line. Olga was enchanting because of her warmth and her shyness. Tatiana was sparkling and outgoing, her delight in life infectious. Marie was a lovely, blue-eyed romantic. Anastasia was a tease and a tomboy.

Olga and Tatiana. Marie and Anastasia. And Livadia, their white palace in the Crimea, to which the whole family repaired as often as they could. There, Alexis and the girls found enchantment and bliss, and the happiness of growing up together, and of disporting together.

Edward was spellbound.

The sweetness of life for the girls was shattered in 1917, when Lenin and the Revolution arrived, and the Tsar and all his family were imprisoned, first at the Winter Palace in St Petersburg, then at Tobolsk in Siberia, and finally at Ekaterinburg in the menacing unfriendly Urals.

Ekaterinburg. Where, apparently, they had all been executed, the Tsar, the Tsarina, the Tsarevich and the four lovely Grand Duchesses. Edward knew of it, of course. Everyone knew of it. But his reading of it became painful. There had been an attempt to rescue them, a failed attempt, it seemed.

In the middle of the book, a selection of photographs held his eyes. They fascinated him, and there was one that brought incredulity to his spellbound mind.

A failed rescue attempt? Edward thought of the young woman who had surfaced in Berlin several years ago, claiming to be Anastasia, a woman ill, with a wandering mind, it was declared, but who had once lucidly said, 'I am who I am.'

Now there was another woman, a woman of secrets. Edward left the library looking as if he had come face to face with the unbelievable. When he arrived at Heriot's, he sat for five minutes, trying to orientate himself to what had been the main purpose of his journey. But incredulity was still uppermost when he got out of his car to look for someone who might help him. He did not go to the hire department office, for he did not want to ask questions again of the man in charge. He began a survey of cars that were available for hire, with or without a chauffeur. He was approached by an employee who doubled as a sales assistant and a chauffeur. Edward opened up a conversation with him. He had his own easy way of communicating with people, and inside a few minutes the man was telling him, yes, sometimes clients who drove themselves were a little careless and did bring back cars scratched or damaged. Not often, but now and again. The winding, hilly coastal road, with its hairpin bends, was a hazard to certain drivers.

Edward mentioned the Citroën that had been damaged several days ago.

Ah, yes, the client had glanced a wall rather badly.

Edward, explaining that his interest was personal, asked what the client was like. His informant, who had dealt with the original enquiry before referring to the manager, was quite happy to describe the man in question. Edward, not completely attentive up to that point, suddenly began to listen and to freeze. The description was unmistakable.

He felt eyes on his back. He turned, his mind in turmoil because of the incredible and, now, the frightening. The manager of the hire department was watching him. He accorded Edward a polite nod of recognition, then disappeared into the office. There had been collusion, thought Edward.

He left in a state of intense, painful urgency. The description he had just been given of the person who had tried to batter him and Katerina over the cliff made him board his car like a man who needed to catch up with time itself. God in heaven, he thought, the lunatic was there, at the Corniche, and Katerina—

My God, I took her to the hotel to be safe, and the tiger's sitting outside her door.

He drove through Nice in a panic. Coming to his senses for a moment, he pulled sharply up outside an hotel. A telephone call, yes. The hotel, boasting a call-box in its lobby, offered a lifeline to his drowning mind. He rang the Corniche. Celeste, a further lifeline, answered.

'Celeste, listen,' said Edward, his chest constricting.

'Yes? Yes?'

'Go to the Countess's room at once, please. Will you do that, will you let me know if she's all right? Quickly, my angel – no questions – go at once.'

'Immediately.' Celeste, leaving the phone off the hook, went. She was back in half a minute. 'She's sitting beside her window, and is only interested in when you are coming back.'

'Celeste, could you sit with her until then?'

'But why, m'sieur?'

'I can't explain, not yet. If you're very busy, then get her to lock the door. Will you do that? It's very important.'

'I see.' Celeste did not quite see, but she did not argue.

'Good girl. I'll be back quite soon – I'm leaving Nice now.'

He returned to the Bentley. The sky was as heavy with clouds as yesterday, and the air cool as he drove out of Nice and on to the coastal road at a speed he rarely permitted himself. He enjoyed his Bentley, his one extravagance, and he handled it carefully to avoid physical stress, and lovingly because of his pride in it.

Compulsively rushing at bends in an attempt to shorten his journey began to do him no good at all. He realised, when his racked mind allowed him a moment of sanity, that his telephone call to Celeste had taken care of any immediate danger. He slowed, forcing himself to settle for his usual steady pace. Common sense, however, did not prevent the drive back becoming a test of nerves and patience. Or ease his lungs.

Having spent almost ninety minutes in the library, it was well into lunchtime when he finally reached the Corniche.

Turning into the entrance that led to the space for cars at the side of the hotel, he saw a knot of people on the front steps. Rosamund was among them, and so was Celeste. Everyone seemed to be talking to Jacques. Celeste, seeing Edward drive in, detached herself and hurried round to meet him as he parked his car. She opened the passenger door and slipped in beside him, her face pale and her eyes big with distress.

'Edward,' she gasped, 'something dreadful—'

'Oh, my God,' he said, and his lungs caught fire. 'Celeste, the Countess—'

'No, no – it's Monsieur Valery. He's dead. He was found at the foot of the cliffs, just like Dr Kandor, only on the beach next to ours.'

'Valery? Valery?' Edward looked at her in stark disbelief.

'Yes. Isn't it terrible?' Celeste was white and shaken. 'He may have been lying there all night, because his bed hasn't been slept in and he never appeared for breakfast. And because it's been such a dull morning, no one has been on the beaches. Colonel Brecht decided to take a walk along the cliffs a little while ago, and saw the body down below. Oh, to have happened so soon after Dr Kandor, to have happened at all – people will think La Roche too dangerous to visit – oh, poor Monsieur Valery.'

'My God,' breathed Edward, 'it's unbelievable.'

It was. The description he'd been given at Heriot's had been unmistakably that of Valery. Slight and dapper, with his long nose, the nose that had pointed so often at the desirable Mademoiselle Dupont, as if she alone represented all he most wanted from life. She, intuitively perhaps, had utterly disliked him. How unlikeable indeed was any man who had deliberately attempted to send Katerina to a terrifying death. Edward decided he would not be at all surprised if the police discovered Valery was not French.

'It's terrible, terrible,' said Celeste. She was trembling. He put an arm around her. She was agitatedly quick in the way she turned and put her face against his shoulder, her young body pressing close. He comforted her. There was no immediate worry about Katerina, none at all. Valery, who was out to murder her, and who had used the Corniche as a base, was gone as dramatically and cruelly as Dr Kandor. And Edward had no doubt it was primitive justice, no doubt it was Valery who had sent the doctor over the edge. The barking Alsatian had signalled an alien presence.

But who had sent Valery over the edge?

'Oh, my God,' he said again.

Celeste whispered, 'Monsieur Valery would surely not have gone walking along the cliff top at night.'

'He might, sweet one, he might have been out before dark. The police will have to find the answer. It isn't for you to worry about.'

Celeste cuddled close, loving his warmth and his comforting.

'Jacques went down with Colonel Brecht to look at the body,' she said, 'and he's just telephoned the gendarme in La Roche before going down to the beach again to guard poor Monsieur Valery until the gendarme arrives. That inspector from Nice will be here again, asking many questions. What will he think? Mama is so upset, for it will hardly do our hotel much good, will it?'

'Your hotel will weather every storm, Celeste, for you and your mother make it a place of warmth and welcome.'

'Some guests will leave, I'm sure. Oh, you will stay, won't you?'

'I'll stay, Celeste. And so will Mrs Knight, I'm certain, and her friend, Colonel Brecht.'

'Oh, I do love you,' murmured Celeste, 'I'm so happy whenever you're here. I haven't told the Countess. She's still in her room and knows nothing of this new unhappiness. She locked her door, as you wanted her to. She said she would hesitate not to do all you commanded of her.'

'I don't think she would have quite said that.'

'Well, perhaps not quite.' Celeste lifted her head and smiled wanly. 'Oh, but it is terrible, isn't it? First Dr Kandor and now Monsieur Valery.'

'A tragic coincidence, my sweet,' said Edward, determined to disclose very little to anybody and nothing at all to the police. If he informed them that Valery was a distinctly murderous character, they would ask a thousand questions, not only of him but of Katerina. Under no circumstances was he prepared to have her drawn into an investigation. He still felt stunned by what he had deduced from that book at the library. As far as he was concerned, Katerina was a woman who should be spared all questions, even his own. All her secrets, whatever they were, belonged only to her. If she ever decided to talk, he hoped it would be to him. If not, there must be no inquisition, no interrogation. He felt now that that was what Dr Kandor had tried to tell him. Dr Kandor had been murdered. That was a tragic fact, he felt. Valery was dead. That was an extraordinary but just sequel.

'I'd better go and comfort Mama,' said Celeste. 'Lunch is quite ruined for everyone, and the whole day quite ruined for her.'

'Celeste, is Monsieur Valery's room locked?'

'Yes.'

'Would you care to open it up for me so that I can take a quick look around?'

'This is to do with Madame, isn't it?' said Celeste.

'To do with our love for her, my infant.'

'You must tell her that,' said Celeste.

'No, no—'

'You haven't seen what I have seen,' said Celeste, 'you haven't seen how she looks at you.'

'I've seen how your tongue wags,' said Edward.

'What do you expect to find in Monsieur Valery's room?' asked Celeste.

'I don't know, but I'd like to look.'

'I'm very upset about things,' said Celeste, 'but such is my terrible curiosity that I'm bursting as well as upset.'

'It's all for the good of the Countess, believe me,' said Edward.

Celeste regarded him in concern. He looked drawn and strained.

'I'm not going to like it if you make yourself ill,' she said.

'Trust me not to make myself ill and not to do anything you wouldn't do yourself. There, Celeste, how's that?'

'Oh, I would trust you always and for ever,' she said.

As they got out of the car, Gregory the gardener appeared.

Edward's eyes fastened on him. Gregory was Russian.

'M'sieur, are you unwell?' said the gardener, drawing his bushy brows together.

'A little short of breath, that's all,' said Edward.

'My arm, m'sieur, to see you into the hotel,' said Gregory.

'Thank you, no.' Edward smiled. 'I've Celeste with me.'

16

Celeste and Edward entered the hotel. The lobby was empty. The guests were in the lounge, and the lounge was a buzz of shocked but active voices. Mademoiselle Dupont came out, accompanied by Colonel Brecht. She looked quite cold. The Colonel looked quite troubled. She gave Edward a polite nod and left the hotel. The Colonel sighed, shrugged and went up to his room.

Celeste gave Edward the pass key to Valery's room, and while he made his way up she went in search of her distressed mother.

The room, on the first floor, was tidy. Edward probed quietly around, looking for something that might confirm Valery's involvement in events concerning the Villa d'Azur. There were no papers, letters or documents of any kind. But on the floor of the wardrobe, partially concealed by a newspaper, was a cylindrical leather case, a foot long. It contained a bright expanding telescope. Edward replaced it, closed the wardrobe and left. He walked slowly downstairs and knocked on Katerina's door.

'Who is there, please?' she called.

'Edward.'

She came at a rush, unlocking the door and opening it. Her eyes were bright.

'Oh, I'm so glad to see you back,' she said.

'May I come in?' he asked.

'Oh, yes,' she said. He stepped inside. She closed the door. 'Edward, Celeste told me—'

'Yes, to lock your door.' He did not want to agitate her. 'I thought of you while I was in Nice, I thought it was something you ought to do, lock your door. It's not only residents who walk in and out of hotels.'

'That is very nice, you know, to have you think of me,' said Katerina. 'I – Edward, it's been such a long morning without you, and you're late for lunch.'

Her tray was on a table beside the window. She alone had enjoyed an undisturbed meal. He studied her with new eyes, the incredulity underlying the fascination. He thought about the book, about the Tsar, the last Tsar of all the Russias, and about the Tsar's family, all supposedly executed in 1918. He remembered a particular photograph. He could not take in all that Katerina appeared to be, all she might be. The magnificent auburn hair, the clear grey eyes, the oval features, her classical beauty and the always natural air of regal elegance. Impossible, impossible. Or could one believe in miracles?

One could when one remembered what had been happening, and when one thought about the high wall Dr Kandor had put around her.

'Katerina—'

'Edward, why are you looking at me like that?' she asked. 'And why are you so drawn and dark?'

'Because no one will paint me in oils, I suppose,' he said. 'No, I was just wondering from whom you inherit such marvellous auburn hair.'

Her lashes flickered.

'From my grandmother, I think,' she said lightly. 'Edward, is something wrong? You really are looking at me very strangely.'

'That's because—' He hesitated.

'Say it, please. If it's something I shall dislike, if it's to do with a fault I have, you must tell me. I do have many imperfections, I know. So please be frank.'

He smiled.

'I was only going to say you're very beautiful. I think you've always been so, haven't you?'

Katerina's sensitive colour rushed.

'Edward?' Little vibrations were perceptible.

'The family you served – the girls were beautiful too? As beautiful as you?' He did not feel they were questions, just expressions of his wonder.

'They were lovely, yes.' Her lashes veiled her eyes. 'Edward, is that what you think, that I'm beautiful?'

'I'm sure you always have been,' he said. 'But you have enemies, haven't you? We both know that, because of what happened to Dr Kandor. No, I'm not going to ask questions. However, I think you're safer now, for the moment. So much so that after I've completed a couple of hours' work this afternoon, I think you and I could go for a little drive. You must hate being confined to your room all day. Would you like to go out later? You can wear your veil.'

'Edward, how good you are to me,' she said. She did not ask why he felt she was safer. 'I've lost my faithful doctor, my guardian, and I'm so grateful that I have you. A drive will be rapture. Yes, really. Thank you.'

'We'll drive and talk,' he said. 'You can tell me about Bulgaria – or Russia, if you like.'

'Russia?' The vibrations were very perceptible.

'If you want to, Katerina.'

Edward did some work. It was difficult to divorce his mind from the unbelievable, but he managed it to some extent. He wrote in short bursts. His flowing pencil halted at times, and he sat looking unseeingly at his notes for long moments.

The police arrived. He heard them. He heard the voice of Inspector Cartier and the voice of Madame Michel. He heard them go upstairs, to Valery's room. They were there quite a while.

Celeste brought him tea at four thirty in answer to his request.

'The police have been and gone,' she said. 'Mama is feeling wretched. All the questions. But what can anyone say? They've taken away all Monsieur Valery's things, all of them.'

'Celeste, nothing must be said that will make the police ask questions of the Countess. You agree, my infant?'

'With all my heart,' said Celeste. 'You haven't told her about Monsieur Valery?'

'No, I haven't,' said Edward. 'The tragedy of Dr Kandor was quite enough for her, even though she didn't know Valery.'

'Oh, yes,' said Celeste earnestly. She poured the tea for him. 'I'm so glad you care so much for her, especially as we've now discovered she has eyes only for you.'

'Dear heaven,' said Edward, 'your imagination will carry you off to the moon one day.'

'Oh, I'm extremely attached to the moon, m'sieur. Do you think everything would be for the best if you and Madame could bring yourselves to make up your minds?'

'I feel I shouldn't ask,' said Edward, 'but I must. Make up our minds about what?'

'About taking care of each other always.'

Edward smiled at her air of innocence.

'Oh, I'm something of a ruin, my angel, as you well know, and could take very little care of any woman.'

'Well!' Celeste expressed disgust. 'Well! Whoever heard such nonsense? Every year you've taken good care of me, and Mama says no one could have been more of a problem than I was as a girl.'

'You're a woman now?' said Edward.

'But anyone can see I've grown, anyone.' Celeste regarded her figure with unselfconscious satisfaction. 'Oh, if you persist in avoiding sweet fate, then a most dreadful one will await you – you will find yourself having to marry me.'

He laughed. Celeste smiled. She liked very much to bring him to laughter.

'That would hardly frighten any man to death, Celeste.'

'I must go and see that Madame's tea is to her liking.'

'Celeste, will you tell her I'll be ready to take her for the drive at five o'clock?'

'Oh, a drive is arranged? A lovers' excursion? I am enchanted for you. I go – I fly – see, I am gone.'

In the most guileless fashion, Celeste advised Katerina that at five o'clock Edward and his carriage would await her in breathless anticipation.

'He said that, Celeste? Breathless anticipation?'

'Perhaps those were not his exact words,' said Celeste, 'but as you know, madame, he's a man most romantic in his speech and I shouldn't think I'm too far out in my interpretation of his message.'

'Thank you, Celeste,' said Katerina gravely. 'But he's better? He looked so drawn a while ago.'

'Oh, he has the healthiest beam in his eye now,' said Celeste. 'Madame, I will tell you, he's always better lately than he wishes us to know. Alas, I'm afraid he puts on an air of frailty in case some importunate lady or other sets her cap at him. He thinks he would make a deplorable husband. There have been ladies here in the past who would willingly have embraced him and taken him to their warm hearts, but no, he has avoided their tender arms—'

'Oh, Celeste!' Katerina laughed in joy. 'You're making this up, you delicious girl. You are as incorrigible as – never mind, you are just incorrigible.'

'No, no,' protested Celeste. 'There's Mademoiselle Dupont now, a lady from Paris. Ah, Paris, that dreadful city. You can imagine, madame, how hungry Mademoiselle Dupont is. Oh, I assure you. She's already made up her mind that Edward is the most interesting man here, and therefore she's very set on him.'

'I'm going to dislike Mademoiselle Dupont,' said Katerina.

'Oh, a covetous woman, most detestable,' said Celeste. 'A spider from Paris. She will eat Edward. Think, madame, of Edward slowly disappearing into her web—'

'Celeste!' Katerina laughed again. 'Stop this. It's more than I can bear. Tell Edward I'll be ready at five, and that I hope he may be breathless but not entangled.'

'Yes, madame, immediately.'

'If not at once,' smiled Katerina.

* * *

Heavily veiled, Katerina left the hotel with Edward just after five, and they drove in the most leisurely way. The clouds had gone, the afternoon sun warmed the Riviera, and Edward proceeded through La Roche and then turned right to take the winding and narrow lanes that led to tiny villages away from the coast. He drove into quietness. Katerina breathed deeply. Again she felt an exhilarating sense of freedom and pleasure. Boris Sergeyovich was a grief still, but Edward was beside her, and Edward was close and caring. The scent of the wild flowers and the pines was a fragrance, a delight, and the world was open to her.

Katerina was set to tease him a little in her pleasure.

'Edward,' she said, 'I'm told you're being pursued by a charming lady from Paris, a guest at the hotel.'

'Am I?' He felt he was beyond all reality. He felt himself engulfed by the impossible. The only reality was in her grace and her enchantment. Everything else was so unbelievable that dreams existed in place of reality.

'You are enjoying the pursuit?' The veil that covered her face fluttered lightly to her breath.

'I'm not even aware of it. What lady in her right mind would want to pursue me?'

'But you are as eligible as any man could be,' said Katerina. 'I was not myself brought up to pursue a prospect, but the war has brought a social change of dire consequences.'

'Dire?'

'Why, yes, Edward,' she murmured, 'for it's possible Mademoiselle Dupont may catch you.'

'Hard luck on her if she does,' said Edward, as they motored gently through a village in which wild vines clung to cottage walls. 'She'll find she's caught only half a prospect. I'm no more than that, and there's an end to it, Katerina.'

'You are ridiculous,' said Katerina.

Edward frowned.

'One should be honest,' he said.

'One should be very honest,' said Katerina, 'but not absurd. I'm sure Emily thought you were not only absurd but unfair.'

'No, I don't think so. Shall we talk about Bulgaria?'

'No,' said Katerina, watching the dusty road and the glint of the sun on the brass of the headlamps. She was out, she was about, she had escaped her walls. And she was so exhilarated that she was teasing Edward.

'Then let's talk about what you're going to do,' he said. 'Have you decided?'

'I have not,' she said. 'Edward, you are my friend, the only one I have, apart from Celeste. You must decide.'

'I?'

'Yes. I'm a woman of my own times, I'm not a – what is the word they use today?'

'A flapper?'

'Yes. In my own times, we were taught gracious and correct ways of behaviour. I can't escape my own pattern. Gentlemen, to me, exist to prevent ladies from drowning. Ladies exist to make their own contributions to life. To expect help from a friend isn't a principle I object to – no, not at all.' She was light of voice, and she was smiling, but she was no longer teasing. 'To me, it's a pleasure to know that one's troubles can be taken care of by one's dearest friends.'

He brought the Bentley to a stop in the narrow road. On either side lay the terraced slopes carrying the grape vines, the crop long since harvested. He turned to her. She was colourful in a light, pale pink coat worn over a white dress that was fashionably short. Her long legs shone in white silk stockings, rounded knees peeping. He was acutely aware of her physical presence, the effect of the slender, shapely body on his masculine consciousness. Despite the veil, she was vivid and alive, and heady in her beauty. The impossible again induced the sense of unreality.

'Katerina, anything I can do, I'll gladly do,' he said.

'I know,' she said, 'and that is precious to me.' She put her veil up, and she was there for him to touch and to kiss, if he wanted to, if he only knew. Her past was her own, locked away, but there were all the years of the future. She suddenly felt almost scalded by the realisation that she did not have to go to America, that she could make her own decision. But her grey eyes, soft beneath the shade of her brimmed hat, carried the message that she would willingly let the decision be his.

'You must leave your villa, you must leave La Roche?' he said.

'Yes, I must at least do that.'

'And I must ask no questions, Katerina?'

'Everyone asks questions, except you.'

'You need a new home, a quiet place?'

'A very quiet place, Edward.'

'Then we must think about it, sleep on it, and talk about it tomorrow.'

'Yes, Edward, very well,' she said, and put out a hand and touched his. It was as much as she could do, because she was a woman of yesterday. It was a light and caressing touch, a momentary one. He smiled, restarted the car, and drove on, making a round tour of their outing.

When they returned to the hotel, most of the guests were gathered in the lounge enjoying aperitifs. Celeste was in the lobby, however, talking to Colonel Brecht. He, fixing his monocle in his eye to peer at Katerina in her veil, gave her a little bow.

'Good evening,' said Katerina. Edward gave the Colonel a smile and ushered her on to her room.

'You'll take dinner here?' he said.

'I would rather,' she said. She would have liked to dine with Edward, she would have liked to have met some of the guests, to have moved among them with Edward and proved to herself that she had not become a recluse. 'If you wish to do some writing this evening, I shall be quite happy. The drive was lovely. Thank you, Edward.'

'Yes, I'll do some writing and thinking,' he said.

'There is—' She hesitated, showing the faintest of flushes. 'Edward, there is more to think about than a suitably quiet place.'

He wondered, as he entered his room, exactly what she meant by that.

Dinner was a quiet meal. Mademoiselle Dupont looked for a moment as if she was about to direct herself towards

Edward's table, but changed her mind. She did suggest a game of billiards afterwards. Colonel Brecht and Rosamund were willing, but Edward excused himself. Immediately after the meal, he returned to his room. He knew he must do some work. He was falling behind. He began to write. But there was no release from his awareness of the unbelievable. He wanted her with him, he wanted to look at her, to indulge the fascination she had for him. He knew that if he knocked, if he took the dominoes, she would be warm and receptive. She would sit at her table with him, laughing and competitive. She would look like a young and striking empress. How strange, that air of being young, as if the joys she had known had placed their indelible mark on her, the mark of years happy and idyllic. Only the shadows that sometimes came to her eyes spoke of other things.

He must stay with his work.

He persevered, although her image floated before him in the light of the table lamp.

For no reason at all, he suffered an attack, a violent one.

Celeste, carrying a tray of empty coffee cups to the kitchen, heard him. She delivered the tray to Marie and hurried to his room. He was sitting on the edge of his bed, his handkerchief to his mouth, his face dark with the pain of squeezed lungs.

'M'sieur, where are your tablets?'

'I've taken one.' He coughed into his handkerchief. He hit his chest with his hand. 'Give me a moment, angel of love and mercy.'

'Oh, m'sieur, even when you're in pain you're sweet to me. Who could wish for a lovelier man?'

Edward managed a smile.

'You could wish for one who didn't creak so much,' he said.

'I will bring cognac, yes?' said Celeste. 'A cognac? Only say, and I will fly for it.'

Edward straightened his back.

'Celeste, you are France's joy. Cognac will be splendid, and with a coffee, perhaps?'

'Oh, at once – immediately.' She turned at the door. 'Oh, first, Inspector Cartier has telephoned. He's coming tomorrow to ask questions of everyone who became acquainted with Monsieur Valery while he was here. But you weren't acquainted with him, nor was Madame. Mama will see to it that you two aren't bothered. M'sieur – Edward – I fly.'

She knocked on the door two minutes later. She opened it. But it was Katerina who entered, Katerina who bore the tray containing coffee and brandy, and Celeste closed the door on them.

'You see?' said Katerina. 'Celeste is so busy. I'm not busy at all. Edward, it was a bad attack?'

'No, not at all. A brief one. Over and done with.' He stood up, clearing papers from the table. Katerina set the tray down.

'I may stay a while?' she said. 'It won't tire you if I do, or be considered too scandalous?'

'I think we'll escape headlines,' he said. 'I doubt if we can compete with the German airship which has just crossed the Atlantic.'

But perhaps she could, he thought. If the impossible was not impossible, she could indeed.

They sat down at the table together. She was quiet for a while, watching him as he drank the coffee and sipped the brandy. The colour returned to his face.

'Celeste told me you'd had an attack,' she said then, 'and that you wished for coffee and cognac, that she was attending to it at once, if not immediately. She's delicious, isn't she, Edward?'

'Celeste stands alone,' said Edward.

'Yes.' Katerina smiled and steadied herself. 'She said she put me into the room next to yours so that you could look after me and care for me.'

'In between my coughing and wheezing?'

'Edward, your pain is my pain. Do you see, you've made me so alive. Edward, I—' Katerina rose to her feet, escaping his eyes. She moved to the fireplace, hiding the flush on her face as she looked down at the laid grate. She was full of the uncertainties of a woman who had never known a lover. There had been many years of trial, many dangerous moments and many different kinds of people. The good and the brave, the weak and the treacherous, the loyal and the helpful, and the cold and the merciless. There had been many men among these. She had been grateful to some, contemptuous of some and defiant of others. But there had been no man she loved, until now. She was not a shy person, not by any means, but nor was she a sophisticate, neither by upbringing nor inclination. What she had to face up to now, by reason of Edward's self-deprecation, touched every sensitive nerve. 'Edward,' she said, 'this is so difficult for me. You must help me.'

'Without Dr Kandor, I know you feel—'

'No, it isn't that,' she said. 'It's us, Edward, you and I.'

'The problem is between us? Katerina, have I said wrong things?'

'You've said nothing. Except that you think me beautiful. That is the problem, that you've said nothing.'

'But we've had so many conversations,' said Edward, all too aware that he was dangerously close to taking a heady leap into the unknown. It was the unknown, Katerina Pyotrovna in his arms.

'Yes, we've talked,' she said. She turned as he approached her. Her eyes reflected the lamplight. The night colour flickered between her unsteady lashes. Her blood suffused her. Love was very painful, very sensitive. 'Edward, it isn't enough.'

'Am I very lacking, Katerina?'

'Oh, no! How can you say that?' She was a figure of light and shadows, an incredible dream to him. Her hands were at her throat, as if her voice hurt her. 'Oh, I had no idea it would be so difficult. Hundreds of times I've had Papa's handsomest young officers declare they loved me, and there was nothing difficult in telling them I adored them all. It isn't like that now.'

'Your father's officers, Katerina?'

She shook her head a little wildly.

'No – no – I mean – oh, there were the officers Papa had command of in those days. Edward, please don't confuse the issue, and please don't avoid it.'

'Katerina,' he said, 'is it necessary for me to say I love you?'

'It's desperately necessary for you to love me very much and to say so.' She clasped her unsteady hands. 'Please, will you say it and make me stop wishing for the floor to open up?'

'Is that all? That you wish to know if I love you? What else can I say except that I simply love you? Do you think it's possible not to love you? You're the most enchanting woman on earth.' Edward smiled into her suffused eyes. 'Without any reservations at all, I adore you. We met only two weeks ago? That's not possible, either. I feel I've known you all my life – you're all my years, all my days. Katerina, you're the loveliest of women.'

'Edward?' Katerina, visibly trembling, drew a long breath. 'Oh, how precious that is to me. I've been looking at you and loving you, and Boris Sergeyovich knew it. Love is a gift of pain and sweetness and magic, and even more than that when it's returned. I've never been seriously in love before, but now, do you see, I've fallen desperately in love in the shortest space of time, a single day. I'll show you.'

She did then what she had wanted to do for many days. She kissed him, on the mouth, and her lips were warm, giving and confessional, telling him in their lingering pressure how much she needed him, how much he filled the life that had been so lonely for her. His declaration of love had been made, and so, because she was what she was, emotionally demonstrative, her response was frank and unashamed. She wound her arms around him, and her warm body pressed very close, communicating its eager life and vitality to his. His blood coursed as he felt the incredible wonder of vigour reborn.

'Katerina—'

'Oh, you're my dearest love,' she breathed, head back and eyes radiant. 'You have brought me to life, you have given me days of sweetness. I used to sit day after day, looking at nothing and thinking only of the years long ago, and now, dear dear Edward, I'm thinking only of the years I shall share with you. I'm disastrously weak with love, quite close to falling down, yet so strong I could fly. Oh, how glad I am you did not marry Emily. You will propose to me now?'

'Katerina, you must think – you can't take an invalid for a husband, you need a far healthier man than I am, a man far more suitable in every way.'

'Far more suitable?' Katerina was visibly shocked. 'Far more suitable?'

'You're not an ordinary person—'

'Stop.' She put a hand over his mouth. 'Don't say such things. I'd never marry a man because someone said he was suitable. Never, never. You must make no excuses for not proposing. You'll break my heart if you do. Yes, that's far more likely to do lasting damage to my health than anything else. Edward, I'm strong, I don't have a weak heart. You know I don't. And you've been wondering why I said I did. You've been thinking things. Edward, they're all irrelevant, all things to do with my past. I'm here, with you, and my heart is beating madly for you. There, do you feel how it's beating?' She brought his hand to her warm, round breast, and a little sigh escaped her at the touch that was a caress. 'Hold me. Put your arms around me, and you'll know how alive and strong I am for you.'

He put his arms around her, and again her body imparted its magical transference of vitality. He felt himself engulfed by the dreams.

'Dear God,' he said.

'Edward?' Her face was against his shoulder, her voice full of faint vibrations. 'I want you to marry me, don't you feel how I do? I beg you, propose, or I shall die a death from burning.'

'Will you, then, will you marry me, my most lovely Katerina?'

'Oh, yes, yes. I want to be with you – every day, every night – I shall care very much for you. Celeste is right, you must have a wife, and I must be the one. It is true you told her I was the most beautiful woman you'd ever seen?'

'Quite true,' he said, in wonder at the turn life had taken.

'You'll always think that, even when I'm old?' she said.

'Even when you're very old,' said Edward.

'Edward, you will have to love me very much,' she said, her arms lingering around him. 'You must, because I'm going to ask a great deal of you. You must never ask questions. You must accept me only as you know me, as Katerina Pyotrovna – oh, but there's nothing in all my years to make you ashamed, believe me. Whatever I tell you about my life you must accept, even though it may not be precisely true. Will you do that, my darling, will you take me as you know me now?'

He might have said he knew her to be far more than Katerina Pyotrovna, that to him she represented a miracle. But he only said, 'Nothing is important to me but you yourself.'

'Edward, I am only as you see me,' she said. 'You must make no guesses and have no worries. We must go far away. Oh, it will be a joy, will it not?'

'We shall find a quiet place, Katerina, and you must have no worries yourself. The man I think responsible for Dr Kandor's death is dead himself. He too was found at the foot of the cliffs.'

Her eyes opened wide. She shivered. She thought of Sandro, who had declared to her that Boris Sergeyovich would not go unavenged.

'Edward—'

'No more, Katerina. You've borne enough. But I gave you that news so that you'll know you can sleep safely tonight. And tomorrow.'

'I must see Anna and Sandro,' she said.

'Tomorrow,' said Edward.

She smiled.

'Yes, Edward. Tomorrow.'

17

Rosamund, Colonel Brecht and Mademoiselle Dupont were quietly conversing in the lounge.

'The poor Countess,' said Mademoiselle Dupont, as Celeste brought the glasses of cognac Colonel Brecht had ordered for her and himself. 'To have lost her doctor, to know that this other gentleman has died in the same way, and she with her weak heart. She's bearing up, Celeste?'

'Yes, mademoiselle,' said Celeste, who would have preferred the Frenchwoman to know nothing about the Countess. But it had got about, the fact that she was resident in the hotel.

'I haven't had the pleasure of meeting her myself,' said Colonel Brecht, 'but saw her enter the hotel with Edward early this evening.'

'If you haven't met her, Franz, how did you know it was she?' asked Rosamund.

'An assumption, Rosamund, an assumption,' said the Colonel. 'I hope most sincerely the tragedies won't bring on a serious heart attack. I have known of people retiring in apparent good health to bed, and failing to wake up.'

'Oh, *mon Colonel*!' Celeste was shocked, and Mademoiselle Dupont cast the German a pitying look.

'That was hardly the most joyful thing to say, Franz,' said Rosamund.

'Ah – most stupid of me,' muttered the abashed Colonel.

'I shall return to Paris,' said Mademoiselle Dupont. 'One cannot in all fairness be expected to relax in this atmosphere, delightful though your hotel is, Celeste.'

'It's as you wish, mademoiselle,' said Celeste, who would quite happily have helped the Parisian lady on her way.

'I shall retire to bed,' said Rosamund, as Celeste departed, 'the day has been quite gloomy. However, there's always tomorrow. Life has its consolation in that there's always tomorrow.'

'Indeed, indeed,' said Colonel Brecht. 'We shall take a brisk walk, yes?'

'Shall we?' said Rosamund.

'If you insist,' said the Colonel.

'I'm provoked into that,' said Rosamund.

Mademoiselle Dupont smiled faintly.

Colonel Brecht coughed.

Celeste could not sleep. She lay awake, tossing and turning. Poor Mama, so unhappy about Monsieur Valery, and about the police returning to the hotel. It was all so bad for the Corniche.

And there was the Countess, so mysteriously a lonely and troubled woman, and so enchanting. Edward simply must look after her.

Celeste loved them both.

It was so late. She must go to sleep or she would never get up in the morning. She turned and reached for the glass of water that always lay to hand on her bedside table. She found it, sat up and gulped thirstily.

She stiffened. Her little bedroom on the ground floor was not far from the staircase. Someone was out there. The tiniest sound had reached her ears. Edward was wandering about? He could not sleep, either? But no, he would not wander about. He would take a tablet and try to relax.

Madame – the countess!

Celeste was out of her bed in a flash. Her eyes, used to the darkness because she'd lain awake for so long, needed no light. She opened her bedroom door very quietly, and just as quietly she walked on her bare feet towards the lobby, then turned to the left. Her heart was beating fast. She reached the door of Katerina's room. It was open, just slightly. She pushed it wide. The darkness of the room was a momentary blackness before her orientated eyes pierced it.

The bed was in upheaval. A body was striving and struggling. A dark, bending form and the glimmer of a white, smothering pillow rushed at Celeste's eyes. The assailant was breathing hard, bearing down and down, but beneath the pillow and the bedclothes Katerina was fighting for her life, because life meant so much to her now. She was neither weak nor swooning. She was strong and frenzied, her smothered mouth open, her teeth tearing at the suffocating pillow, her hands wrenching at the jersey-sleeved arms that were like steel rods in their rigid pressure.

Celeste screamed and hurled herself. The figure came upright and turned. A clenched fist struck Celeste on the temple, knocking her sideways. Celeste pitched to the floor. She screamed again, she came up on her feet like a furious cat, ready to claw and rend. She saw the dark figure vanishing, not through the door but the open French windows.

The bedroom light went on.

'Celeste!'

It was Edward, in his pyjamas, his face drawn and shocked. Celeste flung herself into his arms.

'Edward – Madame – someone was trying to smother her—'

They turned to the bed. Katerina lay trembling, drawing painful breaths, her auburn hair riotous and disordered.

'Katerina – oh, my God,' said Edward, and sat down on the edge of the bed, taking hold of her hands.

'Madame – oh, blessed joy,' breathed Celeste, 'he's gone – you're alive.'

'Celeste,' gasped Katerina, 'oh, my brave and lovely one.'

'My God,' said Edward again, 'what sort of care is this I've taken of you?' He should have guessed Valery would have an accomplice. It was always work for two, this kind of work, the elimination of people.

Katerina smiled. There were two people she loved. They were both here, both close. Relief that was blissful flooded her.

'Celeste came,' she said, 'my sweet Celeste, my brave one. Celeste?' She released her hands from Edward's and put out her arms. Celeste bent and Katerina embraced her and kissed her.

The hotel was alive with the sounds of disturbed guests. Madame Michel arrived in a woollen dressing-gown. Edward crossed to the door and closed it. Celeste, bruised but as intoxicated with relief as Katerina, explained to her mother. A long sigh escaped Madame Michel.

'This too?' she said. 'We are pursued by the devils of darkness. Holy Mary, deliver us.' She crossed herself, regarding Katerina sadly and in shame. 'Countess, what is to be done with such an hotel as this?'

'Treasure it, madame,' said Katerina, 'for it holds my friends, and no harm has been done.'

'Cognac,' said Madame Michel. 'Harm or not, cognac for you. Yes?'

'And a little for Celeste,' said Edward, bitter with himself for taking Katerina's safety for granted.

'Mama, I will get it,' said Celeste, 'while you talk to the guests.'

'A burglar,' said Edward, 'may I suggest that, Madame Michel, an interrupted burglar?'

'Yes, I will talk to them,' said Madame Michel, and she and Celeste left him alone with Katerina.

Edward went to the still open French windows and closed them. He sat down beside Katerina, who lay quite calmly, her hair a spilling mass of dark auburn, her eyes full of shadows. She reached for his hand, her fingers closing tightly around his.

'What a self-satisfied idiot I was,' he said.

'A kiss, please?' said Katerina.

He kissed her, and she felt the warmth and the ardour of his lips, the kiss intense because of his relief that she had survived.

'Thank God for Celeste,' he said. 'I should have guessed, I should have known, there had to be two of them.'

'Celeste has been brave,' said Katerina, 'and God has been good. Do you see, Edward, we've been given life as well as love. Life together. I was determined not to die. I thought of you. I prayed. Celeste answered my prayers. You aren't to blame, my darling. How could anyone have known?'

He regarded her in new wonder. She had just escaped a torturing death. But her eyes were full of light now, her smile a caress. From where did she get her beauty and her courage? From whom did she get them?

'I wonder at you,' he said, 'I wonder why, when there must be thousands of better men, you're so set on me.'

'Oh, I'm very set on you,' she said, 'you will never escape me, never. Edward, you must not put yourself down so much. You are the kindest of men, you are like Papa—' She stopped. She went on. 'I want you. I want you to love me. Will you marry me very quickly, please?'

'I shall love you,' he said, 'I shall marry you.'

Celeste came in with cognac for both of them. She sat on the bed and watched them sip it. She smiled. Her enchanting Madame was warm with colour. They had been kissing. Celeste was sure of it.

'Shall I tell her?' said Edward.

'No, I will,' smiled Katerina. 'Celeste, Edward is going to marry me. He has taken his courage into both hands—'

'Oh, how wonderful!' Celeste flowered into bright joy for them. 'I'm so happy for you, for both of you – there, I knew it, didn't I? I knew you only had to meet, to see each other – oh, blessed Saint Mary, as Mama would say, I'm enchanted and overcome.'

'I share that feeling,' said Edward. Celeste kissed him demonstratively. 'Celeste, you are truly your mama's angel. Were both the hotel doors bolted tonight?'

'Oh, yes,' said Celeste. 'You insisted, and Mama has been very careful about that.'

'The French windows can't be opened from the outside,' said Edward.

Celeste stared. Katerina watched Edward out of eyes that were always drawn to him.

'M'sieur,' breathed Celeste, 'Madame's door – it was open when I came – it was open.'

'And so, having been caught, my little chicken, and the hotel aroused, he escaped by the windows. Celeste, did all the guests show themselves?'

'I'm not sure,' said Celeste.

'Then, with you and your mama, we'll check the bedrooms.'

'Oh,' gasped Celeste, 'you're pointing a dreadful finger, Edward – you're saying one of the guests will be missing.'

'Yes, Celeste. Shall we check?'

'Edward,' said Katerina, 'look for a woman.'

'Madame?' gasped Celeste.

'Her scent is still here,' said Katerina.

Madame Michel agreed to make the check. It meant disturbing some of the guests again.

One was missing.

The room of Mademoiselle Dupont was empty.

Edward, remembering the peculiar relationship affected by Valery and the Frenchwoman, thought with hindsight that this had been the clumsiest way of covering their partnership. That they were French-speaking Bolshevik agents he had no doubt. Some Russians spoke French better than they spoke Russian.

He asked Madame Michel to say nothing. He and the Countess would, with regret, leave after the inquest on Dr Kandor. It was essential, and he begged Madame Michel to ask for no explanations.

'M'sieur,' said Madame Michel, 'we've known you many years. It has been more than a pleasure. You have helped Celeste to become what she is by all the time you've spared for her, and all the kindnesses you've shown her. I am proud of my daughter, and I honour you, m'sieur. I will ask nothing of you except that you regard us always as your friends. The inspector is coming here tomorrow afternoon, to talk to everyone who had some small acquaintance of Monsieur Valery. There's no reason why you need to be here, or the Countess, for neither of you had anything to do with him at all.'

'It occurs to me,' said Edward, sitting with her in her little room, 'that the inspector will concern himself primarily with the sudden disappearance of Mademoiselle Dupont, about whom the less said the better as far as I'm concerned.'

'But she should be guillotined, m'sieur, for what she tried to do.'

'Well, it was a woman according to the Countess. A woman is absent, one Mademoiselle Dupont. That's all we know for certain. Let the inspector put his own interpretation on her absence.'

Madame Michel managed a faint smile. That was almost piquant, she thought. More than one guest would be able to inform the police that Monsieur Valery had cast eager eyes at Mademoiselle Dupont, and that she had responded with quite contemptuous indifference. Her unexplained departure would most certainly make Inspector Cartier concentrate on her, not for her attempt on the Countess's life, of which he would be told nothing, but in connection with Monsieur Valery's death. Yes, it was piquant, almost.

'No guests, m'sieur, are aware of what happened in the Countess's room.'

'Thank you, dear madame,' said Edward. 'I really think she should be spared questions when she's already answered more than enough about Dr Kandor. I'll take her for an afternoon drive, to Nice, I think, where perhaps we can apply for a special marriage licence.'

'Marriage licence?' Madame Michel's eyes opened wide.

'You see in me,' smiled Edward, 'the most fortunate of men.'

'Is that true, m'sieur?' said the astonished Madame Michel.

'Quite true,' he said, and stood up to receive her felicitations. She embraced him with romantic fervour.

'I'm happy for you, most happy,' she said, and kissed him on both cheeks. 'So, a little afternoon excursion in search of a marriage licence. Entirely irresistible, m'sieur. Please, now, return to your bed. The Countess has had a shock, but has borne it bravely. Mademoiselle Dupont, whoever she is, has gone. Nothing will be said by Celeste or me concerning her actions. We all have our secrets. Celeste is going to sleep in the Countess's room. So go to your bed in peace, m'sieur.'

Edward took breakfast early. Even so, Colonel Brecht and Rosamund were in advance of him. No mention was made of Mademoiselle Dupont. Everyone was in blissful ignorance of her flight. Colonel Brecht, finishing his coffee, approached Rosamund with a diffident smile.

'In thirty minutes, Rosamund?' he said.

'For our walk?' she said.

'I shall look forward to it,' said the Colonel, and with a smile at Edward left the dining-room. He paused in the lobby to look around.

Rosamund took up her coffee and sat down at Edward's table.

'There's a mystery, Edward.'

'Oh, there are always mysteries, Rosamund.'

'Do whisper a few words at least?' she suggested.

'Well, the burglar must have decided there were pickings to be had at the Corniche. Fortunately, Celeste was awake, and that disposed very quickly of the intruder. Not much of a mystery, I'm afraid.'

'A burglar?' said Rosamund. 'Dear me. Two suicides and a burglar? We are living, aren't we? La Roche is suddenly the centre of drama. Edward, my dear man, I'm not a simpleton, you know.'

'Well, since you're not,' said Edward, 'the reason why the Countess and I have decided to leave next week—'

'You're leaving?'

'Yes,' he said. 'Her villa has been sold. We're getting married.'

'Heavens above,' said Rosamund.

'It's a shock?' said Edward.

'A shock? No, a lovely surprise. Edward, really, how pleased I am for you. Be very happy, my dear. But such deep waters – how intriguing.'

'And you and Franz?' said Edward.

'Good heavens, no, nothing so romantic,' smiled Rosamund. 'We're friends, that's all. I could never make a husband of him. He's far too set in his ways. Underneath that Prussian exterior, he's not without charm, but a husband? No, I think not. I'll probably marry my gardener. That will be the only real way of making my garden as much my own as his. Tell me more about your intriguing Countess, whom you've never introduced to me.'

Edward talked guardedly to her over the breakfast coffee.

Katerina said coldly, 'You're mistaken, quite mistaken, Colonel Brecht – if that's who you really are.'

'Your Highness,' said Colonel Brecht, no longer a stiff and awkward man, but smooth and self-confident, 'it's taken me a considerable time to convince myself. I am, however, now fully convinced.'

'Then you're deluding yourself. I am not Your Highness.' Katerina stood tall and straight-backed. 'Please leave.'

'A rumour reached us,' said the Colonel, 'and the Emperor—'

'He's no longer the Emperor.'

'He commissioned me to investigate. It hasn't been easy. I'm His Imperial Majesty's aide-de-camp, not a spy. I caught sight of you on one day only. Your protector appeared with a rifle, and I've never seen a man more determined. Fortunately, I managed to conceal myself, and it was the wandering gardener of this hotel who was unlucky enough to have a shot fired at him. I'd glimpsed you. Subsequently, still concealed, I watched your unexpected meeting with Edward Somers, though I wasn't close enough to be positive about you. But since then enough has happened to tell me the Bolsheviks had also heard that rumour. They want you, dead or alive, Your Highness.'

'You're making a mistake,' said Katerina. The confrontation, taking place in her room, and in German, was cold on the one hand, quietly determined on the other. 'I am a Bulgarian exile.'

'Seeing you now,' said the Colonel, 'I'm sure I'm making no mistake. I'm here to offer you the protection of the Kaiser Wilhelm, to escort you to Holland—'

'Stop!' Katerina's eyes flashed. 'Never. Never. Do you dare to come here and offer me the protection of a man responsible for sending Lenin to Russia, responsible by that act for the desolation of Russia and the destruction of so many kings and emperors? And what protection do I need? I am Katerina Pyotrovna, Countess of Varna. That is all I am.'

'I beg you to listen,' said the Colonel, more convinced than ever. 'In no circumstances will anything but complete secrecy and security be maintained. I swear to you that the Emperor was not himself responsible for putting Lenin on that train, that he did all he could to intercede when your family was in captivity.'

'My family has never been in captivity,' said Katerina firmly. 'We have only been refugees, like many other people of Europe. I repeat, Colonel Brecht, I am not who you think I am. Please go.'

'I gave my word to the Emperor to do all I could to find you, to do all I could to persuade you. His life now is quiet and undisturbed, as yours will be. The Emperor's one concern is to find all of you, to redeem any mistakes he may have made, and to offer his love and care.'

'Colonel Brecht,' said Katerina, 'you are a sincere man, I feel, but a mistaken one. I ask you, earnestly, to withdraw from any further effort or investigation. If you'll be so kind as to leave, if you'll report to the Emperor that I'm not the one the rumour said I might be, then I'll regard you as a friend. Do this for me. Do this for my peace of mind, and my happiness. Do you have any assistants?'

'One,' said Colonel Brecht. 'A White Russian, who was to help me identify you. But he vanished. I think he was seen by Bolshevik agents.' He regarded her a little sadly. She was very proud, very fearless, and extraordinarily beautiful. There was mystery there, and strange wistfulness. He made his decision. 'Forgive me, Countess, I have indeed made a mistake. My apologies for intruding on you.'

'You're forgiven,' said Katerina.

The Colonel's smile was rueful.

'I shan't be leaving immediately,' he said, 'I've an appointment with a charming English lady, with whom I'm doing my miserable best not to get too involved. I shall stay a few more days. Countess, let me wish you happiness, and many years of peace. I shall report that the Countess of Varna was a lady so like another in her looks and courage that the rumour was a credible one.'

'Thank you,' said Katerina. She put out her hand. The Colonel took it, bowed low and kissed her fingertips.

'Forgive me,' he said again, and left.

Katerina, a little emotional, sat down. One more small battle had been won. Edward arrived a few minutes later. She came quickly to her feet and swept herself into his arms.

'Edward – oh, I'm so glad to see you.'

'You did see me, just before breakfast.'

'Yes. I know. But. Oh, you see,' she said, 'every meeting is an excitement to me. To be close to you is to feel secure.'

'Watch out for my tottery moments,' said Edward.

'Oh, together we'll be invincible, my darling – yes, invincible. You will see.' Katerina kissed him warmly.

'You realise we must go as soon as we can after the inquest?' said Edward. 'The events here, the deaths, are going to have repercussions, my sweet. Your enemies will be convinced that you are who you are.'

'I am Katerina, only Katerina.' But she hid her face against his shoulder. 'Except that now I'm your Katerina.'

'Yes,' said Edward quietly. 'This afternoon, would you care to drive into Nice with me and help me apply for a special marriage licence?'

'Oh, dearest, dearest Edward.' She hugged him. She kissed him. 'Yes – yes – that will make me so happy.'

When they returned from Nice at five o'clock, the special licence obtained, Inspector Cartier had been and gone. He had, Celeste informed them, asked questions only of Madame Knight, Colonel Brecht and herself, together with Mama, and then searched Mademoiselle's room. He had taken her passport and some papers away. He had not expressed the most faint wish to interview either the Countess or Edward.

'The most faint wish?' smiled Katerina.

'That is really no wish at all,' said Celeste.

'I had a wish,' said Katerina, 'a very dear wish. Concerning Edward. Celeste, we have a licence and are to be married in Nice in seven days.'

'Then we must leave, little angel,' said Edward.

Celeste was enchanted, overwhelmed. She was also sad. She was going to lose them.

At the inquest in La Roche, with Edward and Celeste present, Katerina stood up to answer every question quietly and without a tremor. In a grey costume, with hat and veil, she was impressive. Edward, watching her and listening to her, was in new wonder and fascination. Her demeanour, her poise and her calmness signified, to him, an inherited regality. She did not once falter, though he knew that beneath her composure she was suffering.

In the regrettable absence of the chief witness, one Mademoiselle Dupont, the coroner accepted her testimony as recorded by Inspector Cartier, and returned the only verdict possible. Death by accident or suicide.

Behind her veil, Katerina's eyes misted for the last time in grief for the man who had sacrificed not only his freedom, but his life, for her. Then Edward and Celeste took her back to the hotel.

Three days later, after breakfast, her packing finished, she greeted Edward's entry with an emotional kiss.

'That is for you, my darling,' she said, 'and for my wedding day.'

'Everything ready?' said Edward, lightness covering his own emotions.

'My luggage is ready, and I am ready. Oh, you don't know how ready I am. You have no idea what you're doing for me, how wonderful it is for me. Oh, we must call on Anna and Sandro. They've been so devoted, and must join us when we're settled. You'll arrange that, won't you?'

'Everything, Katerina, my precious, will be just as you want. Always.'

Madame Michel came to say goodbye to them. She wept a little. They promised to write. She embraced Edward. She pressed Katerina's hands.

'God will keep you,' she said. 'But Celeste will miss you both, so much.'

Celeste arrived the moment her mother had gone.

'Madame – Edward – oh, I'm happy for you, truly, but so sad,' she said. 'You see, I didn't think about how it would take you away from me.'

'Listen, sweetest angel,' said Edward. 'Each year you'll take a holiday. Your mama will allow this, of course she will, and you'll spend it with us. I'll arrange it, I'll write – '

'We shall both write, oh, very often,' said Katerina.

'And each year I may really come and stay with you?' said Celeste.

'Each year, Celeste, we shall all spend time together,' said Edward.

'That will make me very happy,' said Celeste. 'Madame – '

'No, I am Katerina, my brave one. Always to you I am Katerina.'

'I'd like to say how glad I am Edward is to marry you,' said Celeste. 'It's saved him the terrible ordeal of having to marry me.'

It was said with a bright smile, but Katerina saw the sadness there, and the love. Celeste had no father. The war had taken him when she was an infant. Edward had filled that role for her.

'Celeste, always we shall think of you,' said Katerina gently, 'always.'

'You must go, or I shall cry,' said Celeste.

'Dearest girl,' said Edward, and kissed her. Celeste clung.

'Oh, I have so much love for you both,' she whispered. 'Write to me, please write, when you're settled.'

'Goodbye, my sweet,' said Katerina, 'you are precious to us, you have given us to each other.'

Celeste stood in the road outside the hotel, with her mother and Jacques. They waved goodbye. Edward and Katerina turned in the Bentley. They waved, they called. Celeste watched them disappear.

'Oh, Mama,' she said, 'how can one be so happy for them and so miserable for oneself? I am breaking my heart.'

'There, my infant, such a gentle one you are,' said

Madame Michel, 'and blessed of God.'

They motored towards Nice. They had not liked saying goodbye to Celeste, but they knew they could stay no longer in La Roche. Edward was sure that the people out of Katerina's past, those who menaced her, would close in on her, and Katerina did not argue. She had placed herself in Edward's hands.

They had called at the Villa d'Azur, where Katerina spoke at length to Anna and Sandro. Sandro said nothing about a man called Valery. He only said, as Katerina made her departure, 'Boris Sergeyovich lies in peace now.'

Nice and the wedding ceremony lay ahead. Katerina, swamped by every kind of emotion, said, 'It's so sad to have left Celeste.'

'We shall part from Celeste from time to time,' said Edward, 'but never for good.'

'No, never. Edward, thank you.'

'For what?'

'For driving me now to our wedding. Where do we go then, where are we to settle?'

'I've thought and thought,' said Edward. 'Katerina, do you know the Balearics, a group of islands off Spain?'

'I've heard of them,' said Katerina, the autumn air fresh around her hat and veil, 'but I've never been there.'

'There's a very small one called Formentera. I went there once, before the war. It's the quietest place on earth. A little steamer puts in once a week from Ibiza, that's all. If you like it, we'll have a villa built there, and a garden. It will suit my chest. And it will give you peace, Katerina, and freedom from worry, I swear.'

'If you like it, then I shall like it,' said Katerina. 'Let us go there at once, if not immediately.'

They laughed then. They knew Celeste would have laughed too.

'We've many things to arrange,' said Edward, driving into the light of the ascending sun. 'First, we must buy the ring in Nice.'

'Yes, my darling. I love you. And one day, after we're married, I will tell you about my family of loved ones, perhaps.'

'I know about your family of loved ones,' said Edward.

Her heart dissolved.

'Edward?'

'I know who you are, Katerina Pyotrovna.'

The Bentley carried them forward, into the future, into all the years ahead.

18

The afternoon sun was sinking.

'Señora?' said Kate. She felt so emotional. The story had taken three afternoons to tell, and there had been moments when the gentle voice had become silent, the narrative lost for a while. And there had been so much that Kate had had to guess at, or imagine. There had been so much that only Edward or Celeste could have told. Kate filled in the voids for herself.

It was over now, the story, and the dreams had come again, putting soft shadows on the aged face.

Who was she really? Kate wondered. She had not once said she was other than Katerina Pyotrovna. And for over fifty years she had merely been Mrs Edward Somers. Yet the story itself, with its suggestions and implications, told Kate she might be far more than she had ever said.

'Señora?'

Katerina looked at the girl, the girl so like Celeste, with blue eyes so like other eyes.

'They are all gone now, my sweet.' The gentle voice was tired. 'All of them. My darling Edward, my bright Celeste and my family of loved ones. But you are here, Kate, and you have my name. You too are a Katerina.'

'Señora, is that what Edward – Mr Somers – called you? Is that really your name?'

Katerina smiled.

'Sometimes he called me Katerina, and sometimes another name. Kate, the world is so beautiful, yet so sad. The ugly is worshipped in place of the good. Love, which is the whole reason for our existence, is treated as casually as a toy. Faithfulness is derided, indulgence deified. Kate, that's very sad, isn't it?'

Kate looked into the eyes which had seen so much and which dreamed so much.

'Señora, I don't think it's as sad as all that, really I don't,' she said. 'Señora, I love you very much.'

The delicacy of the fine face became warm. A slender hand touched the girl's hair and stroked it.

'But I'm so old, Kate, so very old.'

'You're beautiful,' said Kate. 'I should think – well, I should think it was easy for Edward to tell you so, always.'

'Oh, yes, he made his disarming little speeches,' said Katerina.

Maria came out to take a look, satisfied herself that the Señora was as well off as she could be with Kate, and went back to the kitchen.

'Señora, what happened to Celeste? Does she come here sometimes?' Kate was still so absorbed. 'I'd so like to meet her, I really would.'

Katerina turned her eyes on the garden. She felt tired, but could not bring herself to part with the girl.

'Celeste was the bravest of the brave, Kate. It was the other war, the dreadful war. When the Germans invaded France, Celeste was in Paris. She wrote us from there. It was the last letter we ever received from her. In it, she sent us her faithful love. She fought for France, in what I think was called the Maquis. And in 1942, they caught her and shot her. She gave her life for her country. Celeste always gave. She was still so young. Thirty, Kate, only thirty. The world was robbed of her bright courage. Each year she stayed with us, in May and October. I hear them sometimes, Celeste and

Edward. That is special to the aged, Kate, the moments when sweet memories come to life. Today is Edward's birthday, did you know that?'

'No, Señora.'

'This evening, when it's cooler, will you come with me? Always on his birthday, I carry a posy of flowers to his grave. Will you come with me?'

'Oh, yes,' said Kate.

The little Catholic cemetery was a haven of quiet, the gravestones warmed by the evening sun, and flowers for the dead stirred a little in the light breeze. Kate was arm in arm with Katerina, who still walked in the graceful way Edward had thought so regal. Maria was in attendance a little way behind.

Kate saw the grave and the headstone.

SOMERS

EDWARD
and

That was all. It was incomplete. It was awaiting Katerina. Kate felt the anguish of sensitive youth, for she knew Katerina Pyotrovna was ready to lie beside him. That was what her dreams were all about. Kate had never known such love as Katerina Pyotrovna had had for all the years of her life. And because of her son and daughter, and her grandchildren, she still had so much to live for. But she was ready to leave them, to be where Edward was, and perhaps Celeste too.

Katerina saw the anguish plain on the girl's expressive face.

'Kate? You are sad? That is not for you, child – I am so sorry, I did not want you to be sad. It's his birthday, when I come to give him my love.'

'Señora,' said Kate, 'I believe in God, I believe in love.'

'Then you'll be cherished, my child,' said Katerina, and stooped to set the posy of flowers in the stone pot. Kate saw the photograph of Edward in the graveside frame. She recognised it. She had, during these last few afternoons, been shown other photographs of him. Here, in its frame, was one taken of him sitting on the garden patio. It showed him a lean man, and still young, really, with thick hair and a widow's peak, and a smile on his face, which was a little lined but not ravaged. Kate liked his mouth and his eyes. There was faded ink across the photograph.

August, 1931, at home.

'There, my darling,' said Katerina and slowly straightened. Kate filled the pot from the little watering-can, and the posy of flowers drew up the moisture and grew bright. She stood with Katerina for a few minutes, and then Katerina said, quite clearly, 'They are here, they are both here, can't you feel them, Kate?'

'Yes, Señora. They're here because you are here.'

She went daily, every afternoon without fail, to sit with Katerina, to talk with her, and each day the eyes were dreamier and farther away, the fragility more delicate, and Kate knew she was going to lose her dear and beloved friend. Her parents were puzzled by her obsession, and even worried by it, for it seemed so odd, a child of fifteen spending so many hours with a old lady who was over eighty. But they did not protest or interfere. Kate was Kate. And Kate was fortunate, for her parents gave her love, as thye did to her young brother Bobby.

Kate went each day, after lunch, and did not return until six o'clock, when she would spend the time until dinner writing. It was all going down, the story of Katerina Pyotrovna.

Maria, Katerina's servant, watched the girl and her mistress, and saw the love the old had for the young, and the devotion of the young.

They sat, one afternoon, when the sun was mellow and the breeze from the sea stirred the fringes of the umbrella and lightly teased Kate's flowing, blue-black hair. Katerina was at her most articulate, her pleasure in the girl's company bringing smiles to her face and questions to her lips. They shared each other's secrets, though there were some that remained unspoken.

There was a question Kate wanted to ask. There was something she wanted to know about Celeste, something else she could write down about the one who had loved Edward and Katerina so much.

Oh, yes.

'Señora, you've never said – did Celeste meet someone, did she get married?'

Katerina smiled and shook her head, and Kate thought she doesn't look so far away today, she's much more alert.

'Celeste?' said Katerina. 'No, Kate, she never took a husband. There must have been many men, I think, who would have wanted to marry her. But she loved only Edward, no one else. She loved him, my child, and so she gave him to me. Where do such years go, Kate, except into the treasure house of the mind?' Katerina smiled again, and the memories came to lay their soft shadows on her face. 'You are so like Celeste – such blue eyes, so like other eyes. You have been so sweet to me – so sweet – ' Her lashes fell, then lifted, and the smile was there, warm with love and full of dreams. There was the faintest of sighs, and then she sat very still in her chair.

Kate's heart stopped.

'Maria!' She cried out in anguish a moment later. 'Maria!'

Maria hastened out and bent to look into the face of serenity.

She crossed herself.

'She's at peace, señorita, and with God.'

The thick-walled church was comparatively cool. The mourning clothes of the Formenterans were sombre black. Katerina's middle-aged son and daughter were there, also in black, their heads bowed, their spouses beside them. Four grandchildren were present, two of them young women in bright summer clothes that seemed out of place to Kate. But because she was close to the spirit of Katerina, she knew her beloved Señora would not have minded. They had come, they were there. That was all she would have wanted, to have them there.

One of them had marvellous auburn hair.

The church was packed. All these people of Formentera, so quiet in their mourning of her, had come to say goodbye to her. She had wanted to go, she had wanted to lie beside Edward, and she had gone so peacefully.

But Kate's heart was weeping.

The spirit of Katerina Pyotrovna reached out to her and her heart melted.

She dreamed her way through the service. The music was magnificent, a sung requiem to all the years of the Señora's life, the soaring voices filling the church with beautiful sound. And for Kate there were other voices, laughing voices and murmurous voices.

She knelt in wonder and love.

Maria's voice. 'Come, señorita, it's over.'

They joined the people moving out of the church.

In the sunshine, Kate said, 'Maria, oh, the music, it was beautiful, wasn't it?'

'Music? There was no music, señorita.'

'But there was.'

Maria looked at the girl, so young and so sensitive.

'For you, señorita, yes, perhaps there was. But now we must watch them lay her to rest. Come.'

They sat in the morning sunshine, Kate and Maria, on a little seat in the cemetery, waiting for the cortège to arrive, with Katerina's family.

'Maria, when did her husband die?' said Kate. 'I asked her once, and she smiled and said, "Go into the villa, Kate, and you'll find him there." '

'He went ten years ago, señorita, ten years,' said Maria. 'But he lived far longer than he might have done, all because of her care. Seventy-seven, and always afflicted, but never have I known a man so peaceable towards life and people. Never have I known a more loving woman. She gave everything of herself. I grumbled at her many times, and he would protest too. But she said to me once, "Maria, he has given me life and freedom, and I will do for him what I will, so stop your grumbling." And she was almost seventy then. When he died three years later, life for her was never the same. She had no one to give her love to, no one to lavish her care on. Her son and daughter had long since married and gone away. While Señor Somers was alive, for her there was always the future, yes, always. When he died, there was only the past. So many dreams she had, señorita, about her other family, her papa and mama, and her sisters and brother. Who they were, I never knew. There was her own family, there were her grandchildren. But they were not the children of her world. Her granddaughters were divorced almost as soon as they were married, and living with men to whom they weren't married, which was not as God ordained or as she wished. It made her so sad. "Maria," she said, "they know nothing of love, nothing." Señorita, you are to have her villa when you come of age, do you know that? And all her correspondence, all her letters from her husband and Celeste and others.'

'Oh, Maria, no,' gasped Kate. 'Oh, I'd like her letters, yes, I would – but not her villa. Her family will expect it – I'd be so embarrassed. Maria, I can't.'

'Señorita, you must,' said Maria. 'You must for her sake. Her son is a fine man, her daughter kind, but their interests aren't here. They would sell the villa. It was her home for over fifty years. She loved it and every moment she spent in it. She told me she wished it to go into the hands of love. "Kate shall have it, Maria," she said. "It might have been Celeste's, but it shall go to our sweet Kate. Kate will give it love." And she asked if I agreed, and I said yes. Carlos and I – Carlos was my husband who died six years ago – we served her after her previous servants, Anna and Sandro, went to their rest. For thirty years I was with her, señorita. Señor Somers was a man of great kindness. The Señora was a lady of great beauty, which is not something one wears on one's face alone. Señorita, you must have the villa, and old Maria with it.'

'Maria, oh, I'm so confused – you must come and meet my

parents – we must talk about it. They'll help us decide. Maria, she's here – look.'

The cortège had arrived.

A little later, Kate and Maria joined those who wished to spill the earth on to the lowered coffin. Kate bit her lip, fighting to hold back her tears. Hands touched her shoulders. She turned. Her parents were behind her.

'Just to help you say goodbye to her, darling.'

It was through her tears that she saw Katerina Pyotrovna had come to lie beside Edward, for the headstone was complete.

SOMERS

EDWARD
and
TATIANA

In Care Of Each Other

And Kate, who thought little of science or mathematics, but was fascinated by history, knew then who Katerina Pyotrovna really was.

And she knew too that she would have the villa, and dwell there whenever she could in the warm shadows of Edward, Celeste and her beloved Señora, a Grand Duchess of Imperial Russia.